The Hunt

by

Jonas Saul

PUBLISHED BY:
Imagine Press Inc.
Ebook ISBN: 978-1-927404-53-9
Paperback ISBN: 978-1-998047-68-0
Hardcover ISBN: 978-1-998047-69-7

The Hunt
Copyright © 2020 by Jonas Saul

The Sarah Roberts Series

Dark Visions (One)
The Warning (Two)
The Crypt (Three)
The Hostage (Four)
The Victim (Five)
The Enigma (Six)
The Vigilante (Seven)
The Rogue (Eight)
Killing Sarah (Nine)
The Antagonist (Ten)
The Redeemed (Eleven)
The Haunted (Twelve)
The Unlucky (Thirteen)
The Abandoned (Fourteen)
The Cartel (Fifteen)
Losing Sarah (Sixteen)
The Pact (Seventeen)
The Terror (Eighteen)
The Chase (Nineteen)
The Betrayal (Twenty)
Sarah's Return (Twenty-One)
The Hunt (Twenty-Two)
The Delivery (Twenty-Three)
The Trap (Twenty-Four)
The Ultimatum (Twenty-Five)
The Depraved (Twenty-Six)
The Condemned (Twenty-Seven)
Payback (Twenty-Eight)
The Unknown (Twenty-Nine)
Wrath (Thirty)
The Damned (Thirty-One)

The Game (Thirty-Two)
The Decoy (Thirty-Three)
The Disappearance (Thirty-Four)
The Whole Truth (Thirty-Five)
Alex (Thirty-Six)
Parkman (Thirty-Seven)
Darwin (Thirty-Eight)
Aaron (Thirty-Nine)
Remains To Be Seen (Forty)

The Jake Wood Novels

The Immortal Gene (Book One)
The Immortal Target (Book Two)

Standalone Novels

'Til Death Do Us Part
The Drowning
The Woman in the Woods
The Threat
The Specter
The Mafia Trilogy
A Murder in Time
Frequency of the Dead

Co-Authored Novels

Collision Course (Written with Gary Ponzo)
There Will Be Blood (Written with Rania Stone)
The Soulless (Written with Rania Stone)

Short Story Collections

Twisted Fate (Tales of Horror)
Twists of Fate (Tales of Hope)

Chapter 1

For Julie Perkins, it was like deciding who would live and die. This wasn't a joke anymore. She had supported her man, as expected, but their relationship was over if he went through with it.

"You can't be serious," Julie said, her bottom lip quivering. "Please tell me you're joking." She tried to keep the emotion out of her voice.

"Then you tell me what to do," Ron snapped. "I've lost everything."

"This isn't the way to fix it." Her voice cracked.

Ron hit the garage door button and inched around the tailgate of his pickup truck as the door closed.

Julie stared at her boyfriend as she digested what he was saying. She couldn't believe it—refused to believe it. The man she fell in love with had gone batshit crazy.

"Have you thought about your kids?" she asked, knowing even mentioning them would rile him up.

Ron had been strapping a canopy into place over the bed of his truck. He stopped, released it, and placed his hands flat against the truck's side, head bowed. His long hair—one of the things that originally drew her to him, that and the tattooed sleeves that finished at his knuckles—drooped past his shoulders, shrouding his face. There was an aura of energy around him, like he was preparing to explode.

Julie stepped back, easing toward the door that led into the house.

"What's that supposed to mean?" Ron whispered. "Everything I do, I do for them."

"I know that, honey," she said, speaking fast to quell the rising tide of anger oozing off him. "It's just something like this could add to your current troubles with the court system. They may deny access."

His head shook back and forth several times, still bowed, hands still flat on the truck.

"I have lost everything." He raised himself to stand straighter, flicking his hair over his shoulder and easing far enough to the right to stare at her. "They took it all away. And why? Because I couldn't live with an abusive woman? Because I simply wanted out of a relationship—"

"I know, honey, I know." He needed to feel validated, and she was the only one who could do it. She stood by him through it all. "And I'm sorry about everything that's happened. We can fix this—"

"No," he shouted. "Someone has to pay. I built this business. I built that life. My construction company allowed us to buy the house *she* lives in." He moved closer to her. She held her ground, reminding herself she wasn't the enemy. "Family Law? Tell me, why do they call it that? It should be called, Dissolve the Family Law, or Breakup the Family Law."

"I know," she nodded. "I saw it all—"

"Yeah, you saw it all happen while I lost it all." He stopped moving one foot from her, his eyes bloodshot, the strain evident in the vein bulging on his forehead, others pulsing in his neck. "They've taken everything, and you want to know what's worse?"

She dared not speak, so she shook her head, then nodded. Did she want to know or not? She leaned into the doorframe with a hand on her stomach, hoping she wouldn't vomit. Arguing always made her feel sick.

"I allowed them to take my dignity along with the business, the house, and the kids. Children's Aid Society has effectively kidnapped my kids, but they also stole anything I had left in my heart. It's over, Julie"—he leaned closer—"it's *fucking* over." He spit the last word, making her have to blink several times. She almost lunged through the door but held off, knowing this was Ron, her man, and he wouldn't harm her. Would he?

"I can't live with that," she said, pointing at the pickup truck.

Ron glanced over his shoulder at the half-closed canopy. As a peacekeeper for the Canadian Army years ago, he'd done several tours in Afghanistan. When he got home, things had changed. His wife, Bridgette, acted differently, and the kids were brainwashed against him. Julie heard all the stories over a thousand times. But she also heard his stories about the war overseas and what Ron had to deal with. He came back different, too, angrier. But he also came home with new friends, the kind of friends who could arrange delivery of the weapons lying in the back of his pickup truck.

"If you leave tonight," she said, the shake in her voice had gotten worse, "I don't know how I could live with it."

"What's that supposed to mean? You gonna call the cops?" He moved closer again until his face was an inch from hers. One twist of the door handle, she would fall through the doorway and sprawl out on the laundry room linoleum. "You wouldn't do that to me, would you?" Ron's eyes took on a crazy glaze as if madness glistened on them. "After everything else I've lost." He moved away abruptly, placed both fists against the wall beside the door, and then eased his forehead onto it, his breathing coming in fits and starts. "I thought you'd stand with me." He pivoted his head to stare her down, still leaning into the wall. "I thought we'd do this together. I didn't want to lose you, too."

She crossed her arms and brought a hand to her mouth to nip at a nail, her back pressed firmly against the door. "Ron, I didn't think you were serious when you told me your ideas about—"

He smashed the wall with both fists and shoved himself away from her.

"You didn't think," he shouted, repeating her words. "You didn't fucking think. That's the problem."

He clamped down the canopy at the side of the truck, one clasp at a time.

She'd never known him to be physical, to punch walls,

but the immense pressure he was under had to be debilitating. After years of service to the Canadian government and a decade in the construction business, Ron was a reasonably large man, again something she'd been drawn to. Something about her man's weight turned her on when they made love. She wanted to *feel* him on top of her. She wanted to be smothered, consumed, taken. But in an argument, his size, stature, and weight scared the shit out of her. And punching that wall did nothing to ease her nerves.

But she couldn't let him leave without one more plea for reason, one more attempt at sanity.

"Ron?" she whispered.

He clipped the last two clasps on the canopy, then, after a large breath, he faced her.

"What?"

"I love you."

After a moment's pause, he whispered, "I know. And you know I love you, too. But I can't stand by and—"

"Ron?"

He headed for the cab and opened the door, then stopped. "What?"

"Please don't leave."

He seemed to contemplate her words. Then Ron closed the door without getting inside and leaned his forearms on the hood of the pickup.

"Julie, I live for my kids. They're all I have left. I lost custody to that bitch of an ex-wife, and then all her neglect caused Children's Aid to sweep in and take them. And now they won't even tell me where they are. When I called—"

"But this isn't the answer." She fought an internal urge to

remind him that his actions would solidify their position in *never* giving him his kids.

He bowed his head and waited a moment. "When I called and said they could come to stay with their father, the bitch at CAS told me that my babies were a crown ward now, whatever the hell that meant, and if changes didn't take place in the mother's home, they might be given to a foster family, or worse, adopted."

"You'll get them, Ron, but not this way."

"You sound like you're on their side."

She wiped a tear streaking across her cheek. "Ron, you know I'm on your side. That's why I'm fighting for you to stay home. Don't do this."

"The government kidnapped my sons," he said through his teeth. "I've done nothing wrong. My ex-wife fucked up and lost them. All I wanted to do was check on them, visit them, but that's not allowed right now, whatever the fuck that means." He lunged to the side and kicked over a small pile of paint cans. They crashed to the floor, making a racket. "And can you believe when I said to the case worker that I was coming to pick them up—their father, their blood, and remember I've done nothing wrong—I was told that I would be arrested." He grabbed a hammer off the pegboard to his left, leaned down, and smashed one of the paint cans, the clatter too loud to speak over.

After several whacks from the hammer, each one causing her eyelids to spasm, the paint left in the can spilled onto the garage's concrete floor. He tossed the hammer aside and righted himself, his hair a mess.

Ron was always drawn to noise for some reason. When

he'd pull out the frying pan at night before cooking, he'd whack it several times on the granite counter just to hear the intense sound. Like it soothed him somehow, it calmed the noise in his head.

"Arrest me? For visiting my kids? For taking them home to safety? I'm their protector, their blood. I'm their biological father. Ask a bear how it feels about its young being taken from it. How the fuck can they arrest me when they're my fucking kids?" He jabbed at his chest. "How dare they? I'll kill them all. Every last fucking one of them."

He was coming unglued. She'd never seen him like this before. High blood pressure, heart attack territory, aneurism, anything would befall him at any second.

"C'mon honey, come inside," she said in a softer tone. "Let's get drunk. Let's fuck all night. Whatever you want, baby, but just come inside. Think it over. Don't do this. Don't leave. We'll talk about it over coffee in the morning. Just you and me against the world, baby. Like we always say. We'll win the day. We'll get them, I swear, but not this way."

Ron shook his head once, stared at the paint as if surprised he'd spilled it, then strode to his truck and jumped in.

"Leave me, Julie," he shouted from the truck's cab.

Her heart skipped a beat. She couldn't believe what he had just said. It wasn't even possible. Those words cut too deep.

"I'm no good," he shouted. "Get out of my house. Call Annemarie, your girlfriend. Stay there tonight. Be gone when I return."

"Honey," she called, her voice breaking, tears bursting

from her eyes. She clutched at the wall to avoid falling to her knees.

"I said I'm done," he shouted. "Get out of my fucking *house*."

He shouted so loud the last word echoed throughout the garage, reverberating in her head. She never thought this day would come. He was falling apart and needed her more than ever.

"If you're not out of my house by the morning, I'll throw you out on the lawn when I get home. Please, Julie, I love you, but I'm broken. So just leave. I refuse to bring you down with me."

He turned on the truck and hit the garage remote. The door started rolling upward.

Julie jumped to her feet and smacked a hand on the hood. "Honey, please," she shouted. "Don't. You can't do this." She smacked the truck again. *"Please, honey!"*

The door's height cleared the tailgate. Ron glared at her through the windshield. He was crying. This was the second time she'd seen tears in his eyes. The first was when CAS took his kids.

The man could love if he would only set it free.

She pleaded with her eyes. "Think about this. Don't do it. I need you, Ron."

He tilted his head slightly to yell at her out his open window. "I've lost everything already. They've taken my kids. And now I've lost you. I have nothing to live for. Goodbye, Julie. Pack your things and go. You're out of my life."

He dropped it into reverse so fast, there was a heavy

clunking sound, and the truck vibrated, and then he was backing out onto the driveway, turning at the road.

The sound of the pickup truck diminished as he squealed away and drove the length of their street. She didn't chase the vehicle. Even if she wanted to, her legs wouldn't obey a command to run.

She swatted at the garage door opener button on the wall beside her, then dropped to her knees. Finally, she eased down to her side and wrapped her arms around herself as she bawled like a baby.

Ron was going to get himself killed. She was sure of it.

And with all those weapons in the bed of his truck, she was sure other people would die before Ron's last breath.

Should she call the cops and rat out her boyfriend—*ex*-boyfriend—who was just going through an anger phase at the moment? What if he cooled off and came home? What if he did nothing wrong but was arrested for possessing illegal arms?

If she called the cops, that would surely put her on the same side as the people at CAS, the court system, and everyone else out to destroy him, like the Canada Revenue Agency.

That would be putting herself in the crosshairs of his weapons.

But what if she did nothing and he killed someone? Or he killed a lot of someones?

Julie moaned and sobbed on the garage floor, her nose clogged, her bladder full, and her heart broken.

Whatever happened over the next few days, she clearly understood one thing. She needed to leave this madhouse, and she needed to leave tonight. Ron had been serious about that.

She could not be involved with someone bent on murder, whether he wanted her or not.

Somehow, Julie made it inside the house in the next half hour.

Once there, she made one phone call to Annemarie and then started packing.

Chapter 2

Sarah Roberts stared at Parkman from across the table.

"What is it about that toothpick?" she asked. "What's the draw?"

He took it out of his mouth and examined it. "I enjoy fiddling with this small piece of wood as much as other people might chew gum." He raised his right shoulder, then let it settle back down. "No big deal."

"You wouldn't be Parkman without it."

He smiled wide. "I'm always Parkman."

"Okay, well, I declare us officially bored."

"How's that?"

"Listen to us. We're discussing your fascination with toothpicks and whether or not you're Parkman." She sighed and dropped her head onto her forearm.

"Have you been doing okay?"

"Sure," she said, her voice muffled by the cloth of her sleeve. "Why?"

"With what the news has been saying."

"Fuck them. They don't know shit."

After the recent takedown of True Legacy, a human procurement company headquartered in Dallas, Texas, media outlets picked up the story, and even CNN wanted an interview, which Sarah refused. By the time Aaron's chest felt good enough for him to travel home—being shot in the chest hurt bad, even though he was wearing a vest—Sarah had been harassed countless times by the press.

Several of them dug up some of her earlier exploits that had hit the news over the past decade. Stories about the Rapturites, street gangs like the MS-13 in Toronto, the mafia families in Toronto, and even loan sharks in Vegas, plus a couple of her European exploits. One Toronto rag even checked her history in Canada and learned she'd visited a hospital last February. Someone broke a privacy law somewhere, and on the cover of that rag—a name she wouldn't repeat in public until that particular company went out of business one day—was a picture of Sarah with the caption about her losing her child.

If it weren't for Aaron, she would've burned their building to the ground last week. They were considering legal action, but the money her parents gave her several years ago had dwindled. It was too risky to waste thousands of dollars on a lawyer and a case that could go either way. Besides, the newspapers had let up, and she was no longer on the front page. The election in the States was heating up, too. There was much more dirty laundry for the media to cling to than her sordid tale.

"How's Aaron feel about you doing this?" Parkman asked.

"He doesn't like it."

"Because he's not a part of it?"

"He's never liked what I do."

"Does that bode well for your future?"

She suppressed a laugh because it wasn't a funny question, but it was hilarious because Aaron had hated what she did since the get-go. What man would want their partner out dealing with gangs, hitmen, and rogue cops as a job? What woman would want that?

Sarah had support from her team, but she didn't have the law on her side. And understandably, that scared Aaron. It scared him because he loved her, and she couldn't fault him for that. But she wouldn't stop what she did with Vivian for him. She might stop when she became a mother, but wasn't prepared to stop until then.

"In the words of a great author," Sarah said, glancing up at Parkman, "and so it goes."

"Aaron is probably pissed that he can't be here tonight."

Sarah nodded, her forehead still jammed on her forearm. "He is. Although, I don't really know why we're here, either."

"We're having a coffee." When Parkman sipped from his coffee cup, it sounded more like he was eating soup. His toothpick must have gotten in the way. "If your sister tells us more, we act. If she doesn't, we go home and sleep."

A thought occurred to her. She snapped her head up. "Hey, what's your other name? I only know you as Parkman.

Why's that? Why don't I know who you are?"

He frowned, the toothpick rolling around in his mouth. "My other name?"

"Yeah, your other name. Your parents didn't just call you Parkman, right?"

He nodded. "Parkman is my last name."

"What's your first name?"

He shook his head and glanced down at the table. "I'd rather not say."

Sarah sat up straighter. "What the hell," she whispered, then smiled. He had to be joking, playing her. "After all we've been through together? I still remember the first time I saw you—in your cop uniform—when I was fighting that cult in Utah. You chased me, and we entered that abandoned airplane hangar together."

"Yeah, I recall you took off on me again, too."

"And the tracker that you are, you caught up with me in that temple. If I recall correctly, you saved my life, which means you owe me."

"Owe you?" He laughed. "How do you figure?"

"Well, a woman should know who's sticking his neck out for her. I mean, I know you, the man, but I don't know your name." She shook her head, her mind drifting back to those days when she was young and innocent but still driven by a burning need to right wrongs. "I think I was twenty-two years old then, a baby back in those days. And yet, I still don't know your name. Why's that?"

"You never asked."

"I'm asking now."

"Really? Is it necessary?"

"Is it on your passport?"

After a brief hesitation, he nodded.

"And you are an American like me, so you have it with you because we're sitting in a coffee shop in Toronto, *Canada*."

He nodded again. "Observant."

"If I were standing, I'd slap you for that sarcasm." She rolled her fingers in a give-it-me gesture. "Let me see your passport."

"Hotel room."

"Parkman," she whispered. "What is it about your name that bothers you so much?"

"Isn't it good enough that you know me, my standards, my dignity? What does a name matter?"

He had a point. "You're right, it doesn't. And I do know you and love you for who you are, but I still want to know."

"Fair enough, I'll tell you." He paused, flicking his toothpick left, then right. "One day."

"I could ask Vivian."

"You wouldn't. That'd be, like, a violation or something. Bit rude, actually. Harsh."

His humorous tone was easy to spot because he was always so serious. And whether he told her or didn't, it was fun to goad him. Yet, she still wanted to know.

At the mention of Vivian's name, Sarah detected her presence. Her sister drifted through her consciousness, making Sarah hold up a hand for Parkman to wait as she listened internally. Vivian passed on an understanding, and Sarah got it immediately.

"We're in the wrong place." She jumped to her feet.

"And we're almost out of time."

Parkman got to his feet, too. "Where's the right place?"

Sarah shook her head. "Not sure, exactly. But it's that way." She pointed at the road out front.

"That way?" Parkman said, skepticism in his voice. "That tells me a lot."

"Once we're in the car, I'll know more."

They left the small coffee shop and got in the car. Parkman eased the vehicle toward the lot's entrance, and Sarah pointed to the right.

"That way."

Parkman turned right onto Airport Road and started away from Hwy 427. She watched the buildings as they passed by her window. A tall hotel, an office building, and a fast-food drive-thru.

"Anything?" Parkman asked.

"Yeah, but it's weird and makes no sense."

"Try me."

Sarah faced him. "She said we had to stop the matador beside Wendy, or a plane could crash."

Parkman scrunched his eyebrows. "A matador? Beside Wendy? Who the hell is this Wendy?"

Sarah turned to stare out her window again. The sun had set hours ago. The roads were quiet as it was a Sunday night nearing midnight, and school was back in as it was early September. The beginning of a school year had never been on her mind before—until now. By this time, she would've had her baby, and in a few years, he or she would've been starting preschool or kindergarten or whatever kids did in Canada. All the firsts could have been enjoyed together. They could've witnessed the baby's first steps, words, and day of school. But that was a path she hadn't been given. This was, and as much as she yearned for her own child, she would live this way until she got pregnant again—if she got pregnant again. Something she planned on discussing with Vivian when she showed up for a longer conversation.

Perhaps that was why she was strangely absent over the past few months.

"You know," Parkman started, "Vivian hasn't been too clear lately."

"You were reading my mind. She's definitely gone somewhere."

"Any idea why?"

"None." Sarah shook her head, not wanting to discuss it further. She had her suspicions but had no idea what was happening on the other side. "It's like she isn't supposed to be talking to me or something, but she sneaks into my head and tells me tidbits of information. Sometimes just enough to accomplish a goal or enough to stay alive."

"Well, when we were in Texas less than two weeks ago, she wanted you to do something in a month. Yet, she reached out only days later, and you're already trying to stop a matador beside Wendy."

"Sometimes people you trust don't tell you everything when you ask them," she said, staring at his profile as he drove. "You know what I mean, *Parkman*?" The emphasis on his name made him turn sideways to face her. "You know, like what your name is," she added.

"I'll tell you when this is all over. How's that?"

She leaned on the door as she stared out the window

again. "When this is all over could mean tonight, or it could mean this entire case, or you could even mean …" She stopped talking as they were about to pass a fast-food restaurant. Above them, a large airliner was coming in to land at Toronto's Lester Pearson Airport.

"*Stop* the car," she shouted.

Parkman jammed on the brakes, and the driver behind them honked his horn, then jerked around them, offering Parkman his middle finger.

"There's Wendy. Pull in there."

Parkman had to back up five feet to make the turn. Once in the parking lot of the Wendy's restaurant, it dawned on her. In Texas, after shutting down that human procurement company nationwide, Vivian had said something about the hunt starting at an airport and that it involved planes.

"If this is Wendy, where's the matador?" Parkman asked. "And if the matador is walking around with a red flag or something, how dangerous can that be?"

"Look at all these people," Sarah said.

The parking lot behind the Wendy's had at least fifteen vehicles. Roughly twenty people stood around chatting, and as each plane came in to land at the airport, it roared overhead no more than a couple hundred feet above.

"Even though it's dark out, they've gathered to watch the planes land." Parkman turned off the car. "It feels weird. Those planes fly in low overhead, and there's no security of any sort."

"That must be why we're here. One of these people is the matador."

"What does that mean, exactly?" he asked.

"I wish I knew."

Sarah opened her door and got out. In the distance, a line of lights from three planes hovered in the sky, all aimed to land on the runway on the other side of Airport Road. To the right of the Wendy's, there was an automobile repair shop of some kind. Between the buildings, she could see Airport Road and, beyond that, the fence where the airport's property started. Judging by how close to the ground the planes were as they flew overhead, the landing strip would be just beyond that fence.

"Someone is going to try to throw something or shoot something at one of the planes as it attempts to land," she said to herself.

Parkman had gotten out of the car and stared at her over the roof. "Did you just say what I think you said?"

Their eyes met, and she nodded. "And we've only got minutes. Maybe five minutes before it happens."

"You brought heat?"

She nodded and reached around to the small of her back. Her trusty friend was right where she wanted him.

Without needing to form a plan or discuss what to do, they separated and began an examination of the parking lot. She strolled by empty cars to glance inside, passed a few that were occupied—people sitting, drinking coffee, watching the planes—and walked among the strangers who stood around talking as airplanes flew directly over their heads.

They regrouped by Parkman's rental.

"Anything?" he asked.

She shook her head. "I saw nothing weird. No bad vibes anywhere. Although, we caught a few people's attention. We must look like we lost our car keys or something. I'm getting the feeling we're going to miss the matador, and it's freaking me out."

"Can you talk to your sister? Ask her anything?"

Sarah closed her eyes and leaned on the car. Vivian was gone. She couldn't feel a thing. When she opened them, Parkman stared at the plane about to fly over them.

"What are you doing?" she asked.

"Well, the way I figure it, we can't find the matador, and if someone's going to try to hit one of these babies, I want to see where that hit comes from, if possible."

He wouldn't see a bullet, but would a bullet take down a plane?

She grabbed her phone and opened the web browser, her hands fumbling the buttons. This was cutting it too close, and Vivian was absent. It was starting to piss Sarah off, even though she knew half the time Vivian let things follow a natural path, and everything worked out in the end.

She googled matador to see if it stood for something other than what first came to mind. After scrolling several websites, she found one that spelled it in all capital letters with another word behind it.

MATADOR WEAPON.

"Parkman, I think I have something."

He came around the car and stared at her phone screen as she tapped on the link.

Lost momentarily in the words, she read that the MATADOR was a Man-portable Anti-Tank, Anti-DoOR, disposable rocket launcher that someone could fire like a rifle.

"Parkman, it can punch through most known armored personnel carriers and light tanks. It has a warhead that can smash through reinforced brick walls." She looked up at him. "What the hell would it do to the wing of a plane?"

"Or worse, the fuselage?"

Feeling sick and nervous, she clicked off her phone and stuffed it in her pocket. "We need more help. We need the authorities to lock this block down. If someone's here with one of those things, we have to stop him."

Parkman's hand was on the butt of his weapon, which was mostly concealed beneath his suit jacket.

She scanned the area quickly. Everything appeared normal. Only sightseers stood around and chatted, laughed occasionally, and watched as plane after plane landed.

"There's no time to secure the area," Sarah said. "This is going to happen in minutes."

Parkman moved to stand beside her. "Did Vivian say anything else?"

Sarah thought hard about every word, then jerked her head up and glanced over at the automobile repair shop. "Vivian said we had to stop the matador *beside* Wendy."

They broke into a run, both of them pulling their weapons at the same time.

Several people standing around watched as they took off. One man called out, and another said, *what the fuck* as they ran by. Sarah caught someone pointing a phone at them and someone else tapping into their cell phone. Calling the police was a good move. They probably needed the help on this one anyway.

The thought that such a large plane could be in trouble

because she couldn't figure out her sister's message scared the shit out of her and made her fully aware that she wasn't ready for the action just yet. Maybe she'd come back to this too early after her two-year hiatus. Or maybe she just had too much time off and was getting lazy.

None of that mattered now. If someone was attempting to shoot down a commercial airliner with a shoulder-mounted rocket launcher, she had to stop it at all costs.

On the sidewalk of Airport Road, with a four-engine plane bearing down on the parking lot of the Wendy's, Sarah focused on the closed repair shop.

She glanced at the plane, then back to the repair shop. Something glinted near the bay doors, but it was hard to see as parked cars lined the front of the business. Seven vehicles were jammed together along the edge of the sidewalk, with multiple cars parked near the garage doors, probably waiting to be serviced when they opened Monday morning.

She started toward the business with Parkman beside her.

The plane was almost overhead.

She took one last look at the airliner, figured it would be directly above them in five to seven seconds, and then ran toward the line of vehicles.

Vivian showed up and screamed one word in her head, then disappeared from her consciousness.

"Faster!"

Sarah almost lost her footing when her sister screamed in her mind. But she was able to pick up speed, almost tripped again, caught herself, and sprinted with her gun in hand.

She was twenty yards away when she saw the glint once more. There was a blast, a sharp burst of light, and a smoke trail.

The plane flew directly above them, and something chased it with a small fire spewing from its rear.

The man standing in front of the repair shop's garage door had just aimed and fired a MATADOR at a commercial airliner, and Sarah had missed stopping him by mere seconds.

She raised her weapon and fired in his general direction, hoping to plug him a couple of times.

Parkman was firing his weapon beside her, too.

Then someone tackled her from behind, and her weapon was knocked from her hand.

And Sarah screamed as her sister whispered a few more words.

It'll all end in bloodshed and heartache ...

Chapter 3

ONCE SHE WAS PACKED, Julie loaded her car and entered the garage. So many nights, she had woken to find Ron in the garage, tinkering with something. Cleaning one of his guns, researching some other fancy weapon at the desk he had set up in the corner. It was an insulated double garage, and after parking his pickup on the left side, he had plenty of room for his man cave on the right. Rustic desk, beat up office chair, calendar on the wall, complete with over thirty baseball caps he'd collected from some of his favorite teams, it was certainly a man's office.

She stared at those caps as a sadness enveloped her. Ron wanted to continue collecting baseball caps for years and then pass them down to his boys when they were teenagers. He had so many dreams and things he wanted to do with his boys when they grew up. Play ball, take them to the games, teach them to play golf one day. Eventually, leave his construction business to them.

But that was all over now. His construction business was almost defunct as the debts piled too high for him to come out from under it short of a winning lottery ticket.

On the corner tool racks, she opened one of the cases. It held a C4 weapon. Or was that a C8?

She nodded. "C4 is an explosive," she whispered to herself. "This is his prized possession, a Canadian special forces C8 assault rifle."

She recalled it because Ron had said something about it being standard issue to the Royal Canadian Mounted Police, and if the RCMP could have them, he could have one, too.

One case to the right was his M27. Some kind of infantry rifle. The US Marine Corps used them. This one had an eyepiece named a Harris sight or some shit. Ron went on, and on that, it was named by some distant relative of his. For months, Ron had drilled these names into her head for some reason. The man was passionate about his weapons.

The other dozen weapons were unfamiliar to her. An HK-33 or 34 or something like that. Several nondescript rifles, a couple of handguns. Most of it was illegal, and each case was locked, but Ron didn't care. He wasn't on anyone's radar, and no one came around snooping.

Julie was leaving this all behind. The weapons were an easy thing to walk away from. She had no idea why he needed them all. But she loved Ron, truly loved him, and none of his behavior made sense to her. Whatever he saw in Afghanistan while peacekeeping changed him. And weren't peacekeepers safer? Didn't the Americans fight the war?

Weren't they the heroes?

So what the hell happened to Ronald Harris that he came home to Canada so angry, with a burning urge to collect all manner of guns, rifles, and ammo?

She took one more look around but couldn't find his recent acquisition. It was some kind of rocket launcher thing. They'd fought about that one, as there was absolutely no reason for him to have it.

Concerned he was becoming unhinged, she'd reached out to Annemarie, her friend. They'd discussed it at length, and Annemarie's advice was to stay close to him, monitor him, but don't rat him out. Julie did not want Ron to be angry with her—ever.

Reminiscing was only making her want to cry again. Ron's kids were gone. His business was finished. His income all but dried up. Bills had piled in the kitchen, truck payments, mortgage payments, and still, there was no respite. Her job in town covered their groceries, but that was it. Maybe a night out once a week.

And now Ron was losing her, too.

She couldn't stay. Not with him determined to kill himself.

She got behind the wheel of her Volkswagen Bug in the driveway, hit the garage door button, and watched it close on the empty garage.

Was that rocket launcher thing under Ron's canopy in the back of the pickup? Did he take it somewhere?

If he did, why?

He could not find the Children's Aid Society case worker. Ron knew where their office was in Parry Sound, but the case worker wouldn't be there this late on a Sunday night.

He couldn't have gone after his kids because CAS wasn't telling him where they were. And his ex-wife was still in police custody.

"Where are you, Ron?" she asked out loud as her car idled in his driveway.

Should she call the police and let them know what was in the garage and that he'd raced off with a rocket launcher?

She shook her head. No way, because then they'd charge her as some accessory after the fact or something. She knew about the weapons for over a year and did nothing.

Better to distance herself from all this, move on, start over, and find a man who loved her more than weapons.

She reversed out of the driveway, took one last look at the house she thought she'd live in for years to come, and then drove away.

And she cried. Like a coarse blanket of emotion wrapped over her shoulders, weighing her down, she wept for the loss. Not just Ron, but what he represented. Comfort, a man she needed, yearned for, a warm meal together, laughing at a late-night movie, sipping wine. She cried for the loss of companionship and the end of the relationship, which was something she needed in her life.

But most of all, she just cried because there was too much pain in this world, and she heard once that if you didn't heal what hurt you, there was a chance you'd bleed on others, and Ron was bleeding on her, and whoever he was going to hurt tonight or in the coming days.

When this was all over, there would be a lot of people bleeding. She was sure of it.

Her tears didn't stop on the entire drive to Annemarie's apartment, and she wondered if tears ever ran out. She figured she'd learn soon enough if they did or not.

She was wiping her eyes when Annemarie opened the door. Annemarie's hug and warm embrace just brought on another bout.

And Julie wept harder.

Chapter 4

A VEHICLE ON AIRPORT Road bumped into another car, the crunch of metal and the sound of broken glass sharp and distinct. Another vehicle's tires squealed as they attempted to stop.

Sarah listened for anything to tell her the airliner had been hit and was falling to the runway in a heap of flames when airbrakes engaged in the distance. The airliner had landed safely. They'd done it.

"Stay down," Parkman whispered in her ear. "He's shooting at us."

He eased his weight off her and crawled away. She rolled onto her stomach and studied the darkened front of the repair shop. Nothing moved, and there was no glint of light coming from anywhere.

The shooter was gone.

She got up on her knees and saw that three cars had been involved in fender benders, with two of the drivers trying to help the third open their car door. Even from where she was, on the weed-covered grass beside the sidewalk, Sarah could easily see three bullet holes in the front quarter panel of a Buick. A small hole had also been punched through the back window of the Buick.

Parkman was rarely wrong about things like that. When he tackled her, the bullets missed them and hit that Buick.

Sarah whispered a few choice expletives and got to her feet.

Parkman popped up behind a four-door SUV and shrugged. The shooter was gone, just as she thought.

But where?

Sirens screamed in the distance.

Should they stay behind and try to explain this? And be stuck most of the night giving statements to the authorities, who didn't really care for her? Or stash their own guns and slink away to await further instructions from Vivian?

Whatever happened, the airliner wasn't hit. That was the important part, what they were there for.

"Parkman," she called, heading his way.

He started toward her.

"We should just go," she said. "The plane didn't get hit. The asshole's gone. We don't need to stick around unless Vivian tells me where he is."

Parkman nodded. "I agree. Too much trouble trying to explain our presence."

They stashed their guns and started back to their car as the sirens came to a stop on Airport Road.

"He didn't hit that plane, did he?" Sarah asked to be sure. "I mean, it all happened so fast. We would've heard it crash, right?"

"Whatever he shot at, he missed it."

"Because of us?"

"Who knows? Probably. We were there and firing at him. He fired back."

"Then we did what we came here to do."

Parkman glanced at her. "Barely."

"Agreed. Barely."

The people in the parking lot had drawn closer together, their voices louder.

As a unit, Parkman and Sarah gave them a wide berth, trying to keep to the shadows.

"There they are," a man shouted, pointing. "Hey," he added, breaking away from the crowd. "Who were you shooting at? The plane?"

With each word, his voice rose in volume, a challenge.

Several other men advanced on them as they tried to get around the group.

"Hey, we're talking to you," a taller man shouted, moving even closer to them. "Did you cause that car accident? We saw you run by us, and you had guns."

They were fifteen feet from the car when the taller man started running toward them.

Here we go, Sarah thought.

"You're not going anywhere," he shouted. "You can fuckin' wait for the cops."

Sarah spun around, drew her weapon, and ran several steps toward the man.

"Back the fuck up," she shouted. "This is none of your business."

Like a strong wind had hit the group, they all moved back and ducked down as if she was going to shoot. They probably believed she would if they thought she'd shot at those cars on Airport Road.

The tall man had stopped running toward them. He held his hands out at the side and tilted his head, a cocky smile pasted on his lips. She already understood what he was thinking. How could he save face after a woman had challenged his bravado?

She'd make it easy on him.

"Parkman, get the car."

"Already on it," he said, a distance from her.

Sarah stashed the weapon back in her pants.

He lowered his hands. "Big tough girl with a gun."

She crossed the six feet separating them in two strides and glared at him, a foot from his nose.

"When you were a little boy"—she kept her voice low so only he could hear—"didn't your mother tell you to pick your battles? This isn't your battle. You have no one to save here. I get it. I really do. You want to do the right thing." Parkman's rental started behind her. They'd be gone in seconds. "You don't need to know what we just did. All you need to know is that we're the good guys, just like you."

He blinked like he understood something. His eyes went distant briefly, then he focused on her and took her all in.

"Shit, you're Sarah Roberts. I saw you on the cover of —"

"Shh," she blurted, "don't say the name of that rag."

"And you were here?" He hesitated. "Saving someone?"

She nodded. "And now we're leaving."

He gave her a short nod. "Go, I've got you covered."

That made her frown. Covered? How?

A door opened behind her, and Parkman shouted for her to get in.

One step back, then two, and she slipped down into the passenger seat. She mouthed the word, *thanks*, to the man, and Parkman hit the gas, slamming her door shut with the force of the acceleration.

At the exit, they turned left away from Airport Road as two cruisers drove into the Wendy's parking lot.

Parkman hit the gas because, within seconds, one of those cruisers would be redirected after them.

A block down, he hooked a left, then a right.

"What did you say back there?" he asked.

"Just that it wasn't his fight. And then he recognized me."

"Recognized you?"

"Yeah, the media and shit. Posting all those photos of me."

"Sounds like it worked in your favor here."

"How so?"

"He wasn't a bad guy. I'd hate for you to have to shoot him."

"I wouldn't've shot him." She leaned down and looked in the side mirror. "Maybe an uppercut or something. A kick to the balls so we can take off, but nothing permanent."

Parkman took a couple of more turns, and then they were on Goreway Drive. She studied the little mirror on the side.

Only one pair of headlights followed them, and it wasn't a cop. Too high. An SUV or a pickup.

Parkman turned right. She caught a glimpse of the sign as they turned onto Rexdale Blvd.

"You're heading to the highway?"

"Yeah, so we can get lost in traffic and get you back out to Mississauga."

"Is anyone following us?"

Parkman checked his rearview mirror. "Not that I can tell."

"Watch that truck back there. I think he took several of the turns we took."

Parkman signaled to access the ramp onto the 427, heading south. Minutes later, they'd pass the 401 as they continued south to the Queen Elizabeth Way, which would take them to Sarah and Aaron's apartment.

"Is he still there?" she asked as Parkman merged.

"He is."

"That's a tail."

"You sure?"

"On a Sunday night? He happens to be going the exact way we're going—"

A siren started up behind them somewhere, cutting her off. She spun in her seat as Parkman cursed. About a hundred yards back, an Ontario Provincial Police cruiser moved into the lane beside theirs, his lights flashing, siren on.

"That for us?" he asked.

The truck behind them eased off toward the shoulder.

The cruiser moved in directly behind them and drove up only ten feet from their bumper.

"Looks like it."

Parkman signaled and started toward the curb.

"Now what?"

Sarah yanked her gun out.

"Wait, Sarah," Parkman blurted.

"You know me better than that," she said, stashing the weapon under the seat. "Sometimes I hate cops because they always find a way to fuck with me, but I wouldn't kill one. You know, unless he deserved it. Just don't let them search the car."

They stopped, and Parkman rolled down the window.

Sarah checked the mirror. The OPP officer just sat in his cruiser.

"What's he doing?"

"Probably waiting for backup."

"That doesn't sound good."

Behind the cruiser, the pickup that had been following them pulled back onto the highway. Sarah turned around and watched it drive by the cruiser and then pass them.

She could tell the driver was staring at her, but that was it. It was too dark inside his cab to see anything else. It looked vaguely like a female driver with all that long hair, but it could've been a man.

Then, the pickup was by them, and they headed south. On the side of the truck and the tailgate, black letters advertised a construction company called Ronald Harris and Sons.

"There goes that truck that was following us."

"Or it wasn't." Parkman placed his forearm on the door where his window was open. "Ronald Harris and Sons doesn't sound too ominous to me."

"Me either," she said softly, her mind racing.

"Another cruiser arriving—oh, scratch that, two more cruisers."

"This sucks. We could be detained all night. And what if our shooter does something again at another roadside stop where planes fly low enough for his weapon to hit them?"

Parkman glanced at her. "Vivian around? Is she saying anything?"

Sarah shook her head. "Gone."

"Well, sometimes we live by our own code, and other times we're like regular citizens. We can't go racing around Toronto firing weapons at rocket-launcher dudes without the cops wanting in on the action."

That made her laugh. "You make it sound so hip, so seventies. I could just see you in those days, rockin' it with bell-bottomed pants, kicking your arms out at the side, and talking about how groovy everything was. You'd say it's in the groove and dyno-mite." She used voice inflection on the word *groove*. "I've seen some American Bandstand on YouTube."

"That was never me," he said, still staring at the rearview mirror. "Now they're talking by the first cruiser. I don't like this."

Sarah peered over her shoulder through the back window. Five officers advanced on their car, four of them with weapons drawn.

"This doesn't look good."

"Agreed."

The OPP officer stopped by the back window without a

weapon in his hand.

"I'm going to need both of you to step out of the …" he called.

A large rig passed them two lanes over, obscuring some of his words.

"Step out of the car now," he repeated, much louder this time.

Parkman opened his door, showed his hands through the window, and used his knee to open the door the rest of the way.

After a moment, he was standing beside the car, and three officers circled him, placing cuffs on his wrists.

"You too, ma'am," the cop said.

Sarah cracked her door and repeated Parkman's procedure. They'd stopped the airliner crash. Vivian had given her nothing else so far. Neither she nor Parkman had jobs to go to in the morning—*this* was their job. So, there was no reason to fight or attempt to bolt. They'd talk to the cops, get released, and go home.

Once their story checked out and the rocket or whatever the fuck it was that guy shot at the plane was located, this chapter would be over.

Sometimes, it was better to work with the cops, even though she still struggled with that.

When they placed the cuffs on her, they weren't too gentle, but that didn't piss her off. She was learning empathy and understood that they were scared, too. They wanted to go home to their wives and children at the end of their shift. This might be considered a high-risk traffic stop, which is why the first officer waited for assistance.

"You have a weapon of any sort on your person?" one officer asked over her shoulder.

"No," Sarah said.

"Policy dictates we have a female officer check you, but none are available. So I will ensure you're not carrying anything that'll be a problem for myself or my fellow officers. That okay with you?"

Sarah nodded. "Go ahead."

The officer was kind and gentle. He kept his hands away from her crotch and breasts, only going where weapons were commonly concealed and easily grabbed. Once he found nothing, they spun her around to face the cruisers.

They were searching Parkman. She watched as an officer pulled his weapon from the holster strapped to his chest.

"You want to explain this?"

"I've got the permit."

"Sure you do." The officer was shaking his head. "This is Canada. You must have an Authorization To Transport to have this in your vehicle. And if you did, it would have to have a trigger or cable lock on it, have no ammo, and be in a locked box. The ATT authorizes you to transport it to one of five places, and I doubt you were on your way there with it in a shoulder holster."

The officer handed Parkman's gun to another cop, who slipped it inside a large plastic bag.

The officer moved back in front of Parkman. "Sir, carrying a concealed weapon here is a federal offense."

"You're wasting your time preaching to me about that weapon. I have an Authorization to Carry. I was able to demonstrate an imminent danger to my person a few years back that the authorities weren't able to protect me from. Guys working up in the wilderness get the same permit. Also, armed guards. I'm just an armed guard."

A couple of them laughed. "Okay, I'll bite. What was this imminent danger that we can't protect you from?"

Parkman looked over at Sarah. "I work with her."

Everyone was staring at her now.

"Is that Sarah Roberts?" one of the other officers asked.

"Damn, it is," the cop beside her said.

"Okay, that makes sense." The cop in front of Parkman nodded. "I could see that. But still, we have to check it out."

Parkman's weapon wasn't the one to worry about. The issue would be with the gun Sarah had. It was something Darwin had arranged for her a while back. No serial number, no ability to trace it. No permit to carry, either.

"You want to tell us why you stopped us, Officer," Parkman said. "I wasn't speeding."

The two cops handling Sarah started walking her to one of the cruisers. She allowed them to escort her without struggle.

One of Parkman's officers said, "You were both witnessed at the scene of a car accident on Airport Road." Then, as if an afterthought, the cop added, "With guns. And there are bullet holes in one of the vehicles."

"We were there, but we didn't fire at the car," Parkman said loud enough that she could still hear him. "We can explain."

"You'll get all the time you need to explain in a holding cell."

Before Sarah was placed in the cruiser's back seat, she

glanced back at Parkman. He was being escorted to another waiting cop car.

Two officers were leaning inside the rental. At any second, they would find the gun under Sarah's seat.

Things were about to heat up and get much worse for them. Something told her they were in trouble and that the pickup driver had something to do with it.

Before the driver of the cruiser she sat in pulled away from the curb, one of the officers examining the interior of their rental stood up, holding Sarah's weapon in his gloved hand, another officer supporting a bag to place their evidence inside.

Bagged illegal weapons at a roadside stop wouldn't bode well for them. Calling Darwin or Aaron wouldn't really do much.

Maybe Casper was around to help, but she doubted it. Last she heard, he was on a boat catching fish bigger than him in Lake Michigan, which wasn't far from Toronto, but he was taking time off. She couldn't ask him to come and work any magic to get them out of this jam.

Was Detective Marina Diner back from Texas yet?

Already trying to figure a way out, she was starting to feel there wasn't one. The only play was to play it out and see what happened.

Or Vivian would have to show up and fix this because she was the one who started it all.

Otherwise, they could stay in a Toronto jail cell for a long stay.

Chapter 5

JULIE HAD LEFT HER bags at the door as Annemarie poured two huge glasses of red wine. They retired to the living room, where Annemarie hit the mute button on the TV. Citypulse 24, Toronto's main news station, continued on soundlessly.

"Tell me what happened," Annemarie said, her tone soft and gentle.

Julie told her everything, leaving out a few of the bits regarding the weaponry. She didn't want Annemarie calling the cops.

"And he just left?" she asked.

Julie nodded, sipping from her wine glass. The tears had stopped shortly after getting inside Annemarie's apartment. They'd known each other for years, and Julie knew she could stay with her until she found a place of her own.

"Do you know where he was going?" Annemarie asked.

"Do you have any hints whatsoever? A name, a place, anything?"

Julie shook her head and studied the wine in her glass as she swirled it. "He didn't say, but I know it's not good."

"Because of that thing you said to him when he was leaving."

"Yeah, I told him not to do it, and he left anyway."

"When you say, '*not to do it*,'"—she used air quotes on those four words—"what are you referring to?"

"You see, that's the thing, I don't know. He's been wrapped up in finding his kids, and CAS won't tell him. Actually, he was told he could apply to the court, something about a motion to file. Anyway, he said he was going to make them listen. Then he spent all of yesterday afternoon in the garage working on something. When I came to get him for dinner, he had all his—" She stopped talking before she said *weapons*.

In one large gulp, she finished her wine.

"You were going to tell me what he had in the garage," Annemarie prodded, waving a hand in a come-on gesture.

Julie held up her glass. "Another one of these would help with the nerves."

Annemarie grabbed the bottle off the kitchen counter and returned with it, pouring Julie another glass, then she topped hers off.

"So what did he have?" she asked.

Julie drank more, then held up her free hand. "Okay, listen. I will tell you, but you must swear you won't say anything to anyone."

"Who would I tell?"

Julie waited a moment, her gut roiling, then glanced up and stared at her friend.

"Ron is a weapons collector."

Annemarie frowned. "So what? Big deal. Lots of guys are into that shit. My brother included."

"No, not like Ron."

Annemarie got serious, her face expressionless. She leaned forward on her chair, elbows planted on thighs, sipped her wine, then said, "Do tell."

"He collects illegal weapons."

"What's an illegal weapon? You mean the kind without a permit? Not such a big deal. Again, many people have illegal weapons."

Julie shook her head. She needed something stronger than wine for this. "Nothing Ron has would ever come with a permit."

"Okay, I get it, a scythe or some blade that's longer than the allowable length. I mean, that's what you're talking about, right?"

Julie shook her head one more time. "I'm talking rocket launcher, heavy artillery, assault rifles that only tactical units with the RCMP use. Something called an HK-33 and some other gun called a C8."

Annemarie's mouth dropped open. She held that pose until her mouth closed on the lip of her glass, and she swallowed the rest of her wine like water.

"You're joking," she whispered after a moment.

"Wish I was."

"What's he got all that shit for?"

"I don't know. To feel safe. I mean, something happened

to him on one of his peacekeeping missions, and now, he's just …"

She drifted off, not knowing what to say about how Ron had been changing.

"He's just what?" Annemarie grabbed the empty bottle, shook it, and got up. "One second." She ran to the kitchen and returned with another bottle, her glass full.

"He's just scary now. I begged him to stay. Don't do it, whatever *it* is. I could just feel he would do something, and it wouldn't be good. I can't go back." She lowered her head and stared at her lap. She didn't want to add that he told her to leave him, that he was no good. "I can't go back. His fanaticism or radicalism, or whatever the fuck*ism* it is, has destroyed what we had. Wherever he's going, he's on his own."

"Does he know you're here?" Annemarie asked.

Julie looked up. "That wouldn't matter. You're safe. His anger is aimed at CAS, his ex-wife, and the court system. Family law preaches fifty percent equalization, but it's bullshit. I watched as everything was stripped from that man. Then, when he ran low on money and couldn't even pay his suppliers, his business suffered." She took a breath to calm herself before getting too worked up. "And he prides himself on paying child support for two kids. But *she* got the house, and they assessed him on income for the past three years when his business was doing well. Now that he's behind, they want to take his driver's license. How the fuck can he work without his truck?"

Annemarie shook her head. "That makes no sense. Cripple him, then take his business, his truck, and let the bills pile up until what, he offs himself.”

Julie gasped. She hadn't thought of that. What if he was on a suicide mission of some sort? That would be a way out of the pain.

“Julie, I'm sorry,” Annemarie said, rubbing Julie's arm. “I shouldn't have said that.”

“It's okay, really—”

The phone rang.

“Who could that be at this hour? It's after midnight on a Sunday night.”

Annemarie picked up the phone gingerly. “Hello?” She listened momentarily, turned to Julie, and stared at her. “Yes, she's here.”

Could Ron be calling? Asking her to come home?

“He wants to speak to you,” Annemarie said, holding out the phone.

At first, she wanted to refuse. One night to cool off, one night to think about what was said in the garage. But if this was a call for help, a plea with an apology, she had to take the call.

One intake of breath, and she was ready. With the phone in hand, she placed it at her ear.

“I'm here,” she whispered.

“Julie, just know I'm truly sorry and love you.”

The tears started again, and she fought to keep the crying out of her voice.

Staring at Annemarie's carpeted floor, she said, “I love you, too.”

“But we can't carry on the way we were.”

More tears.

"Before I go underground, I wanted to—"

"Underground?"

"Off the grid, disappear."

"Oh, right." She set her wine glass down to wipe at her nose.

"Before I disappear, I just wanted you to know that I intentionally missed the plane."

"Missed the plane? Ron, what are you talking about? You were going to fly somewhere?"

"Just know that I missed the plane because I wanted to get Sarah's attention."

Her gut twisted up further. Who the fuck was Sarah?

"Ron, you're not making any sense. Are you seeing someone named Sarah—"

"Julie, listen to me. There was only you and me against the world. That's it. When this all comes out on the news, I didn't want you to think I tried to do what they said about me. I needed Sarah's attention. I got it, but then fucked that up, too. So, now I'm on my own and going off the grid."

Was he crying? She swore that the last sentence sounded strained.

"Ron, it's okay, just come home. We'll work it out. Together."

"Goodbye, Julie. You were the love of my life. Always were, always will be. This is the one time I have to go against the world alone. I'll see you on the other side. We'll be together again then. When we wake up at home, where we belong."

"Ron, don't talk like that." The line had died. "Ron!" she shouted into the phone. "Oh, Ron …" She let the phone drop from her hand as she bent over and rolled out of her chair.

Julie curled up on Annemarie's carpet and felt the world's pain in her soul, trying to crush her.

Life has become a nightmare. Maybe Ron was right about one thing. Heading over to the other side sounded good.

Perhaps death was the answer. At least then, this would all be over.

There was nothing left inside her but the tears.

Her Ron was gone. Her life was gone.

And who the fuck was this Sarah bitch that he sought her attention?

Chapter 6

UPON ARRIVAL AT THE police station, they'd placed Sarah in a small interview room. They'd removed the restraints and left her alone. Her cell phone and ID were taken, and all her loose change was removed from her person. There had been no phone call and no contact for over three hours.

Then the door opened, and a man and a woman stepped inside.

"About fucking time," Sarah whispered.

"Your schedule full or something?" the woman asked. "Gotta be somewhere?" The woman wore glasses and was dressed nicely, but she had a look in her eye that warned people not to mess with her.

The man was an attractive black man. He had a body like Terry Crews, with a face like Denzel. He pulled out a chair and plopped down, then tossed a pad of paper on the table with a couple of pens.

The woman leaned against the closed door. "You'll be with us for a while, Miss Roberts. No need to worry about your time."

"Yeah?" she said, sitting up straighter. "How's that?"

"My partner will fill you in."

The man stared at her. "I'm Detective Dover, and this here's Detective Vicky Budnack. We've been given this case because of who you are."

"And who am I, exactly?"

"An American visiting Canada. While here, you broke several serious laws on our soil."

"An international criminal, eh?"

The detectives exchanged a glance, and then Dover faced her again. "You've been here for some time, years, in fact, running roughshod over our city." He leaned forward and clasped his hands together on the table. She wondered if his sleeves would rip as his bulging arms fought for release. "Tell us what you're working on. Make it something worth taking to the judge upon your arraignment in the morning."

"I don't know what I'm working on." That was the truth, as Vivian hadn't been forthcoming, but it didn't sound good.

Budnack laughed as she pushed off the door, stepped behind her partner, and moved toward the other chair.

"How could Sarah Roberts," Budnack started, spun her chair around, then dropped onto it, "not know what she's working on?"

Something about Budnack bothered her. Maybe it was the cocky smile. Maybe it was how she tried to make it look like she was impressing her partner, yet she was in control of this interview. Sarah could tell Budnack was much more confident and disciplined. Her eyes, how she held herself, her poise, and even her strong hands. Her partner was a giant of a man, but there was a gentleness about him. Detective Budnack, on the other hand, was probably paired up with Dover because of how strong she was. As soon as she entered the room, she had commandeered the conversation, warning Sarah about time and how long she'd be with them. Was Budnack trying to scare her? Detective Dover—she kept seeing Denzel in her head—was playing to Budnack's lead.

Or was she falling for the age-old routine of good cop, bad cop?

"Has anyone spoken with the witnesses on Airport Road?" Sarah asked.

Dover nodded. "We have, and they paint an interesting picture."

"How so?"

"Parkman does, too," Budnack added.

Okay, Detective Vicky Budnack wanted to play hardball. Sarah respected her strength and would have to watch herself with this one.

"Of course he does." Sarah snickered. "Because Parkman would've spilled everything."

Budnack leaned farther over the back of her chair and smiled, showing teeth. "He did. And we hope your story matches his."

"You're too good, Detective Budnack." Sarah watched the woman's face to see if she detected the sarcasm. "This your first interrogation?"

Budnack glared at Sarah, then turned to Dover, but

Dover looked down at the pad of paper on the table, fiddling with his pen.

Budnack was in charge. Guaranteed.

Sarah waited a heartbeat, then said to Dover, "So, you spoke with the witnesses."

Dover looked up, and she was sure she saw a slight uncertainty on his face about how to conduct this interview with Budnack in the room.

"A small group of people stayed behind to speak with us. Allegedly, they saw you and Parkman get out of your car, glance around as if you were expecting to meet someone, then start running after you checked your phone."

"With your weapons drawn," Budnack added.

That warranted a glance from Dover.

"Who were you there to meet?" Dover asked.

"We don't know."

"Sarah," Dover said, releasing his hands and leaning back in his chair. It creaked under his bulk. "You'll have to give us more than that. Several cell phone cameras recorded you two running. We saw the weapons. Witnesses said you made it to the sidewalk on Airport Road, then started firing your weapons. Several cars got hit, Parkman tackled you, and then you both ran for your car. After three cell phones recorded most of that, we saw it as it played out, and so will the judge. The laws you two broke are quite serious. Talking is your only way out of five years as a minimum."

At the mention of five years, she felt physically ill. It wasn't the time as much as her biological clock. She'd be thirty-five in five years, and with each consecutive year, her chances of a healthy baby and healthy pregnancy decreased.

She'd already had a problem at the age of twenty-nine. Imagine the challenges at thirty-five.

"Do you know me?" Sarah asked.

Dover waited a moment, then lowered his head in a soft nod.

"And you know what I do, how I get my information? Have you read the tabloids, the rags out there?"

He nodded again. Even Budnack nodded.

"So you're aware I hear my sister?"

One more nod.

"Good, that'll save us time in unneeded explanations."

"The judge won't get any of that, though," Budnack cut in. "He'll be following the rule of law, and with both of you violating federal laws …"

She gave Budnack credit. This was a great time for her to add some piece about doing time and how they nailed her. The cops finally got Sarah Roberts on something that would stick.

"My sister gave me a message."

"What was it?" Budnack asked, leaning forward.

"Stop the matador beside Wendy. It wasn't stop the guy about to fire a MATADOR at a commercial airliner beside the Wendy's restaurant on Airport Road. He's hiding in front of the repair shop. No, it's never that clear. All she said was, the Matador beside Wendy."

Budnack cleared her throat. "So, that's why you appeared to be looking for someone?"

She nodded. "We wondered if we were looking for someone with a red flag or something."

"Until you looked up Matador on your phone?"

"Right."

"And found out it was a shoulder-fired rocket launcher?"

"Exactly. And then I recalled Vivian's words were, *beside* Wendy. So we ran as I understood we were running out of time."

"And you found him—"

"And fired at him toward the front of the repair shop where he was standing with the MATADOR, hence the discharging of our weapons."

"So if you fired at him toward the repair shop, how did those cars on Airport Road manage to drive into your bullets? Did you run across the street?"

She shook her head. "They weren't in our crossfire. When we shot at the perp, he shot back at us at least three times. That's why Parkman tackled me to the ground. So I wouldn't catch a bullet to the face."

Detective Dover picked up one of the pens on the table and tapped it several times. "Let me get this straight. If we pull ballistics on the bullets found in the cars in the accident, they won't be from your weapons?"

She nodded. "They won't be."

"That'll help some. I mean, it removes half a dozen charges from the long list still building at this time."

"You're joking, right? Is this some kind of interview technique?" Her anger was surfacing. She pushed it back down. They weren't the enemy. The situation was bad, but it could be fixed. At least, she hoped it could be.

"I wish I was joking. You've done a lot of good, but we can't sit by and allow vigilantism to go unchecked. What would the rule of law look like if anyone could take it into their own hands? That would be lawlessness."

"Yeah, you're done in this town," Budnack added. "Especially with what Parkman is saying. His story doesn't even come close to yours."

Sarah ignored her. Budnack was trying to goad her into talking. Parkman wouldn't say a thing. He probably stayed quiet the entire time unless he was to utter the word, lawyer. But then, his weapon was registered with the Canadian government. Parkman would check out. An old cop friend of theirs, Spencer, who was dead now for over a year, had vouched for Parkman's applications to be able to carry a holstered gun on Canadian soil. It took forever, but he got it.

Sarah, on the other hand, could not legally carry a gun. And they supposedly had it all on a cell phone recording. The ball was in their court because she actually had nothing more to offer them.

Unless …

"Did you catch the guy by the repair shop?" she asked.

Dover shook his head.

"Any evidence he was there?"

"We found the MATADOR. It had been fired once."

"Spent shell casings?"

Now Budnack nodded.

"The plane get hit?"

He shook his head.

"So, we did something right. Parkman and I shot at the guy, probably screwing up his aim, and then he got away. You know I'm on your side. Where's the problem?"

Budnack cleared her throat again. "How do we not know that it's your MATADOR and you and Parkman argued about it? One of you fired your weapon, creating the car accident. Then you had to abandon the idea and leave the MATADOR behind?" She shrugged. "Knowing you and some of the things we've read about, I could see you wanting a rocket launcher. I mean, everyone knows you hate cops."

Detective Budnack curled up the right corner of her top lip. It reminded Sarah of an image of Billy Idol for a moment before Budnack eased it back down.

"You're a fucking piece of work, you know that?" Sarah reminded herself to stay calm, but it wasn't working. "Why the hell would we ever need one of those things? And yes, the authorities and I haven't had the best relationship in the past, but I only kill the ones who deserve it."

Budnack didn't flinch, but Dover jerked back in his chair.

"Did you just threaten us?" Dover asked, acting surprised. Or was it the shock he was trying to portray for Budnack's sake?

"If you think that was a direct threat to your person, you should drop that police ID in your wallet and go get another job. That, or an education."

Budnack raised her hands. "Okay, calm down. No one's threatening anyone. And Sarah, you're not helping yourself by talking like that."

There was no denying Detective Budnack was the one in charge here.

Sarah leaned back. "You *suggested* that thing was ours. I could've just said, fuck you. Might've been easier."

"Again, not helping yourself."

She tapped the side of her head and glanced up to the corner of the room. "Wait, my sister's saying something."

She closed her eyes to listen, then opened them and stared at Dover. "Vivian says the same thing."

"What's that?"

"Fuck you." She leaned across the table. "I told you the truth. Twist it around all you like. Make up stories and create evil plots, but at the end of the day, the ballistics will match, the story on my end won't change, and we saved an entire commercial airliner from being hit by a rocket launcher tonight. Maybe he would've missed anyway, but surely he missed due to bullets rushing by his head like pissed-off hornets. I can live with that."

Dover studied her face for several seconds, and Budnack stayed quiet.

"Write it all down here," Dover said, spinning the pad of paper toward her. He shoved it across the table, then rolled the pens over. "We'll come back when you're finished to take you to meet the judge. If you want to make a call, you can do that then."

They stood up to leave. Budnack got to the door first, her hand on the knob.

Heat rose to Sarah's face as she realized Aaron would wake up alone, wonder where she was, and then make calls. When he found out, he'd come down to the station, bruised ribs and all, and end up going home alone. It was more ammo in his argument that she calm this life down.

Dover turned back before Budnack opened the door.

"Think about your words carefully, Sarah. Make it a truthful statement, and we'll see about getting you out of here for the weekend."

"This is Sunday night, well, Monday morning now."

He nodded. "I know. It'll be a week before you leave, and that's if you leave. Being an American, they'll press to detain you until trial. Probably seize your passport."

"Try and take my passport. My one phone call will be to my embassy in Toronto. Americans don't like their citizens detained on trumped-up charges. Sure, I carried a weapon illegally, but under the circumstances, it was warranted. No one got hurt, and people were saved. I have a solid reputation south of the border. Fine me, then. I'll pay it. Charge me, then. I'll fight it in court. But detain me for a week or longer?" She got to her feet, knowing they had gotten under her skin, and she allowed it to piss her off. She was more mature than that but found her mouth wasn't stopping. "All you're doing is letting that asshole with the rocket launcher try again."

Budnack stepped closer. Dover moved by the door. The woman had seen battle or something. Budnack wasn't intimidated in the least. She was all business. For that, she garnered Sarah's respect.

"Did you see the perp?" she asked. "Can you tell us anything about him? That would help your situation."

Sarah recalled the pickup that followed them, the female driver. Or was it a man with long hair?

"There was a pickup truck."

Budnack crossed her arms but didn't say anything.

Dover blinked, and he rubbed his chin once. "A pickup?"

"Yeah, it followed us from the parking lot."

"Did the officers see it?"

She shrugged. "You'll have to ask them. Check their dash cams if they were turned on."

"What can you tell us about this pickup?"

Budnack was smiling now. She could easily read her mind. Budnack thought she was making this up to create a story. Have the cops chasing phantoms. Smoke and mirrors shit. The old Sarah would've smacked that smile off her face, but she restrained the urge, fully aware she had to think about the future. One that was on the outside of these walls and included Aaron and possibly a baby one day. The attitude of one cop couldn't be allowed to take all that away from her.

"I can't tell you much, but it followed us until we were pulled over. Then, while parked on the side of the road, it drove by us slowly."

"Parkman didn't talk about a pickup," Budnack said.

"Yeah?" Sarah blurted. "Parkman didn't talk at all, and you know what I think about your—" She cut herself off before making it worse. She really had to work on those responses. Thirty was around the corner, and maturity came with it. Responsibility, too.

Dover leaned forward, whispered something to Budnack, and faced Sarah again. Budnack's face reddened, and Sarah smiled.

"You were saying," Dover said, "about it driving by slowly."

"Just that I didn't see much."

"How about color?" Budnack asked. "Size? Make? Model? Driver description? License plate, if we could be so lucky."

"I think it was white, but it's hard to tell in the lights on that section of the highway." She wouldn't tell them what she read on the side of the truck and the tailgate. The black letters that advertised a construction company called Ronald Harris and Sons. "The driver stared at us as she drove by slowly. Whoever it was paid extra attention to us on purpose."

"She?" Dover asked.

"The driver was shrouded in the dark. It was either a female with long hair or a man with long hair."

Budnack cleared her throat again. "Now we're getting somewhere. A white pickup followed you, and after you were pulled over, the long-haired driver passed your vehicle, paying extra attention to you. That about sum it up?"

Sarah nodded. "There was another small detail, but until I offer that, I want to speak with Parkman. You're going to want to let us know when we can leave this place, and then —"

The door smashed open so fast it caught Dover in the left shoulder. He was shoved sideways, lost his footing, and almost kissed the floor.

It was Budnack who saved him. She had jumped at the intrusion and dropped sideways, grabbing her partner a foot before he face-planted the tile.

Sarah had jumped, too, into a defensive stance Aaron had instilled in her years before. More of a reactionary thing now, hands up, feet spread, center of gravity low. In the brief moment it took to drop into the stance, she saw more cops entering the room. She lowered her fists, brought her feet back together, and stood to her full height.

"What the fuck?" Budnack shouted.

Dover brushed the front of his suit as he moved closer to the intruder, his chest not needing to be puffed out—it was already about to break the center buttons of his shirt.

"Who the hell are you?" Budnack asked. Her deep growl of a voice gave Sarah chills. The woman was all alpha, and she knew it.

"This prisoner is no longer your prisoner," the man said. "Sarah Roberts, please come with us."

A thousand questions raced through her mind. Was this Darwin's doing? Parkman called a lawyer? An old cop friend, someone she saved once?

But the most important question on her mind was the one Budnack asked. Who was this guy?

Detective Budnack brushed her hair out of her face. "You're not taking her anywhere until we know who you are and what gives you the authority to barge in here and claim our suspect."

The man yanked a folded piece of paper from his inside breast pocket.

"Your boss signed transfer papers. Call him if you want, but he didn't take too kindly to being woken up at four in the morning." The man turned to Sarah and waved his hand. "Sarah Roberts, please come with me."

"Detective Budnack?" Sarah said as the woman unfolded the papers and glanced at them. "That thing legit?"

After a brief moment, Budnack glanced over at Sarah.

"It appears to be real."

"Who are you?" Sarah asked the man.

"Sutton is my name, although I don't see how that matters. All the documents are in order. I have a vehicle waiting, Sarah. As you say, this is legit and fortuitous for you as you won't be going to any arraignments in the morning."

"Then where am I going?"

"For a short ride. To hear our deal. I will drop you off at home once we finish discussing terms." Sutton pulled a cell phone out of his pocket and extended his hand. "Here's your phone back. During the ride, you can have the police on speed dial if you need their assistance. In fact," he reached into another pocket, "here's your loaded illegal weapon."

"Hey," Budnack shouted. "Do not give that to her."

Sutton handed it over. Sarah took it, checked the chamber, and then slipped it into the back of her pants.

"What the fuck is this?" Dover asked.

"Yeah?" Budnack chimed in.

"This is my show," Sutton said, his volume increasing. "I'd suggest you go back to being detectives and work on another case. If you don't like what you see, look away. If you don't like what you hear, don't listen. If you don't like my methods, take it up with your boss." Sutton addressed Sarah. "We must leave."

With her weapon and cell phone back, she nodded at Budnack, then followed Sutton out of the building.

With that much sway, he had to have some kind of case that needed her unique help.

What mattered to her was the *going home* part. That clinched the deal for her. The phone and gun were extra icing and gravy.

Whatever Sutton wanted, there was probably no way she could help him.

Vivian gave her nothing and was still gone.

She wondered how the arrangement would change when she informed Sutton she wouldn't help him.

Would she have to hurt him?

She hoped not.

Chapter 7

THEY TALKED FOR SEVERAL hours into the night. Annemarie cracked open a bottle of Irish whiskey around two in the morning and microwaved several pizza pockets for each of them.

Julie felt better but knew it was the alcohol talking. Ron had left her and gone after some girl named Sarah.

"What did he say exactly?" Annemarie asked. "I don't understand that part about the plane."

"He said something about missing the plane on purpose and wanting to get Sarah's attention."

"Where was he going to fly to? And you don't know who this Sarah girl is?"

Julie exaggeratedly shook her head, her hair flying around her shoulders. "He said the news will lie about him and not to believe it."

"The news?" Annemarie sat up straighter. She lunged sideways across the loveseat she sat on, grabbed the remote, and hit the volume button. CP24 was covering a cooking show. There had been an accident, and someone got burned.

"Nothing there about planes," Julie said, her eyes closing. She needed sleep. And water. Maybe water first. Then sleep. She rarely drank this much, but it helped her get through the night.

Maybe just a little sleep first. And a pee. Wait, piss in the morning. Sleep.

"Tell that to the bladder," she whispered, her eyes closed.

"What?" Annemarie said.

Julie shot up. "Oh, shit, you scared me. I think I was drifting off, talking to myself. Damn, I have to piss." She got up, wobbled once, stabilized herself, and then waddled to the bathroom.

When she was finished, she grabbed a cup in the kitchen and poured a glass of water from the sink.

"Thanks for letting me crash at your place, Annemarie," she shouted into the other room.

"No problem. You're always welcome."

She drank the entire glass, then poured more.

"I know I just sprang it on you—"

"*Julie!*"

Annemarie's scream was so loud, even from the living room, that Julie's glass jerked in her hand, and she dropped it into the sink, where it broke into jagged shards.

"Holy fuckstick," Julie whispered.

"Get in here," Annemarie shouted again. "Someone tried to shoot down a plane with a rocket launcher."

Her eyes widened, and she lurched away from the kitchen counter. She turned around and ran right into the wall.

She moaned and rubbed her nose. Her knee ached, too.

"Hurry," Annemarie said, urgency in her voice.

Julie rubbed her forehead now. "I'm trying," she muttered. "Shit, that'll leave a mark."

She moved into the living room and stared at the TV screen, her hand still rubbing her forehead.

"… Police are unclear what caused the accident and aren't offering too many details at this time," the news anchor said, "but an inside source claims witnesses saw the American vigilante, Sarah Roberts, along with someone else, at the scene. Police have arrested her while fleeing the area. We'll have more on this breaking news story as it develops. We'd like to repeat no harm came to the aircraft that an unknown suspect attempted to shoot down with what some are calling a surface-to-air missile. Teams are scouring the area around the airport. At this time, Pearson will remain closed with no flights in or out for at least another hour until the authorities reopen it. That's your Breakfast Television news for this early Monday morning …"

"Holy shit," Julie mumbled.

"I know, right." Annemarie nodded as she hit the mute button again. "He tried to shoot down a fucking airliner at the Toronto airport. Why Julie? To get Sarah's attention? Sarah Roberts? *The* Sarah Roberts? Holy fuck, Julie, what's Ron up to? When he said he missed the plane, that's what he meant. He wasn't flying anywhere. He was trying to shoot one down. And to get Sarah's attention? Well, shit stick, he got more than Sarah's attention."

Julie dropped into the easy chair, misjudged how far it was, and slid to the floor off the front of it.

"What has he done?" she mumbled to herself. The room wasn't spinning anymore. The news had sobered her up enough to feel fear and anxiety. Ron was dead, or he would be soon. The best-case situation would be jail. But how long would he be gone? His boys would be full-grown by the time he got out after what he'd done.

In one crazy moment, Ron destroyed his entire world. It might as well have been suicidal because he will leave behind so much pain. Her loss, her pain, and the boys that need him. Everyone hurting while he's dead or in jail. How could he do it? *Why* did he do it?

To get Sarah's attention? Sarah Roberts?

Who the fuck is she to him?

Annemarie was already on her computer, typing like a stenographer in a courtroom.

"What are you doing?" Julie asked.

"Reading up on Sarah Roberts."

"Why?"

Annemarie blinked, pulled back from the screen, and stopped typing. "Because I've known Ron a long time, and I have no idea who this Roberts woman is." She met Julie's gaze. "Why would Ron want her attention?"

"I have no idea." She pushed up off the floor. "Got any more of that Irish shit?"

Annemarie nodded. "It's on the counter in the kitchen over the dishwasher. Pour me a double."

"Let's just finish it. I won't sleep much now. Need

medicating."

Julie found the bottle, poured four fingers into two glasses, left them neat, and returned to Annemarie at the computer.

They clinked their glass once, then sipped from them. The whiskey burned fresh, and it calmed her nerves.

"You're not going to believe this." Annemarie pointed at the screen.

"What?" Julie leaned in closer to read what Annemarie was pointing at.

"Sarah had a miscarriage last February. It's all over the news because she was recently in Texas working with the FBI to bring down a human"—she moved closer to the screen—"procurement company." She turned to Julie. "What the fuck is that?"

"Organ donor shit."

"How did you know?"

"Look." Julie pointed two paragraphs down. "See? Organ donor shit."

"Oh, my fuck." Annemarie was back reading the screen. "Apparently, she saved some kids on a van and then fought something called True Legacy because they took limbs from a young girl."

Julie stepped away from the table. "Do you think Ron wanted to meet with her to talk about getting his kids back?" She frowned. "Man, that sounds so stupid. Why the hell would Sarah help him with his kids?"

"Too late now," Annemarie said. "Sarah's in police custody."

Julie turned back to face the screen. "Is Ron mentioned

anywhere on the news?"

Annemarie typed Ron's full name into the search engine. After scrolling through a few articles, she stopped and grabbed her whiskey.

"Nothing on Ron. Just the usual stuff. His construction company, his website. That's it."

"He got away with it." Julie moved back to the easy chair. "He got away with it, and now Sarah's been arrested."

"You think she had nothing to do with it?"

"Annemarie, Ron said on the phone not to believe what they said on the news. He intentionally missed the plane. It was only to get Sarah's attention. He said he fucked that up, too."

"Looks like he got a lot more attention than he bargained for."

Something was missing from the equation. Ron had a plan of some sort, and sure, it got screwed up, but why reach out to Sarah? She'd heard the vigilante's name in the past but didn't think much of it. She had been at a concert at the Roy Thompson Hall when something happened at the Roger's Centre. Some professional hitman was trying to take out a guy in the stands. The baseball game ended when the fans stampeded out of the place. Then cops stormed the CN Tower. The band she was watching was told to end a few songs early so everyone could be escorted out of the building.

But that was years ago. Many years ago. Since then, she'd seen Sarah's name in the news here and there but didn't think much of it.

So why now, Ron? Why Sarah?

After a couple of sips of whiskey, a piece fell into place. While Annemarie quietly scoured the internet on her computer, Julie examined their relationship, Ron's slow downfall, the loss of his kids, and the anger, the fanaticism.

She fought for a connection to Sarah Roberts, and one came up. It was weak, but it had to be right.

Ron was just crazy enough to do it, too.

He was a fan of Stockholm Syndrome. He'd read every book on the topic a year ago. He was a military man, über disciplined.

The weapons weren't to go after the Children's Aid Society workers or anyone at the Canada Revenue Agency. They were for Sarah.

Once he had Sarah, he would plead his case and convince —no persuade, order—her to help him.

Apparently, she was psychic. There's a chance she'd just know where his kids were. Sarah was the only one who could find Ron's kids, fight to retrieve them, and not only have the balls to do it but the heart as well.

She'd just lost a child herself. Of course, she'd be on board.

But Ron forgot one thing. And that one thing might get him killed.

He had a woman like Julie who would do the same things for him if he'd just asked—minus the psychic part.

She drank back the last two fingers in one gulp.

A plan of her own had formed.

She was ready to take back her life and her man and win his freedom.

"After all," Julie said, staring at her empty glass, her eyes swimming. "No one knows who he is."

"What's that?" Annemarie asked.

Drunk talking out loud was something she'd have to watch going forward.

"Sorry, talking to myself about Ron. I just can't believe what he did, is all."

"Me neither." Annemarie shook her head. "Me neither."

She'd sleep. In the morning—probably lunchtime—she'd head back home.

There were weapons in the garage that she needed.

Someone else was looking for Sarah Roberts now—Ron's woman.

Without Ron, what was she anyway? Self-worth was hyperbolic shrink talk. Together, they were a team, unbeatable. Together, they were *us*.

They'd always called themselves *us*.

His call tonight wasn't about saying goodbye again. It was code. A message. To follow him down the rabbit hole.

He told her to leave him and move out, but that was Ron's way of protecting her. He was still protecting her from afar, from the damage he was about to create. But it didn't work out in his favor, and he called her to let her know.

Because Ron loved her and needed her.

And she would answer his call for help.

He knew her better than anyone and knew that phone call would clinch the deal.

Julie rose from her chair and started down the hallway.

"I'm coming, Ron," she whispered as she made her way to the bathroom. "Just hold on, baby. I'm coming because it's always been us. Us against the world. Us against the world, baby."

On the toilet, while leaning against the bathroom counter, she rested her head on the folded towel Annemarie had put out for her. She finished thinking about her plan as she peed.

Every last weapon in that garage could fit in her bug. She'd drive to Toronto and find Sarah and fix this.

She'd fix it all right.

"Uth againth the worlth," she muttered, her mouth pressed into the towel. That last bit of whiskey had been too much for her small frame, and she needed sleep for her plan to work.

Hours later, she woke with a splitting headache and sore back muscles, still sitting on the toilet.

Chapter 8

"You want to tell me more than just your name, Sutton?" Sarah followed the man up the stairs to the main level of the OPP building. "Like who you are, who you work for, and how you have the power to grant me release."

"Gratitude," he said over his shoulder.

"Excuse me?"

"Just be grateful. You're free of these pencil necks and in our custody."

"I have gratitude coming out of my ass, but I still want to know who I'm leaving with. You know, stranger danger and all."

He looked back at her but kept walking.

She stopped at the doors that led outside. It had to be less than an hour before daybreak. The building was mostly empty, with only a few officers in uniform coming and going.

Sutton had gone through the first set of doors before realizing she had stopped. He glanced back at her. To his credit, he didn't beckon or wave. The man stared for a count of five, then pivoted on his heels in a way that reminded her of a military about-face and came back to stand in front of her.

"Okay. What do you want to know?"

She stared up into his eyes. "Are you a threat to me?"

"No. And why ask such a question, Sarah? Even if I were, I wouldn't tell you."

"You may lie, but your eyes won't. Where's Parkman?"

"At your apartment with your boyfriend."

She frowned. "Why?"

"Why is he there specifically? Or why is he not here?"

"Both."

Sutton inhaled, held it, then said, "Parkman was released shortly after arriving here"—he jerked his arm up, glanced at the watch on his wrist, and dropped his arm back to his side —"approximately four hours ago. His information checked out. Yours didn't. He's at your place explaining to your boyfriend, Aaron Stevens, that you'll be held for several days, if not longer."

She crossed her arms and took a step back to evaluate the man.

Vivian? You wanna tell me what this is all about?

"Anything else?" Sutton asked.

"Yeah, where are we going?"

"To talk."

"I get that. But where?"

"I don't care. Anywhere but here."

"Talk about what?"

Sutton glanced around the building, his eyes roving past her shoulders, then refocusing back on her.

"Not here. Confidential."

"Confidential?"

As if this was some cloak-and-dagger DND game, he leaned in closer and whispered, "Top secret shit."

His smile won her over. The man wasn't all machine, all robot, even though he'd come across as a military leader of some kind. He had heart and was willing to play by her rules, at least a little.

"Okay," she said. "I'll go. But one more question."

He nodded, his eyes never leaving hers.

"How long?"

"One hour. Tops. After that, you go home. This," he gestured at the interior of the police station, "becomes one more page of your history. Or, you might agree to work with us for a few days. That's it."

"Work with you for a few days? On what?"

That smile again. "Top secret shit."

"We're going in circles," she said, acknowledging the truth out loud.

He nodded. "Circles."

"You have a vehicle?"

He was still nodding. "Three, in fact."

"Three? Wow, you must be somebody high up in the military to commandeer three."

He blinked. Not a normal blink, one heavy with understanding, leaden with awareness.

"Shall we?" he said, holding the door open for her.

Sarah stepped outside. Three black SUVs were parked at the curb, idling.

"Shit, had I seen these, I would've guessed FBI, but this is Canada, and the FBI rarely work up here driving those things."

They strode across the concrete walkway toward the waiting vehicles.

"You're not an FBI wannabe, right?"

He just kept walking without answering verbally or otherwise.

"You remember you gave me back my weapon, right?"

Still no answer.

"And I have my cell phone. I could call Aaron so he wouldn't worry."

"You could," Sutton said. "But wait an hour. Chat first. Better for you."

They stopped outside the middle SUV.

"Better for me? How's that?"

He appraised her, arching one eyebrow high. "You have an odd way of responding by always repeating a small portion of what I said."

"Huh, get to know me. There are a few other oddities you wouldn't like much."

The door opened. Inside were two heavily armed men.

"SWAT team let out early today," she said to Sutton. "Giving them a ride home?"

"I realize this may seem like overkill, but the people we're hunting are extremely dangerous."

"Hunting?"

"Please, Miss Roberts, I implore you. Get in the vehicle

so we can discuss your potential involvement."

Both armed men wore green combat fatigues and vests equipped with dangling grenades, sheathed knives, guns strapped to their thighs, helmets, mouthpieces, and everything else imaginable, plus an assault rifle on their laps. That gave her pause. Vivian wasn't there to tell her if they were friends or foes. She had to go on gut instinct, and her gut was telling her this was okay—marginally.

She climbed in to sit beside the shorter of the two men. Sutton climbed in and took a seat opposite her. The short man slammed the door closed, reached over his shoulder, and tapped the wall behind his head with his knuckles. The SUV skirted away from the curb. In the back window, the other SUV followed, and she assumed the one in the front was leading the way.

"One hour," Sarah said. "So, what's this all about?"

"It's all about you, Sarah," Sutton started. "And how did you come to know about that MATADOR tonight? There's an international arms dealer in Toronto, and he's moving millions of dollars of merchandise across the province. When your name came up in connection with the MATADOR found at the scene after the attempt to shoot down an airliner, we thought we'd have a chat." Sutton leaned forward and clasped his hands together. "So tell me, Sarah Roberts, what do you know about the MATADOR and this arms dealer?"

This wasn't starting well. Her hand twitched. She wanted to reach for her weapon, order them to stop, get out, and Uber home. But they'd come for her. They knew too much. It wasn't hard to recognize powerful men when she met them.

The man to her left adjusted himself. She caught a

glimpse of him moving his weapon in her direction.

"You've kidnapped me?" she asked.

"Quite the contrary. You came of your own free will."

"Then stop the vehicle. I want out."

"That's not possible." Sutton checked out the side window. "It appears we're on the QEW. We couldn't leave you here as it's an elevated highway."

"And if I draw my weapon?"

"It's been rendered useless."

Without missing a beat, she asked, "My cell phone?"

"Useless. A fake sim was put in it. Upon cursory examination, it would look the same to you as it's actually your phone, but it doesn't work."

"And if I throat punched you, then killed these two?"

To his credit, Sutton didn't blink this time. "There are two other vehicles full of armed men. You wouldn't get far." He sat back in his seat, appraising her. "I appreciate and respect your talents, but I don't fear you, Sarah. You'll do the right thing."

"And what's the right thing?"

He smirked quickly, then it was gone. "Tell us everything you can about the arms dealer, the weapons, the MATADOR. Help us stop them."

"What if I don't know about any arms dealer?"

"Ask your sister."

"She's been strangely absent lately. Looks like I'll be of little help after all. You can just drop me off at the nearest corner, and I'll catch an Uber home."

"But Sarah, you haven't heard my proposal."

"Proposal?"

That smirk again. Right, because she's repeating his sentences. *Shit, is that a nervous twitch I've developed?*

"Help us, and we'll help you."

"I don't need any help."

"Of course you do. My superiors have been tracking you as you walk that fine line between the law and the lawless. Sometimes, like tonight, you needed a hand. My bosses have the power to give you that hand."

"Who are your bosses?"

"They prefer to remain nameless at this time."

"Right. Confidentiality and all."

He nodded. "I'm sure you'll be able to meet them one day. But for now, we must chat about the weapons and the arms dealers. We are hunting dangerous people, and what you did tonight put you on their radar."

"What I did tonight was stop a madman from—"

"We know," Sutton said. "And all we want to know is how you came to be there. Although we listened to your entire chat with Detectives Dover and Budnack, you didn't finish your description of the driver of that pickup. He's the party we need to know more about."

"I told them everything I know." *Except the construction company name on the side of the pickup.* But why tell these guys after they kidnapped her?

"Sarah, I hope you don't mind me using your first name."

She shook her head. "No issue."

"Sarah, you're holding out on us. You know something else about that pickup truck. I've interviewed a lot of people, and I recognize the tells. Dover and Budnack missed it, but in that interview room, I saw something. Call it a flicker in the eye, a twitch of a facial muscle, but there's more you're not saying. And it's information we need."

The armed man beside her clutched at his earpiece, then nodded.

"Sir, permission to speak."

Sutton nodded.

"Echo Foxtrot spotted a tail, sir."

"Echo Foxtrot?" Sarah said.

Sutton jerked a hand over his shoulder, his thumb pointing backward. "The vehicle behind us," he said to her, then addressed his man. "Off the highway. Next exit."

The man spoke the order into his mic, and then the SUV sped up and moved to another lane. No gradual lane change was involved. Sarah had to grab the door to avoid shouldering into it.

"We'll continue our discussion in a moment."

"I'm going to need a gun. One that works."

"No. You will not."

The SUV had to be going a hundred clicks as it descended an exit ramp. Her stomach lifted like falling from the crest of a rollercoaster. Although the windows were heavily tinted and it was still quite dark out, Sarah could recognize Spadina Avenue.

"How dangerous are these people?" she asked. "Tell me something about them. I mean," she pointed at the two heavily armed SWAT team members in the SUV with them, "they have to be dangerous if we're running from them."

"They're a group of ex-military mercenaries. They formed their own team and operate out of a Toronto location, which we're still trying to pin down. They're all dead men."

"Dead men?"

"Faked their deaths. Fingerprints burned off. They don't exist. We tried to tail one once. Didn't work out."

The SUV took a hard right. To his credit, the armed man beside her didn't fall into her. He clutched at the door and held his position on his side of the seat.

"Fuck," she whispered. "This driver have a license?"

"The best driver we've got."

They hit another turn hard. All four of them swayed to the right, then left, then back again as the driver raced through the circuitous streets.

"Mercs, eh?" she said. No one answered her. "Dangerous? Why didn't the tail work out?"

"Made him within a block. He was dead on the second block."

She did not like the sound of that. "These guys don't fuck around."

Sutton met her gaze and shook his head as they rounded another corner.

She tried to glimpse the SUV behind them through the window while they were turning, but it was up too close. All she saw was their back end.

The roar of an engine caught her attention. It wasn't their engine—someone else was close.

After another high rev, she scrunched up her face at the window as she tried to see where it came from.

A large Hummer was tailing the rear SUV with men suspended on the outside of it, weapons strapped to various parts of their body.

This was downtown Toronto, but that image made her

think of Humvees racing through villages in a foreign land. It was like a war was raging around them.

The engine revved again, followed by the sound of crunching metal.

"I'm not enjoying the ride, Sutton. Any chance you could drop me back into police custody?"

The man beside her had his hand at his ear again.

"Sir," he said, his voice sharper, more severe now. "Echo Foxtrot has been hit, sir."

"Hit?"

"They're out. We need to evacuate immediately—"

Something exploded behind their vehicle. The back end lifted, then dropped, tossing them off their seats. Sarah grabbed the door and held herself in place with a hand pressed firmly against the roof.

The rear window shattered inward as their SUV connected with the asphalt again, fishtailing back and forth as the driver attempted to regain control.

"Find a park," Sutton shouted over the wind rushing through the back window. "Avoid residential areas."

"I need to be armed," Sarah yelled at him.

"No," he shouted back.

Another explosion shoved the SUV a few feet to the left. It rocked hard, knocking Sarah into the man beside her. He must've anticipated her smashing into him as his right arm wrapped around her, steadying her.

There was no time to thank him as another explosion blew out several of their tires. Both armed men prepared their assault rifles as the SUV bumped along on its rims. When it crawled to a halt, they swung the doors open and jumped out as if they'd done it a hundred times, like from helicopters behind enemy lines. No thought, nothing to it. Engage the enemy and pray you live through another day.

Sutton was tapping something on his phone.

"Got a way out of this?" she asked.

"Two vehicles have been—"

Weapons fire outside the SUV cut him off.

"Fuck," he swore. "How did they know we were there?" He set his phone down on the seat beside him and glanced up at Sarah straight-faced. "It was you."

"Me? Fuck you. I had nothing to do with this." She took a breath. "How do you figure?" Her nerves were firing, and her heart was racing. Whoever was attacking their entourage was executing Sutton's men one by one. Something told her she should've stayed at the OPP station and avoided this ride. Where was her sister to warn her? Although she had said bloodshed and heartache. Maybe this was the bloodshed part.

More weapons were fired outside the SUV. Someone grunted close to the open door. She thought about closing it but realized she might have to dive out at a moment's notice.

"The MATADOR is linked to you now," Sutton was saying. "Your name is all over it. The morning news mentioned you by name. These guys probably had a team outside the OPP station waiting for you. They watched when we left. They watched you get in the middle vehicle. They've come for you, that's why the other two"—more weapons fire interrupted him—"SUVs were destroyed, but this one hasn't been torched yet."

"Well, that's just great. I know nothing about that MATADOR thing, and these guys can go fuck themselves."

Sutton was shaking his head. "These are the kind of men who don't care what you say. They know pain. They'll learn everything they want, then dispose of you."

"You're not making them sound too friendly."

"Sarah, I'm sorry." He leaned forward, extending the hand with the cell phone in it. "Take this. If I don't make it out of here, call General Whyte. Tell him who you are and what happened here. He'll get you out, providing you're still alive."

The armed man who sat beside her in the SUV moments ago crawled into view at the open door. His face was covered in blood, a wound in his neck spurting what was left of his life into the grass.

His eyes were already glassing over, and his movements were restricted by lack of blood and the realization he had seconds left. He withdrew the handgun strapped to his thigh, pulled back his arm, and tossed it at Sarah. The strength needed to lob the weapon was incredible in his condition. Sarah caught it before it smacked her ankle.

When she looked back at him, his forehead rested on the grass, the one eye she could see was closed, his throwing arm outstretched on the grass.

The man was gone.

Sarah jammed Sutton's cell phone in her pocket.

"I removed the password," Sutton was saying. "The phone is ready to use. Call General Whyte. He's on speed dial in the contacts."

Then Sutton withdrew two small weapons from inside his jacket and moved to exit the SUV.

Outside, a tall man, fully wrapped in protective gear,

stepped into view, wearing a motorcycle helmet. He gazed at Sarah, then down at the man with the neck wound who lay at his feet.

His right hand held a large handgun. He aimed it at the back of the man's head and fired two rounds into his skull from two feet away. The man's body barely jerked as he was already dead.

All this happened in the space of no more than four seconds.

Then Sarah was raising her weapon, and the helmeted man was turning toward her.

She'd forgotten the safety. That thought raced through her mind as she pulled the trigger, and nothing happened.

But it didn't matter.

Sutton was already firing both of his weapons in rapid succession. The helmet didn't break as bullet after bullet deflected off it. But Sutton got lucky. One of his first shots hit the man's exposed wrist where a small area had opened between his glove and his sleeve.

The man moaned and tried to raise his weapon again, but his hand wasn't obeying.

Sarah frantically searched for the safety on her weapon.

Sutton shot by her in a flash, diving from the van. He tackled the man to the ground.

The safety now off, Sarah raised her weapon, her heart in her throat. She hadn't been through a high-adrenaline gun battle like this in years. For her, it wasn't a learned skill, exactly. Sometimes, it was a matter of outthinking the other guy, something you made it through on instinct, luck, or a combination of both. Everyone wanted to stay alive, and that's what was at stake here. Who would walk away, and who wouldn't?

Another gun fired close to the open door.

Sutton pushed upward. The helmeted man wasn't moving. Behind the SUV, through the broken window, another helmeted man was approaching with a large device strapped to his shoulder.

"Sutton," she shouted. "Behind you."

She lifted her weapon, but the man walking their way fired his before she got a shot off.

Sutton dropped with half of his head disappearing in a mist behind his body. His legs and arms jerked and spasmed on the ground.

Everyone was dead. All of them. She was the only one still breathing from all three SUVs.

"Holy fuck," she whispered to herself.

She aimed carefully through the broken rear window and emptied the weapon in the man's direction.

His body jerked with the first few bullets as they bounced off his protective wear, but one must have gone through because he dropped to his knees, grasping at his chest near the neckline.

Seconds later, he fell flat on his face.

Car doors slammed from somewhere near the front of her SUV. More men were coming.

This wasn't over, far from it.

Sarah dove out the side, rolled in the grass around the dead SWAT guy until she was at the rear bumper, then peered around the edge. Four fully armed men in motorcycle helmets had exited another Hummer and were walking toward her vehicle with assault rifles aimed from their waist.

"What the fuck is going on?" she whispered.

Her adrenaline was at an all-time high, and she was firing on all cylinders, but her legs shook, and her stomach was flipping a toxic stew. She hadn't feared for her life like this in years.

There seemed to be no way out.

So she stayed low and ran in the opposite direction of the on-coming assault team. She made it fifteen feet before they began firing into the SUV. Glass shattered, the metal made thunking sounds, and Sarah kept running.

At a large tree, she huddled behind it, looking back.

The men had stopped shooting, and one of them jumped inside the SUV. It was completely ruined, the side of the SUV looking like pointillism gone mad.

The man jumped out and said something Sarah couldn't hear from where she was, and then the entire team turned in slow circles, looking for her. They all moved several feet away from the ruined SUV as if preparing to begin a search in grid formation but then stopped.

Sarah didn't move. She wasn't about to let them know where she was that easy.

One of the men stepped forward, then spoke over his shoulder to his team.

In the distance, sirens screamed in the early morning calm. Of course, someone called the police. What took them so long?

The entire attack probably lasted no more than four or five minutes, but it was enough to kill every single member of Sutton's team, him included.

After speaking among themselves for another few seconds while still scanning the area, they started back toward the Hummer as a unit. They were inside and driving away before the first siren was a block away.

They'd be back. Whatever Sutton was hunting had been hunting him in the end. And now the crosshairs were on her back.

She couldn't go home. They'd be waiting. She couldn't go back to the cops. If Sutton's team lost that easily to these mercs or whoever the hell they were, going to the police would only result in the death of cops.

No, she had to do this on her own, whatever *this* was.

Or maybe with Vivian's help. Although, her sister couldn't be counted on lately.

Would this General Whyte do something for her?

She eased away from the tree and started walking, stashing the weapon Sutton's man tossed her, the grief at the loss of life filling her heart with sorrow.

Alone, three blocks from the site of the attack, Sarah dropped onto a park bench as the sun rose and cried for what she had just endured. It all happened so fast. Everyone reacted, the men from years of training, her by gut instinct. So many lives lost. Too many.

She wept for what she had to do and the bullseye Sutton had put on her back.

Or was it all Vivian's fault?

After all, she was the one who sent them in search of a MATADOR beside the Wendy's.

Her head shot up.

Parkman.

They would know about him. He was at the Wendy's with her. There was cell phone coverage of them together. Sutton said the news had the story.

Parkman was with Aaron at their apartment.

She had to warn him.

Now.

It all ends in bloodshed and heartache, Vivian said. Was that the bloodshed?

If so, she couldn't imagine the heartache if the mercs were already at her apartment.

Her fingers trembled as she dialed Parkman's number.

Chapter 9

"And that was it," Parkman said.

"So what's next?" Aaron asked. "They're going to hold her in jail because she's an American?"

"That's basically what they told me." He lifted the coffee cup to his lips, supporting it with both hands. "We'll find a lawyer, at least work on getting her out of there. She has friends here. I'm confident we'll get her out soon."

Aaron stood by the stove after placing several bacon strips in a cast iron frying pan. He grabbed a spatula and positioned each piece to cook evenly, then grabbed his coffee and spun around to face Parkman.

Parkman eased sideways to look at the counter. "Why are you cooking so much food?"

"The boys are coming for breakfast."

Parkman glanced up at the wall clock. "This early? I

woke you at five after they released me."

"I was up most of the night waiting on Sarah. When she didn't show up and I saw the news, I called them. They should all be here any moment."

"There's nothing we can do. Sarah's in a holding cell."

Aaron nodded and sipped his coffee. "Having friends around helps. We'll figure something out for Sarah."

Parkman drank from his cup as the bacon sizzled on the stove.

"I don't know," Aaron said. "For me, it seems like a big waste of time going out on a limb like that if Vivian isn't more forthcoming. She has to give Sarah tangible information so you guys can avoid using guns and running from crime scenes."

"If Vivian had told us everything, we could've been waiting for that guy to drive up, had a word with him, and it would've been settled. Sure, running up to him at the last second isn't good for anyone. But we can't lose sight of something here."

"What's that?" Aaron turned back around to tend to the bacon.

"Vivian always has a plan. It might look like she's absent, but she's always there, on the sidelines."

"Yeah, while Sarah takes the fall."

"She's never actually taken the fall."

Aaron shot him a glance as he cracked an egg into the pan beside the bacon.

"Seriously," Parkman said. "For a decade, she's been shot at, stabbed, incarcerated, attacked by thugs, street gangs, cops, you name it, but she's spent no time in prison, other than holding cells, and even traveled the world dealing with human trafficking and cartels."

"I know about most of that and even the cartel." He held up the hand with the missing finger. "All I'm saying is, why can't Vivian just tell her more? If the phone line from Heaven is already open, tell Sarah all of it at once."

"I get it, and all I'm saying is sometimes that wouldn't work. Vivian knows what Sarah will do. She knows what'll happen and gives her just the right dose of psychic knowledge when needed. Back in Los Angeles, when Sarah was helping the LAPD stop some guy who was killing priests —"

"I remember that one, too," Aaron cut in. "She saved us from that church explosion."

"Yeah, and saved herself by hunkering down in the crypt of that church while it burned. Anyway, in a parking lot off Sunset Blvd, a guy pulled an M1911 handgun on her. He had it in her face, and Vivian described the make and model and how to disarm it because, on the M1911, the slide stop can be depressed from the reverse side to incapacitate the weapon. Sarah didn't know any of that on her own, and we were able to walk away. She's always there when needed. Somehow, this is all Vivian's plan."

"Could Vivian have fucked up this time, and Sarah's lost without her? I mean, why not just make it easier?"

Parkman thought back to that night in Los Angeles. They'd been looking for a Mercedes but then found out at the last minute that Mercedes was a woman. Maybe Aaron had a point, but Parkman still believed Vivian had Sarah's back.

"You watch. Sarah won't spend a week in their holding

cell. She'll be out in no time." He drank the rest of his coffee as Aaron put the bacon and eggs on plates. "In fact, she'll be out today. I'm sure of it."

"And if she isn't?" Aaron said.

"Then we'll speak with a lawyer."

Aaron set the plates down and turned back to get utensils.

"Look, I know you love her." Parkman set his coffee cup down. "I do, too. We all do. And you want to take care of her, get married, have kids." They exchanged a glance. Parkman regretted saying the word *kids*. It had been a hard time for both of them. "It's just, this is Sarah's life, her thing. And until she stops for good," Parkman shrugged, "it will be the way it will be. Even if she heard a whisper from Vivian to stand on the corner of Yonge Street and Bloor downtown for three hours, she'd do it. That would be all she needed to know. Her trust in Vivian runs thick, even if her sister pisses her off half the time."

They ate in silence for a minute before Aaron said, "Ever since we've been together, I've known what she does, and still, I can't seem to get past it."

"My first response is, then maybe you're with the wrong girl, but I won't say that because you two are made for each other."

Aaron stopped chewing and stared at him. "But you said it anyway."

"Well, yeah, but not officially."

"Okay, by that rationale, I will unofficially say you're a dick. I didn't actually say it …" He burst into laughter.

Parkman joined him, a hand on his stomach. "Oh, man, it's good to laugh. Sometimes we take all this shit too seriously."

"Yeah, adulting is great, but it sucks, too."

Parkman's phone rang. He frowned, retrieved it from his pocket, and stared at the call display.

"Who the fuck would be calling me from something called the CDS?"

"CDS?" Aaron said as the phone rang for the third time. "Maybe someone is selling old CDs? Sounds pretty stupid to me."

Parkman set down his fork and answered it on the fourth ring.

"Hello?"

The second he said hello, someone knocked on the apartment door. Aaron got up to get the door when Sarah's voice filled Parkman's ear.

"Are you out of breath?" he asked.

"Where are you?" Sarah asked.

"Your place. Breakfast with Aaron."

"No, no. Oh, my shit. Get out, Parkman. Get out now!"

"What?"

"Get out of the apartment," she screamed. "They're coming, and they'll kill you both. Take Aaron. Run, Parkman. Run and hide somewhere. I'll call you back on this phone in ten minutes."

The deadbolt clicked in the other room as Aaron was about to open the door.

"*Aaron*," Parkman shouted, jumping up from the table. His thighs smacked it so hard that the two untouched orange juice glasses tipped over and spread juice across the table. "Don't open that door."

Before Parkman could move one step from the table, the apartment door burst inward, knocking Aaron off his feet. Even through the noise of people stomping inside, Parkman heard Aaron's grunt when he fell. That had to hurt those tender ribs. The man was in no condition to fight.

The frying pan filled with bacon fat sizzled beside him as a man ran through the kitchen door. Parkman turned away, clutched the frying pan's handle, and continued turning, torquing at the waist for speed. He swung the bacon grease and hot cast-iron pan toward the intruder's head.

The pan made contact with the man's headgear with a heavy thud, stunning him to his knees. For the next trick, he swung his arm underhanded like lobbing a ball in a softball game and brought the frying pan up into the man's chin.

He dropped like dead weight at Parkman's feet.

Aaron was still moaning out in the foyer as another man entered the kitchen.

He glanced at his colleague on the floor, then at Parkman.

The gun in the stranger's hand came up, aimed at him.

He let the pan drop to the kitchen floor, where it clattered loudly.

The few seconds they stared at each other felt like an hour. He'd stopped breathing and didn't move, waiting for bullets to spit out of the man's weapon and into his chest.

The apartment door moved behind them as more men entered.

What the hell was going on? Parkman thought.

Before he could fire his weapon, the man lost his balance and dropped to one knee, his gun dislodged from his grasp.

Now on his knees, he tried to spin around, but something hit his head so hard it bounced off the wall, and he dropped to the kitchen floor, unconscious.

Parkman realized in the seconds that followed that Alex and Daniel had arrived and made quick work of the intruder.

Aaron groaned from the other room. Parkman stepped over the unconscious intruder and ran to him.

"What the fuck, man?" Aaron grunted. "Being smacked around with an apartment door fucking hurts."

Daniel stepped into view. "What is it with you? Come for breakfast, he said. Sarah's in trouble." He shook his head. "Looks like the trouble found you."

"Yeah," Benjamin added, entering the apartment from the hallway.

Parkman stared at him.

"What?" Benjamin said, shrugging. "I was watching the hall in case more were coming."

"And they had guns," Daniel added.

"Well, yeah. I mean, I've had my fair share of that shit. Any of you could take a turn." They all looked at him. "I mean, not that I want any of you shot. Just that, you know, I've had my fair share—"

"We need to leave," Parkman interrupted. "More may be on the way."

"What he said." Benjamin moved back to the hallway.

Daniel helped Aaron to his feet. Parkman glanced around for Alex and found him scrunched by one of the men, examining his weapon. He was probably staying close to them in case one of them woke up. No one liked surprises. That Alex had the best instincts of them all. Either that, or he had some kind of prior military training, and none of them knew about it.

"Was that the phone call?" Aaron asked.

Parkman nodded. "It was Sarah. She said run, get out of the apartment."

"She knew they were coming?"

Parkman held up the phone. "She called, didn't she?"

"Yeah, but that proves my point from earlier. Ten minutes' notice would've solved all this."

"You don't know she called because of something Vivian said. She could've called because she was told they were coming by some other source or learned about it after beating it out of someone. Shit, she could've just guessed it."

"Guys." Benjamin stuck his head back in the doorway. "We're going, right? Sarah said *run*, so I vote we leave."

"Yeah, we're going," Aaron said. "Alex, can you drag those guys into the hallway? Benjamin, help him. Daniel, help me get dressed. We leave in less than five." Daniel helped Aaron down the hall. At his bedroom door, he turned back. "Thanks guys."

Parkman nodded. "I'm going to call the cops. I'll tell them these guys were caught breaking into an apartment. We should take them down on the elevator and hand them off."

Aaron nodded, and everyone got to work.

Parkman moved out to the balcony and eased close to the edge to peek over. He couldn't see any emergency vehicles or anything else suspicious on the ground.

Just a quiet Monday morning with a few early risers driving to work.

He called 911.

Back in the apartment, Aaron was already coming out of the bedroom, and Alex was putting the last man over his shoulder. The counter was covered in weapons and knives. They'd disarmed the men before placing them in the hall.

The kitchen floor still had the frying pan and the remnants of the grease.

Parkman moved closer to the pile of weapons and grabbed one of their guns, appraising it. "Sarah said she'd call back."

"We'll be in the car in minutes," Aaron said. "Everyone, take what you need, and let's go."

They loaded up and got to the hallway. At the elevator, one of the men was stirring. Alex fixed that with a solid jab.

By the time the elevator stopped in the lobby, a cruiser was pulling in. By the time the officer was inside the first set of doors and waiting to be buzzed into the apartment building's lobby, they had unloaded the intruders. The doors closed, and they descended one more floor.

They all piled into Parkman's rental in the garage under the building. He synced his phone to Bluetooth as he drove to the exit. Up the ramp, a quick turn to the right, and they were gone with no one blocking their exit.

"We leaving our car behind?" Benjamin asked.

In the mirror, Parkman saw Alex and Daniel glance at him.

"What? I'm just asking." Benjamin shrugged.

"What next?" Aaron asked.

"Breakfast. You boys need to eat. Wait for Sarah's call. Then we'll find out what's going on."

They didn't have to wait long. Four blocks later, on

Tomken Road, the phone rang as Parkman headed toward the 403. CDS showed up on call display on his dash.

He pushed the button on the steering wheel.

"Parkman?" Sarah's voice came through loud and clear.

"I'm here."

"Oh, thank God. Aaron with you?"

"Yes, and the boys."

"Everyone's there?" She sounded surprised.

"Without them, we'd be in trouble." He stopped at a red light on Burnhamthorpe, watching his mirrors while quickly explaining what happened in the apartment. "How did you know?" Parkman asked. Aaron was staring at the dash, waiting for that answer.

"Some kind of Canadian military execs, or whatever the hell they call themselves, dropped paperwork on the OPP and walked me out of the building around four in the morning. I was told my name was on the news, and it was connected to what we did last night near the airport. So, I had a gut feeling these people might come after you, too, since you were with me. I was going to call Aaron next as they might use him to get to me."

Parkman glared at Aaron as he started forward when the light changed to green. "Smart play. What's Vivian saying?" He faced the road.

"Nothing since last night."

"So, that was just lucky timing when you called this morning?" Another look at Aaron. He was staring out the window now.

"Yes, and I need to be picked up. Get me out of downtown."

"Where are you?"

"Hiding in a dumpster off a one-way street called Richmond, right in the core. It connects with Spadina."

"I know where that is," Aaron said. "But it's about an hour from us as it's right downtown, and traffic will be stop-and-go heading into Toronto on a Monday morning."

"And Sarah, with Aaron and myself in the front and the three guys in the back, there's no room."

"Just drop us off downtown," Benjamin said. "You guys carry on. We've got classes to teach anyway. We'll grab an Uber."

Daniel and Alex stared at him again.

"Parkman," Sarah said. "We have somewhere to be. I'll fill you in when you get here. I have a lead on where this is all coming from, but I won't say it over the phone."

"Who's phone do you have anyway?"

"Sutton's. It's a long story. And I have to make another call. We'll talk when we're together. Just come get me out of here."

"On my way. Call back in forty-five minutes. We'll be able to give you a better ETA. Oh, and just so you know, the guys who went after us at your place are in police custody."

"That's good. That'll play well for my next call. Thanks."

"Who are you calling?" Aaron asked.

"Someone named General Whyte. Sutton said he'd be able to help."

"General Whyte," Parkman repeated. "*The* General Whyte? He's the second highest in the Canadian military. The Chief of Defense Staff."

"Could that be what the CDS stands for," Aaron blurted.

"CDS?" Sarah said.

"Your call display says CDS."

"Sutton and his team were well-trained operatives, soldiers."

"I don't like any of this," Aaron said. "One minute, I'm cooking breakfast, sipping coffee, and the next minute we're fighting mercenaries in my living room, and now you're chatting with General fucking Whyte. Sarah, this may be too big. Even for us."

"Welcome to my life," Sarah said. "Shit, half the time, I don't even know what's coming next. But this is some high-level shit. Arms dealers killing Canadian soldiers. We need my name off this. So, now, I've got no choice. I'm in this until the end. Too much heat otherwise. I'm going to call this General Whyte guy, then we need to look into one more thing, Parkman, and that's it. Too dangerous for us. Once it's all dealt with, I'm out."

"Call us back," Parkman said. "We're just getting onto the 403."

"Got it."

The line died.

They all remained quiet for several kilometers.

Benjamin spoke first. "When Sarah says it's too dangerous and that she wants out, that's a good sign. I'd say we could consider this as basically over."

He glanced around for support.

No one responded.

"What?" he said. "I'm just saying. This might be a case where no one needs to be shot."

He looked at each man in turn. No one returned his gaze.

"I'm thinking about you guys this time," he added. "Well, me included. You know."

Alex elbowed him in the arm.

"Okay, okay. Fuck." He rubbed the area that received the smack.

Aaron turned to face Parkman. "You were right."

"About Sarah's call?"

Aaron nodded. "And you said something about her getting out of custody soon, probably even today. While you were saying that, she was already downtown."

"Yeah." Parkman let out a sad laugh. "But I didn't expect her jailbreak to include a body count."

"This is just … shit."

"It is, it is." Parkman nodded.

"You know what my problem is?"

"Tell us."

"I think I love her too much."

"We all do, Aaron, we all do."

"Will it ever end?" he asked. "I mean, we took off for almost two years. It seems she can't catch a break now. First Texas, and now this. It's like the bad guys were just waiting, and now they're lining up for their pound of Sarah's flesh."

"You might be misreading it." Parkman changed lanes to get in position for the 427 South to start toward the downtown area. "She took some time off, but Sarah never catches a break. As long as she's alive, Vivian will be in her head. And as long as you love her, you will be there, too."

Aaron stared out the window, a hand on his ribs. "Yeah, if it doesn't kill me first."

He'd never heard Aaron sound so dejected in all their

time together. There was something about it that was starting to upset him. If he weren't grateful that the best human being they'd ever known—Sarah Roberts—loved him and had chosen him as her life partner—she even wanted to have kids with him—then maybe he was the wrong man for her.

His depression or anxiety or whining or whatever the hell it was needed to stop soon because it was getting on Parkman's nerves.

When this was all over, he'd take him to a ball game, go out for drinks, shoot a round of golf at Copper Creek, one of his favorite courses, and figure out what was truly bothering Aaron.

Otherwise, this might fester and grow into something no one wanted—their separation.

Chapter 10

JULIE SPRAWLED OUT ON the couch and moaned, holding her stomach. Annemarie woke her after a long spell—too long— on the toilet. Now her neck was crooked, her back ached, and her stomach threatened to expel all of last night's beverages.

"Annemarie," she croaked. "That was stupid."

Her friend had passed out on the floor in front of the TV last night and only woke Julie because she needed to pee.

"It's not even nine in the morning," Annemarie whispered, her body aching, too. "On a Monday. What were we thinking?"

Julie forced herself to sit up. She needed to eat, drink water, and get ready to leave. Ron needed her help. Most of last night was fuzzy, but she remembered his call and his plea for help.

Us against the world.

Annemarie's living room spun when she sat up. She leaned back and closed her eyes.

"Irish whiskey be damned."

"Yeah, we're not even Irish," Annemarie said.

Julie forced her eyes open. When her man relied on her, she had to answer the call.

She pushed herself off the couch and held her stomach with both hands. "Shit, I don't feel so good."

"Then go back to sleep. You have nowhere to go. Relax. We'll feel better by dinner, then we can drink again."

Julie laughed. "Yeah, cool. Nope, not me. No more drinking for me."

"Famous last words."

She started down the hall toward the bathroom.

"Don't fall asleep in there," Annemarie called after her. "Gotta use that myself soon."

Julie didn't respond. She did her business, washed her face, and got to the kitchen without throwing up. Step one completed.

Now, to keep something down.

She grabbed a box of muesli, poured it into a bowl, added almond milk, poured juice, and sat at the table.

From Annemarie's snores, it was obvious her friend was back under.

Once the cereal was done and the urge to vomit had dissipated even more, she felt confident enough to drive home.

She placed the dishes in the sink, grabbed her purse, and headed out the door, leaving it unlocked as Annemarie hadn't given her a key.

The drive to her house was easy. Even though her eyes were heavy and she felt she needed sleep, this was something she had to do.

Once the car was loaded, she could be in Toronto by mid-afternoon. Several large coffees on the way, plus a solid breakfast at the McDonald's on the highway. It would all work out.

She exited 654 south of North Bay and headed up her street. At her driveway, she saw it was empty. Ron's pickup wasn't there.

After hitting the garage door button, the door eased upward. Inside, the garage was empty as well.

Ron never came home last night.

So, she parked inside the garage, closed the door behind her, and rested her head back to close her eyes for a moment.

The cereal wasn't sitting well. She waited two full minutes, then opened her eyes and the car door. Gingerly, she exited her bug and popped the trunk. Before she did anything else, she needed to pee again.

Inside the house, she ran to the bathroom, sat down, and peed. Her kidneys were still trying to flush the alcohol. At this rate, after adding large coffees on the road, she'd have to stop every half hour to pee unless she ate something heavy and took a couple of Advil. Painkillers took the edge off her bladder urges.

Back outside the bathroom, she started for the garage when she saw something that made her stop.

Someone had left the kitchen cupboards open.

She turned around and saw all the couch cushions were on the living room floor.

"What did you do, Ron? What were you looking for?"

He wasn't here now as his truck wasn't in the driveway. He must've come back last night, trashed the place, then left again.

But why?

It didn't matter. She had to go after Sarah Roberts, get her attention, then lead her to Ron somehow.

She got back to the garage and grabbed the first assault rifle she saw, placing it gently in the trunk. It fit nicely. The next one, the HK-33 one, wouldn't fit. So she placed it in the back seat. A blanket would have to cover everything in the back seat against prying eyes.

At Ron's shelf, she randomly picked up boxes of ammunition, unsure which ones worked on which weapons, and stashed it all in her trunk. She grabbed three bulletproof vests stored on hooks and covered the items in the trunk, then closed it firmly. Once more, back at the rack, she surveyed all the handguns. A couple were antiques, a few were a decade old, but the five new ones were polished and clean. She recalled Ron saying one was nickel-plated, but they all shined and looked nickel-plated. Except the gold one. Was it a magnum? A Glock?

"The names don't fucking matter," she whispered, grabbing four of the newer ones and placing them in her back seat.

In the far corner of the garage lie several blankets from a couple of their picnics by the lake this past summer when he was granted access to his boys for the day. She used the largest one to cover the weapons in the back seat.

The sound of a vehicle pulled up to the front of the

house.

Julie stopped and listened. The garage door had no windows. It was impossible for anyone to know she was here, but also impossible for her to see who pulled up.

At any second, she anticipated the garage door opening.

While she waited, she quietly picked up the gold-plated handgun. Remembering Ron's few lessons, she clicked the side to check the chamber. It was loaded.

Wasn't he supposed to keep these things unloaded and in locked boxes? Maybe that was only the weapons with permits. He locked the garage and didn't let anyone inside, especially when his boys were over for a visit. That was probably good enough.

The front door of the house opened and closed.

"Holy shit," she whispered. "Ron's home."

So why didn't he park in the garage?

Should she go in and see him? What if she misinterpreted his message on the phone last night? He could be seriously angry that she showed back up to the house.

Now she felt sick all over again.

The crumpling sound of a bag came from the kitchen area, easy to hear through the thin door separating the main house from the garage.

He'd gone out to pick up food. That's why the kitchen cupboards were all open. He'd been looking for something to eat.

But they had a lot of food.

Something wasn't adding up.

She felt Ron was looking for something in the house last night. That's why it appeared ransacked.

But what if it wasn't Ron? What if someone else had ransacked their house, gone through everything? But why would they do that? And what were they looking for?

The gun in her hand made her feel safer.

But none of that mattered if she couldn't leave. As soon as she opened the garage door, whoever was in the house would hear it and come running.

If it were Ron, they'd talk, argue, or both.

If it wasn't Ron, then it was an intruder.

She glanced down at the gold gun in her hand. After a moment, an idea came to her.

Julie clicked off the safety, eased her finger inside the trigger guard, and then strode to the garage door opener beside the door to the house.

She got down on her knees, breathed in, breathed out, then hit the button.

The door started up.

She smacked the button again.

The garage door stopped a foot above the ground.

Footsteps bounded toward the door from inside the house.

Whoever was in there was running.

They made it to the door.

She pushed herself flat against the wall, the gun raised to where she supposed the chest of the person would be.

The door swung open fast, and a man filled the doorway with a large weapon.

Before she fired the gold-plated handgun repeatedly, the word Uzi raced through her mind. The fucking guy had an Uzi, and it wasn't Ron.

She pulled the trigger on that handgun until it was empty and clicked on nothing. Then, a couple more times.

The first bullet had hit the man dead center in the chest. His Uzi hand had been sweeping the garage, heading her way. The second, third, and fourth bullets kept entering the man's body about the abdomen. His Uzi didn't get to finish the full sweep. He didn't even get a chance to pull the trigger as his legs gave out under her barrage of ammo, and he fell to the floor of the garage.

Before he stared at the garage's roof, his eyes looking at nothing, he'd turned her way, blinked twice while trying to catch a breath, and coughed.

Blood oozed from his mouth.

The look of abject surprise was all over his face while she finished clicking the empty gun. Then she heard a final breath, like an exhausted huff, and his eyes stopped moving.

She had killed a man.

The gun dropped from her grip. Not because she let go but because her hands were shaking too badly.

She caught herself moaning but didn't try to stand up. Still on her knees, she turned away from the dead body on her garage floor and got two paces before falling forward. Before her face hit the floor, her hands broke the fall.

She rolled onto her back, a soft wind ruffling her hair.

The garage door was still open a foot.

Their neighbors weren't too close, but they were close enough to hear gunfire.

Was it hunting season? Would anyone care?

She sat up and used the wall to get to her feet.

She had killed a man.

Without thinking about it, Julie turned and stared at the dead intruder. The blood had stopped flowing. Probably because his heart had stopped. Was he in the house earlier? Could her timing be that fortunate that she arrived back when he was out getting breakfast?

It would be her body lying on the garage floor if she'd shown up fifteen minutes later.

She leaned on her car, holding her stomach.

Another look at him, and then she couldn't hold it any longer.

Julie's stomach clenched, and she vomited all over the floor by the drain. At least there was that. A quick hose down later would make the floor as good as new.

Well, unless blood stained a concrete floor.

Should she take his Uzi?

Julie shook her head. She needed to leave. She had what she came for. It was time to get on the road and leave all this behind.

Find Sarah Roberts, find her man, and do whatever Ron had planned for part two.

Julie got behind the wheel of the bug and hit the garage door, praying no one was randomly walking by out front.

In her mirrors, the road was deserted.

She turned on the car, exited the garage, and hit the button.

The garage door lowered at an agonizingly slow rate.

When it stopped at the bottom, she exhaled.

She'd killed a man and gotten away with it. Well, maybe. She'd left the gold-plated gun on the floor. Her prints were on it.

But they were on everything. She'd lived in the house. Didn't mean she was the shooter, even though she was.

"He's the one who broke into *my* house," she said to the rearview mirror. "With a motherfucking Uzi to boot!"

Julie reversed out of the driveway, feeling better now that she'd vomited, but she was shaky. She needed food. She needed coffee.

Then she'd take the large HK-33 thing and figure out how to work it, walk into a large shopping center, and aim it at a bunch of people. Just like Ron did with that plan to shoot down an airliner.

He didn't really *mean* to shoot down a plane. He just wanted Sarah's attention.

And Julie didn't really *mean* to shoot people at the mall.

She just wanted Sarah's attention as well.

Or maybe she could do something worse. Why stop at a mall? Why not go to a school and threaten to kill kids? Of course, she'd never do it, but didn't it have to be big to catch someone like Sarah Roberts's attention?

Then it hit her.

The biggest idea yet.

"Oh, Sarah, you're going to come running my way. Just you wait and see."

Julie floored the little bug en route for Highway 11, taking her south toward Toronto and the killing fields.

After actually taking a life in her garage, faking it for real would be easy.

But she still needed to eat first.

Chapter 11

PARKMAN HIT THE BUTTON on the steering wheel to answer Sarah's call.

"Where are you?" she asked.

"Less than five minutes out. Getting off the Gardiner Expressway now."

"Okay, I've moved locations."

"Tell me where to go."

"I'm in a dollar store at the corner of Adelaide and Spadina. Carry on up to Richmond, go left, and come around the block, as Adelaide is one-way."

"I know where it is," Aaron said.

"Aaron's with you still?"

"Yes, the three in the back are getting out when we grab you."

"Aaron's gotta leave, too," Sarah said. "Where we're

going, we can only do it alone." Then clicked off.

Parkman hit the turn signal and waited at the lights at Richmond.

"She's not going alone again," Aaron said. "I'm in."

"Even with your ribs as bad as they are?"

"I'm in," Aaron repeated.

"You tell her, then. I won't."

"Oh, I plan to."

They made it to Adelaide and stopped in a no-parking area. Sarah exited the dollar store as the three teachers got out of the car. They hugged on the sidewalk, and Sarah thanked them.

Aaron's door was opened from the outside. Sarah leaned down.

"You need to go with them," she said.

"I'm staying," Aaron replied. "I go where you go on this. You could use my help."

Sarah leaned down farther and glanced in at Parkman. He shrugged.

"Aaron, your ribs ache too much to be of any use to us. You need rest and time to heal. Go with them, rest at the dojo, oversee the classes, whatever you want, but you can't come on this trip."

He kicked his legs out, rose to his feet, and stepped away from the car.

"You can have the front seat, but I'm coming," he said. "You could use a lookout or something. I can cover your backs. I know how to use weapons."

"Aaron." Sarah's voice took on an edge, and Parkman wondered if Aaron would regret fighting her on this point.

"There is nothing you can do on this one. Look, what we're going to handle isn't all that hard—"

"Hard? Like last night's incarceration, hard? Or like surface-to-air missiles and being arrested on federal weapons charges, hard? Come on, Sarah, let's get in the car and go home. Let's go back to the way it was on our time off. Let the world figure out its own shit."

Parkman leaned down in the front seat to see Sarah's face. Her eyes seemed to radiate heat as she glared at him. He'd never challenged her like this before, at least not in front of anyone. From the corner of his eye, he saw the three teachers moving a few feet down the sidewalk to give the couple their space.

He'd give them a minute to iron out their issue before hitting the horn. He couldn't stay where he was parked for long.

"Aaron, this isn't the time or the place. I am leaving with Parkman and will return soon. We will talk then."

"What's going on that my help isn't needed—"

"Aaron." Sarah cut him off, her voice rising. "You weren't supposed to come to Texas, but you came anyway and almost got killed. Listen to me." Aaron bumped into the car as Sarah pushed into him. "Stay the hell away from this one. It's too dangerous. We will be back soon. Then, whatever issue you have, we'll deal with it then, but you are not coming this time. It's not even open for discussion. I'm sorry."

"Fine." He pushed off the car. "Go then. Hit me up when you get back."

Aaron strode away. In the mirror, Parkman saw Daniel on

his cell phone, probably summoning an Uber. Benjamin was beside him, but Alex had stepped farther down and was now about five cars from them on the sidewalk. He probably wanted to avoid listening in on the confrontation involving the people he loved.

Sarah dropped in the front seat, then twisted back. "Hey, Aaron."

Parkman didn't move. He didn't breathe. *Here we go.*

"Don't go home. More men will show up. Stay with your team until this is over. It won't be long." She twisted back forward. "Go," she said, slamming the front door. "Fast, before I get out and bitch slap him. Fuck, sometimes he infuriates me."

Parkman exhaled heavily, hit the gas, stopped at Spadina, and then turned right.

"Get on the Gardiner eastbound. Head toward the Don Valley Parkway."

He glanced over at her. Sarah turned on a cell phone.

"That the phone you used to call me?" he asked.

"Yeah."

The phone's screen lit up. Sarah checked the mirrors, leaned back in her seat, and held the phone tight.

"You okay?" he asked.

"Yeah, as soon as we deal with this phone, we'll be fine."

"Deal with the phone? What's going on?"

"In a minute. Just get us on the ramp to the Gardiner."

They had to hit every red light, and at each one, Sarah seemed more and more fidgety.

"What happened last night?" he asked, hoping to get her mind off whatever bothered her.

"Can't talk. Not until this is dealt with." She lifted the phone, turned it in her hand, then set it on her lap again.

Parkman nodded as he turned left on Lakeshore Blvd. He followed it to the next lights, then stayed in the right lane to take the ramp onto the Gardiner Expressway. Halfway up the ramp to the elevated highway, Sarah lowered her window and held the phone outside the car. After several seconds, she pulled it back inside and clicked the power button to turn it off.

"Okay, shit, I'm glad that's over." Sarah opened the center console, stowed the phone, and closed her window.

"What's over?" he asked. "You gonna fill me in?"

"Yes, but exit up here on Jarvis and get us back on the Gardiner going the other way. We need to be heading west to access the 427 to get out of Toronto." She turned to Parkman. "Get us on the 400 heading toward Barrie as fast as possible without alerting a traffic cruiser."

"I can do that."

"Good. While you drive, I'll talk."

"Sounds fair. Shoot."

Sarah told him about the police interview with Detective Dover and Budnack, how they lied about what Parkman was supposedly telling them, and how Sutton strode in and took her away from them. Then, the deadly ride from the police station, and finally, the call she made on Sutton's phone.

"Holy shit," Parkman said. "You got lucky. What the hell was that all about? You could've been killed."

"What happened at the apartment?"

"When you called, Aaron was answering a knock at the door. We were lucky he'd had the teachers on their way over.

We sure needed their help."

"The real luck is that I chose to call you because you were there last night, and you happened to be with Aaron at the apartment when they arrived. If you were anywhere else, what would've happened to Aaron?"

They sat silently for a few moments as Parkman navigated the 427's wide turn by the airport as they continued north.

"I shudder to think," he said. "In Aaron's current condition, he couldn't even attempt to fight them off."

"Which is why he's safer at home." She glanced at Parkman. "Well, not exactly at home, but you know what I mean. Not with us."

"What was that all about, anyway?"

"He's whining. It's bothersome. Ever since Texas, well, even before Texas, that's why I left him here when I went to the States. I asked him to stay home. Well, that and Vivian warned me he'd be in trouble in the States. For some reason, his head isn't straight right now. He's not the same Aaron from Europe, Los Angeles, or Mexico."

"He loves you, that's the problem."

"Yeah, well, that's great, but love isn't enough."

"It's not?" Parkman's voice rose a notch to show his surprise. "I thought the Beatles had it right; love is all you need."

"No. You have to show it, too. He's showing disrespect right now."

"I don't know if I'd go that far."

"Parkman, he challenged me in front of everyone, and fine, I'm not his boss, but I do get to have a say in who I want to put in harm's way."

"Gee, thanks."

"You know what I mean. I love him, too, but I didn't want him in Texas for obvious reasons, and I don't want him here. These people are too dangerous. I can't lose Aaron. If I have to fight him to keep him, I'll do it. But anyway, Aaron's got to find a way to go back to the way things were. Along with love, I need understanding, too, with a little validation mixed in for good measure."

"He validates you." Parkman tried to keep his tone even as he wasn't going to bat for Aaron as much as he was for their relationship. It would be a tragedy if they were to ever split up after all they'd gone through.

"Sure, he does, most of the time. But when it comes to Vivian, he feels like he's taking a back seat, but he's not. This is just what I do. I was doing it when he met me, and I'm still doing it. It's not about Aaron as much as it may seem so."

"It just seems crazy that the one thing you two bonded over is the monkey wrench causing you two issues."

"And I get that it bothers him, and I get that he wants me all to himself so we can be a regular couple, and I love that about him, but this isn't the time. Right now, today, I have something I need to handle. Maybe next week, maybe next month. Maybe not. Shit, I could be doing this into my forties. All I know is I love that man with everything I have, and I want to knock a tooth out of his head once in a while, too."

They rode in silence for a few kilometers.

Parkman changed lanes and cruised north in the center lane.

"I'm not sure if Aaron'll make it to your forties with

what you do. All I'm saying is, I'm seeing cracks in his resolve."

"That's what I'm worried about."

"Are you choosing Vivian over Aaron?" Parkman asked. "I mean, could you let it all go and stay home, get married, build a family?"

Sarah fidgeted with her hands. He felt a sadness ooze off her and wondered if she'd cry.

She nodded, then stared up through the windshield. "I think that might be the issue."

"How so?"

She focused her attention out the side window. "When we took that time away, we got closer than ever before. When we lost"—her voice caught, she swallowed—"when February happened, we struggled for a bit. Aaron wants what we had before February. But now I'm busy again. This is what I want. I feel this is my life. I love to be tackling something. I *need* to be busy. And sure, there was Texas and now an arms dealer without much of a break in between, but it'll calm down. We have plenty of time to try for a baby again. We have the rest of our lives. I'm just busy right now and feeling good about it. I need this right now."

"To take your mind off …" he paused, then said, "other things."

"Yes. Other things."

"Have you told him that?"

"No."

"Maybe you should."

"I'll think about it."

They rode in silence again until Parkman noticed Sarah's

eyes getting heavy. He still had a couple of questions for her.

"Moments ago, you said these people are too dangerous. If so, then what are we doing exactly?"

"We're going to talk to a few people at a construction company called Ronald Harris and Sons."

"And why's that?"

"The MATADOR shooter was driving one of their pickups last night. That truck was following us when the OPP pulled us over."

"Sounds safe enough. What was it with that phone?"

"That was Sutton's phone. He gave it to me to call General Whyte."

"And you called him?"

"I did. The general spoke to me like I was one of theirs. He asked questions about the attack. He said, 'Were my soldiers dispatched?' and stuff like that, all official and serious. He told me he was sending a team to pick me up. He wanted to bring me in. He said something was happening behind the scenes that I wasn't privy to and that he would explain it all when I came in. I don't know who this general is or even what the hell's going on, so I said no. General Whyte said I would probably get myself killed if I didn't come in and get his protection. The men Sutton were hunting would have a bullseye on my back."

"Maybe you should have listened to him."

"Not a chance. I was fine until I was with Sutton. This Whyte guy wants to send more like Sutton? Fuck that. I'll take my chances on my own."

"Why turn it off then?"

She hit the seat button to recline it back and twisted it

slightly to the side. "I didn't sleep in that interview room and then Sutton, a shoot-out, and then waiting for you guys. I must catch a few hours' sleep before we reach North Bay."

"No problem. I drive, you sleep. But tell me about that phone first."

"They were tracking it. After I spoke with you, I called Whyte, and then I moved position, thinking about where a good spot for you to pick me up would be."

"And?"

"A small team of men in two vehicles, this time, stopped in front of a Starbucks. I knew they were after me, so I bolted out the back and climbed a fire escape ladder to the roof. I was able to jump from roof to roof until I was far enough away to climb down and disappear. While up there, I turned off Sutton's phone." She cleared her throat, her voice already slowing down as exhaustion overtook her. "From that rooftop perch, I saw two Hummers, one at either end of the block watching Whyte's team. They were waiting for visual confirmation that his team had me before engaging. Then they left the Starbucks and drove around the block, presumably waiting for me to turn on the cell phone again."

"Holy shit, Sarah."

"I know. Freaked me out. So, I turned it on briefly to call you, then off again. The dollar store offered me an easy back door to leave through if I saw them approach again, but no one did this time."

"And that's why you turned it on as we were headed east."

"Exactly. And got you to head west once the phone was turned off."

"And what about this General Whyte? Gonna deal with him again?"

"I don't work for him. He spoke to me—no, ordered me —to come in. He wanted a full briefing on the attack. Granted, I understood that, so I gave him the watered-down version. Everyone was dead. Two H2 Hummers with heavily armed assholes murdered his men. I told him to bring more men—a lot of them—look for Hummers, but I'm going back to my life."

"How did he take that?"

"Not well. Told me I'd be killed if I wasn't under his protection. But I already said that, didn't I?" She adjusted herself in the seat. "After reminding him what happened with Sutton's team, I said I'd take my chances."

"And that's who came to your apartment to attack us? More Hummer guys?"

"The way I figure it." Her voice was slowing, becoming slurred.

"You sleep. No one knows where we are or where we're going."

"That's the … plan."

Parkman put his cell phone on silent as he headed north on the 400 highway. Their destination was about three hours away. Plenty of time for Sarah to sleep. He'd wake her at the coffee stop in Huntsville.

She'd been through enough since last night, and who knew what the day ahead held for them.

With Sarah's prophecy of these people being that dangerous, he didn't feel their prospects looked too good.

Parkman didn't have to be psychic to know the future

held dark days ahead.

He also figured Aaron and Sarah were in for some devastating arguments if they were still alive when this job ended.

Something told him the future wasn't so bright after all.

Chapter 12

AARON WATCHED THE CAR turn right at Spadina and felt a sharp pain in his gut. Not the kind of pain from a punch or a jab. A different kind, the one that hurts when you're in love and confused.

Scared, too.

What if he couldn't deal with his feelings regarding the danger Sarah always put herself in? What if they spent a life together with her always gone, off helping other people, routine hospital visits, attempts on her life, until one day someone got lucky and the police came to his door asking for a positive ID?

He had often wanted to be rid of this lifestyle, let it all go, and just enjoy themselves, but that wasn't up to him. As much as he thought it might be, Sarah clarified that when she took off to Texas weeks ago. They'd had so many years together, and he was left with the proverbial fork in the road. Continue this life on Sarah's terms and learn to accept it, regardless of what happened. Or let her go to do as she wanted without holding her back.

But could he let her go?

Staying seemed to be hurting him more at the moment.

All this also made him feel vulnerable and feminine. He was the one with *feelings*. He was the one wondering about their future. It made him feel needy, and he didn't want to be needy as he thought it was unattractive in a man, not to mention a horrible way to live.

There was no way to ignore how he felt because he wanted Sarah all to himself, which was selfish, but sharing her with the world, with strangers, was overwhelmingly dangerous.

Maybe he was afraid to lose her. Although, pushing Sarah was a surefire way to lose her.

The internal conflict drove him mad with worry and indecision. It caused an internal agony that Sarah would see him in a weak, little boy light when he wanted to be her man.

But who was he kidding? He was the counter to her masculinity, her strength. A strong, dominant, confident woman was attractive to him. That was the most beautiful kind of woman, in his opinion. That's why he wanted to spend his life with Sarah.

"Aaron," Daniel said, breaking his reverie.

He blinked twice, then turned around. "Yeah?"

"We might have some trouble."

He frowned. "Trouble? No, that just left in Parkman's car."

Daniel fixed him with a hard stare. "That's not funny. If you have a problem with Sarah, fix it because no one else does."

Aaron nodded, feeling horrible at his choice of words. "Sorry, I just want it to go back to the way it was for those two years off. We need each other."

"Sure you do, but she needs her sister. You knew it going in."

Aaron held up the hand with the missing finger. "And I'm reminded daily."

Daniel stepped back and regarded him with a look Aaron hadn't seen before.

"I'm going to say something that would normally elicit a violent response."

Aaron nodded. "Go ahead."

"Get the fuck over yourself. Can you count how many times Benjamin has been shot? The danger to me is what Alex has endured for this team. Sure, you lost a finger, but Sarah has lost so much more. Dear friends like that guy Dolan Ryan and Esmerelda. People Sarah has talked about with fond memories. They'd be alive today if Sarah didn't do what she did. And how about Drake Bellamy, who changed his name and resurfaced with Spencer to help Sarah but ended up getting killed?" Daniel leaned in closer, and Aaron felt sick hearing the truth. "How do you think Sarah feels right now with all that weighing on her head, not to mention a million other lives affected by what she does? And you're concerned about some alone time? Let's get married, settle down, shit? Right." Daniel nodded twice. "I can see that with Sarah." The sarcasm in the last sentence hit him in the solar plexus.

"All right, all right, I get it. Fuck, I'm sorry, man. Just going through some shit, you know."

"No, I don't know. And while we're chit-chatting about your shit, Alex is gone."

"What?" Aaron glanced over Daniel's shoulder. "Gone where?"

"Don't know, but we have to find him. Benjamin's at the next corner waiting for us." Daniel pointed.

Aaron followed his finger but didn't see Benjamin.

"Where?"

Daniel looked, too. "He's gone."

They broke out in a run simultaneously, but Daniel easily overtook Aaron due to his rib injury. He had slowed halfway to the corner and clutched at his ribs, wincing in pain as they expanded and contracted with each agonizing breath.

Daniel hit the corner jogging and disappeared around it. Moments later, Aaron got there.

He stood at the corner of Brant and Adelaide. A tall building sat to his left, and a fenced-in schoolyard was on the right, but no sign of his three friends.

The idea that they'd play some kind of stupid joke on him crossed his mind before he realized something was actually wrong.

He scanned the area for trouble, letting his hands fall to the sides. The constant pain in his chest, a reminder his ribs needed much more time to mend, was forgotten for the moment.

With each tentative step forward, his senses on high alert, he moved along the sidewalk until he came to a ramp that led to an underground parking for the building to his left. A small guard shack sat unoccupied.

To his right, the public school was jammed with kids out on recess.

Where the hell did they go?

He debated heading down into the darkness of the parking garage, then decided to continue another hundred yards before retracing his steps and investigating the garage.

An alley separated the two buildings to his left, with graffiti tagged on the walls. Seven vehicles were jammed into the small alley, all lined up along the side.

He stopped again to scan the area and debated calling their cell numbers. He checked his phone but saw no messages, no missed calls.

"Don't move," a man said behind him.

Aaron jolted at the voice and started to turn around, his hands rising in a defensive gesture, but stopped midway when something cold pressed into his left cheek.

"You don't listen well."

"Who the fuck are you?"

"This way," the man said, yanking on Aaron's sleeve.

He took a step, then another, turning around all the way to go where the man wanted him to go.

The alley's seven vehicles included a Hummer. The man pointed toward it, lowering his gun to the side by his thigh.

"Where are the others?" Aaron asked.

The man didn't respond.

Aaron stopped walking five feet from the Hummer and faced him. If something had happened to any of his friends, he'd have no choice but to hurt the man in front of him, gun or no gun, bruised ribs be damned.

"What's going on?" Aaron asked.

The man was dressed in all black with thick shoulders. Several knives were strapped to his person at various places, with what looked like pepper spray clipped to his waist. The empty holster at his thigh would hold the gun in his hand. How could this man not be worried about being seen dressed for combat near a public school?

"We don't care about you," the man said as doors opened behind Aaron. "Or your friends."

Aaron watched as Benjamin and Daniel were paraded out from behind the Hummer. Four other men dressed like the one in front of him walked them to the center of the alley. His friends' wrists were strapped together with white ties, and a strip of duct tape muted them.

Aaron's anger doubled. He clenched his fists, doing everything in his power to deny the urge to attack the man in front of him. There were five of them against his three. Even handicapped as Benjamin and Daniel were with their hands tied, he knew they'd fight better than these armed men.

But where was Alex?

"What do you want?" Aaron asked, his tone even, his heart racing into the red line.

"Your stupid bitch. She has something of ours. We want it back."

"Well, whatever it is you think she has, good luck. I can't even get ten bucks out of her."

The man smirked. "Jokes? At a time like this?"

"Where's the third one?" Aaron nodded toward Daniel and Benjamin.

While Aaron thought about Sarah on the corner of Adelaide and Spadina and argued with Daniel, they'd taken Alex and then Benjamin. Aaron would never forgive himself if anything happened to Alex because they were delayed and couldn't help him.

But wasn't this Sarah's fault in some way, too?

"Your other friend wasn't a good listener."

"How so?"

The man nodded briefly at his crew. They opened the back door to reveal Alex. Blood covered his nose and forehead.

"What have you done to him?" he asked, his body twitching to attack.

"Calm down, little puppy." The man leaned in closer, raising his weapon to Aaron's ribs. "An ounce of pressure and you're done with this world, on to the next." He lowered his voice and moved closer to Aaron's ear. "Your friends are free to go. It's you we want. You're the asshole who fucks the woman who fucked us. So now—"

Aaron had heard enough. Odds be damned. He couldn't listen to any more of their shit.

His right hand came swiftly. It was so fast and clean that the sound of the man's wrist snapping upon contact fueled him into a wonderful rage. The weapon was lost to the air as the hand that held it could no longer hold anything.

Even before the man was able to formulate a physical response to the first hit, Aaron's left hand flattened and shot up into the underside of the man's throat for a violent jab.

In a marionette parody, the man was about to lift his injured hand to inspect it, but that floppy broken wrist ended up at his throat as he choked on a collapsed trachea. Aaron figured the trachea had to collapse on the violence of that one hit because the man's head snapped back hard with the force of the blow.

Then the man dropped to the alley's dirty concrete.

Aaron stepped forward as two of the heavily armed men placed weapons at Daniel's and Benjamin's heads.

"Stop," the driver of the Hummer said. He opened the door and got out, leaving the door ajar. A monster of a man, he was at least a foot taller than Aaron and double his thickness. "No one else needs to die today." He waved a hand, and the two guns at Daniel's and Benjamin's heads lowered.

The sounds of traffic and kids playing in the schoolyard behind them were broken by the gagging of the man dying on the ground behind Aaron.

"We just want what's ours," the driver said. "And we understand your girlfriend has it."

Aaron seethed anger through his nostrils, his clamped teeth. Everything in his body was fueled with adrenaline, the kind that felt good and made him want to hurt people. Before he could think rationally, the driver motioned toward his fallen man.

"Get him out of sight."

Two of the four men watching Daniel and Benjamin rushed over, lifted their comrade, and carried him to the rear of the Hummer, where they placed him inside.

"One each is fair," the driver said. "We'll find and deal with Sarah on our own, but it would be better with you." He waited a moment, then added, "Alive."

Aaron contemplated Daniel's ability to fight with only his feet. And what about Benjamin? What kind of effort would he want to expend? These guys had guns.

"Better to find Sarah with me," Aaron said, repeating the man's words.

"What about them?" He torqued his waist slightly to point with his bulging arm.

"Take me," Aaron said without hesitation. "You don't need them. They barely know Sarah."

Daniel shook his head and glared at him.

The driver studied his face. After a moment, he nodded.

"Let them walk away. Untie their wrists so they can carry the other skinny one."

The men obeyed their leader without hesitation. Once Daniel and Benjamin were untied, they grabbed Alex by the shoulders and pulled him out of the Hummer.

When Aaron saw the full extent of Alex's injuries, he was horrified at the extent of them. His nose had to be broken, for sure. The swelling was rising all over his face. The ragged breath from his open mouth escaped in fits and starts like breathing was painful.

He had cuts and gashes on his arms and hands. Even his thigh was bleeding where his jeans were torn, and a blade of some kind had sliced deep enough to need several dozen stitches.

"We didn't want that," the driver said. "But he wouldn't stop fighting. Three of our men left in another vehicle to head to our doctor." The man sounded like he was appraising Alex. "Without a weapon, whoever trained this small lad taught him well. I've never seen what he could do. Three of my soldiers left here with broken arms, one with a snapped kneecap, another with his elbow popped the other way. The screams were too much. I had to stop it with a tranquilizer. Your boy is sleeping now but will wake up within the hour. I would've killed him, but I needed to know if he was Sarah's man. Once we determined he wasn't, we kept him alive to wait for you." The driver turned back to the Hummer and stepped up to the open front door. "I trust you're a man of your word."

Daniel and Benjamin had carried Alex to the mouth of the alley and stopped to set him down and watch.

"Get in the back, or I will order my men to open fire on those three. And you're still coming with us."

Aaron stared at his friends, wondering if this were the last time he'd see them. The men who had flanked his friends moved into position around him, all waiting for instructions from the driver.

"Aren't you coming, Sarah's boyfriend?"

Aaron nodded at his men and his teachers, then climbed up into the back seat of the Hummer.

The driver jerked his head for the others to follow suit.

Once everyone was inside and the doors were closed, the driver pulled away and stopped beside Daniel, Benjamin, and a sleeping wounded Alex.

It broke Aaron's heart to see the look on their faces. He'd let them down. Sarah had let them down. They were beaten, wounded, and divided. Whatever it was she had taken from such dangerous men was going to get him killed.

And maybe it was better that way. He didn't want to die, but what would his world look like without Sarah? Did he even want to live that way? The love of his life gone from him was too much to bear. But the way they were living was driving him mad. It led to these kinds of things, and this wasn't his discipline. Martial arts was about self-defense, but Sarah was always on the offense.

She'd be happier without him. The nagging and his soft, feminine side wouldn't bother her anymore. Or was that self-pity talking?

There was no mistake that this was a suicide gambit. He had no intention of dying or getting himself killed, but it had just become a reality. These men would take what was theirs, kill Sarah, then kill him, too.

And this all had to fall onto Sarah's shoulders. Or perhaps Vivian's.

Either way, Sarah chose this life, and he had to understand that he chose it, too, by being with her.

But fault didn't matter anymore.

As the Hummer eased out into traffic, the man beside him laid out his hand.

"Cell phone."

Aaron retrieved it and gave it to him. The man passed it through to the front, where the passenger tapped on it.

"Passcode?" he said without looking back at Aaron.

He told him and watched as the man scrolled through his contacts.

"Where's Sarah's number?"

"It's listed under *my dream*."

The man laughed. "Fuckin' romantic. Pathetic, too."

He tapped her number and held the phone to his ear. After a moment, he lowered the phone to his lap.

"She have a different number?"

"No."

"She didn't answer that one."

"Well, she should've."

Was Sarah not taking his calls now? What the fuck?

The passenger turned around to look at Aaron. "You two have a fight or something?"

He glanced out the window as they turned onto Lakeshore Blvd.

"She was with someone else. The second guy we grabbed said his name was Parkmen or something." The passenger scrolled on Aaron's cell phone again. "Here it is. Parkman."

He tapped the call button and placed it to his ear.

Aaron watched out the window and thought about what would come in the next few hours. These guys were military-grade, through and through. He could fight, but they had better discipline and better weapons.

"No answer," the passenger said, interrupting his thoughts.

Aaron continued to stare out the window.

"You'd better hope someone picks up their phone before the day ends."

Aaron Stevens knew nothing mattered anymore. Pick up the phone or not, he wasn't going home again.

As the Hummer left the downtown area, the ache in his ribs intensified as the adrenaline wore off.

The pain would be over soon because this was probably the last ride of his life.

Beyond all the bullshit, the neediness, and the arguments, he loved Sarah—deeply.

When they found his body, he wanted her to know he died standing up, on his feet, fighting like a man should to protect his woman.

He'd find a way because he wouldn't die without a fight. Injuries or not, he planned on going out with a bang. Something even Alex would be proud of.

Chapter 13

Julie had avoided two calls from Annemarie. She was supposed to be hungover. Annemarie would have to assume Julie went home and was in bed with the phone off.

There were a few moments when Julie thought about pulling over and resting because she was shaking so much. Killing a man in her garage had taken its toll on her weakened body. She'd felt like shit after all that drinking, and then to go home and shoot a guy, only to vomit, made her feel even weaker. He had a family. Someone loved that man. She wasn't a murderer. Would she go to jail? So many thoughts raced through her mind as she drove south out of North Bay.

She'd stop in Huntsville soon. Grab some McDonald's, a Coke, and a large coffee. Fill up and juice up on sugar and caffeine.

Maybe even grab a small nap in the car somewhere off the road, where a curious cop wouldn't peek in her back seat and ask what was under the blanket.

She watched the signs and saw that Huntsville was another fifteen minutes away.

Would she make it safely? Falling asleep was becoming more of a risk as her head lolled forward.

She lowered her window and leaned over to let the wind blow in her face.

Without thinking too much, she dialed Ron's number and connected it to the car's speakers.

He answered on the second ring.

"You shouldn't be calling," he said.

"Why?"

"Because, Julie, it's dangerous."

"What? Because you tried to shoot down a plane last night?"

"Are you driving? Is that the sound of your car in the background?"

"Yes."

"Where are you?"

"I left town. I'm heading south, near Huntsville."

"Oh, good." Ron exhaled audibly on the phone. "It's better if you're gone. Then they can't come after you. Don't go back to the house."

She let that one go for now. "Come after me? Who? The cops?"

"No. Worse."

"What's worse than the cops?"

"You don't want to know. Look, Julie, why'd you call?

This isn't a good time, and we broke up, remember."

"We didn't break up. You walked out, angry. We'll fix this together, get through whatever trouble you're in together."

"Julie, you're not listening to me. You can't *get through* anything with these people. There is no negotiation. Even the cops can't fucking do anything. I tried to reach out to that Roberts woman because I've read about her. I was hoping she could help or at least tell me what to do, but that got all fucked up. And now I'm in this alone."

"You've got me." Julie signaled to get off the highway one exit early. Highway driving was putting her to sleep. She'd drive into Huntsville using the road that came in from the north. There was a McDonald's on the right as she entered town. After she ate, there was a Tim Horton's within a block. One extra-large, black coffee, and she'd be ready for the longer drive to Toronto.

"Julie, if you want to live to see the end of the week, hang up and forget my number."

"You threatening me?" she screamed at the dash, much more awake now.

"Not me," Ron said, sounding pissed off. "The people who are after me will come for you. Keep driving. Take a couple of weeks in Ottawa. Better yet, drive to Montreal or go the other way and hit Windsor. Cross over to Detroit. In the States, you'll be safe until this blows over."

"I'm not worried about your friends with the Uzis."

She slowed to take the turn on the exit. Ron didn't speak for almost half a minute. She might have thought he hung up if she didn't hear him clear his throat.

"What friends?" he asked. "And you said Uzis?"

"I went to the house."

"You didn't." His voice rose.

She could picture him leaning forward, staring at nothing, waiting for her response.

"I have a plan, too."

"What did you do at the house?"

"I killed a man."

"*What?*" he shouted. Then, in a lower voice, said, "You're joking."

"I'm not. I entered through the garage, packed all your weapons in my car, went inside the house to pee, and saw that someone had been there since last night. He'd gone through everything and made a bloody mess. When I went back to the garage to leave, he showed up."

"And?"

"When he was in the house, I opened the garage door a notch, stopped it, and waited for whoever it was to investigate. I ambushed him at the door. He was carrying a weapon that resembled an Uzi." Even though she'd killed a man, and it made her sick, she was proud of herself. Telling Ron made her feel good.

"Oh, baby, you shouldn't have done that. What if it was a cop?"

"It's fine. He was an intruder. And he was carrying a scary weapon, an automatic machine gun thingy. Total self-defense. In my own home."

"If it's who I think it is, I'm not worried about cops, baby. The men he works for never stop hunting their enemies."

That didn't help the pit in her stomach. She felt sick again, but a part of her remained defiant.

"Doesn't matter who they are. Shouldn't be breaking into people's houses."

"Oh my fuck, Julie. It's good you left town."

"I only left to meet up with Sarah Roberts."

"You what?" he shouted again. "Sarah? How?"

"You wanted Sarah, and I'm going to get her."

There was a pause as she assumed Ron was putting it all together.

"What are you going to do?"

Yup, he now understood.

"You'll see." Julie eased to a stop at a red light. "Watch the news this afternoon."

"Julie, please don't. You're already in over your head. Just drive somewhere safe. Dump the weapons. Let this go. You can't do what you're planning."

It hurt that Ron didn't think she could help him. He didn't believe in her. Sure, she killed an intruder, but she had no plans to kill anyone else. She just wanted to stage something huge that Sarah had to show up. Then Sarah and Ron could meet, and he could talk to her.

"I gotta go, honey. Gonna hit a drive-thru on my way to shooting up a police station with that HK-33 thing you have." It was out before she could stop it.

"You're going to do what?" Ron screamed so loud, his voice distorted on her speakers.

"Don't worry, honey. I'm a capable woman. Sarah and I will figure out the next step."

She clicked the button to end the call, grabbed her phone,

and turned off the ringer to avoid taking his calls.

She'd help him with or without his blessing. And since Sarah was psychic, she'd know what to do about their future.

The idea wasn't a good one. Walking into a police station to use some kind of automatic weapon would make them all drop to the ground, sure, but when they got off their feet, every single human being in that building would have a weapon trained on her. The probability of success for her plan to break Sarah out from the holding cell of a police station and survive to talk about it was probably extremely low. The last she saw on the news was that the OPP had Sarah in custody, which probably meant their downtown location. It would be easy to get inside, shoot a bunch of bullets into the roof, and demand they release Sarah. But she'd probably never make it out alive.

There were other things to consider, such as the cops not negotiating with someone holding a weapon on them. And not getting shot by any of them would be difficult to avoid.

Sure, it was a dumb plan and one she wasn't actually going to do. She probably had to think of something else. Yet, there was something attractive about telling Ron that crazy story. It would make him see the length she'd go to for him. She'd killed a guy, and now, loaded with all his weapons, she was on her way to break out Sarah and deliver her to him.

What man would not want that kind of commitment?

Food first. She needed to eat.

She pulled into the McDonald's parking lot and killed the engine. She'd order inside and eat in the car. The legs needed a stretch, and her bladder needed emptying.

Then off to the Timmy's and back on the highway. Think about her final details, then.

She'd be willing to do it if it came down to shooting someone to get Sarah's attention. Anything for Ron and his boys. Just not shooting cops. That was stupid.

When this was all over, they'd all live together. No more Children's Aid Society, no more tax people calling Ron and seizing his bank accounts, and no more shit to deal with.

Just them as a family.

Although, maybe they could live in another house.

She wasn't sure she wanted to remain in that house anymore after killing a man in the garage.

Overall, her plan sucked, and she knew it, but she had nothing else to go on, no idea what else to do.

Outside the car, the mid-September heat warmed her, while the knowledge of what she would do in the hours to come made her feel cold on the inside.

She'd killed already.

She could do it again if she had to. There was no doubt.

Hostages would get Sarah released. Maybe take a classroom hostage.

It was the only thing she could think about.

If the cops didn't let Sarah out, they would be dead in the public opinion polls.

They would have to do what she wanted.

She was the one with the weapons.

Chapter 14

"Sarah?" Parkman called. "We're stopping in a few minutes for coffee."

She opened her eyes, feeling the weight of fatigue. She stretched, pushing the seat back to its limit. Then, she blinked a bunch of times and rubbed her eyes.

"I could sure use a good night's sleep soon."

"I hear that."

"Where are we?"

"Huntsville. We're still about an hour to North Bay. Thought you might want a coffee. This'll give you some time to wake up before getting there."

"Yeah. I'm in. Let's do it. Coffee." She yawned and stretched again. "Heard from Aaron?"

"Haven't heard from anyone. My phone's on silent."

"Good. Don't worry about it, then. Maybe I'll call him

on the way north." She watched the tree-lined shoulder race by outside her window. "I need to be more awake to deal with his whining."

"Whining?"

She looked over at Parkman. "I guess that's a bit harsh. What would you call it?"

"Well, it is whining, but—"

"See."

"I was going to say, when it comes to Aaron, he's just *feeling* more than he's ever felt before."

They turned off the highway and started up a ramp. A Tim Horton's was right in front of them.

"Feeling? You mean he's in love with me, but now he's even more in love or something?"

"Something like that. Hey, I don't claim to know what you two are going through, and I won't speak for him, but I feel Aaron wants changes. He wants you to stop what you're doing and stay home more often."

"He knew what—"

"I know, I know. But people change." Parkman looked at her. "He's never really liked what you do. And now that he's massively in love with you, he wants you all to himself. In and of itself, there's nothing wrong with it. The guy's madly in love with you and only wants the best for you. His heart is in the right place."

"But he's missing several vital pieces."

"Which are?"

Parkman made a right and then a quick left and eased into the parking lot of the coffee shop. It was busier than she thought it would be for a school day.

"How about what I want?" she asked. "How about asking me, then deciding what you want to do next? And once he found out that I will not stop listening to my sister, he could accept me for who I am—because I haven't changed one bit—or leave now." She crossed her arms at the thought of Aaron leaving her. What would a world without her man look like? She shuddered at the thought. "He has to make a decision before we, you know, have another baby on the way." She turned to Parkman as he turned off the car. "If I get pregnant again and then he leaves, you know I'd have to kill him, right?"

Parkman smiled. "If you got pregnant, Aaron wouldn't go anywhere. He's in love with you and has enough honor to see that through. He just doesn't like this stuff."

"Do you?"

Parkman stared out the windshield for a moment. His eyes tracked a dump truck as it exited the parking lot.

"I wouldn't say I like it." He lowered his head, then faced her. "But I'd never stop, either. And I don't begrudge being a part of it. You have become such a huge part of my life, Sarah, that I think it would be boring without you."

"Good." She nodded. "Before I get turned into a sappy, tear-filled ball of emotion-fuck, let's get coffee."

"Deal."

Once inside the coffee shop, they got in the line that was coiled around the counter.

Sarah elbowed him and pointed at the washrooms. Parkman nodded, and she bounded off.

When she came out, Parkman was at the counter. She motioned with her hands that she wanted an extra-large, then found a small table by the window overlooking the highway.

Parkman was at the table minutes later with two huge coffees. Sarah got hers open and started sipping.

"Do you think Aaron and I have a future?" she asked.

"Of course I do."

"Other than the obvious, what's going on with him?"

He shrugged. "No idea."

She glanced out the window and saw an OPP cruiser with its lights on and immediately thought they were coming to nab her, but it was pulling over a Volkswagen Beetle.

The vehicles stopped, and the cop got out, adjusted his hat, and started walking toward the Beetle. He stopped near the rear of the Bug and touched it.

"That's weird. Don't think I've ever noticed that before. That cop touched the back of the vehicle."

"Some police departments still train them to leave a thumbprint on the rear of the vehicle in case something happens. He's already logged in where he is, the license plate, and the reason he pulled them over. Dispatch will have everything. That fingerprint marked the car for added protection."

She sipped more coffee, watching the cop as he leaned down into the driver's window from the side.

"Something's going on," she whispered.

Parkman watched, too.

"He appears to be getting frustrated," she added.

The OPP officer stepped away from the window with his hands up at the side. A woman exited the Beetle and motioned for the cop to move toward his cruiser.

"Oh, shit," Sarah said. "She's got something in her

hand."

"Looks like a gun to me."

Sarah got up and stood at the window. She could've sworn the female driver just looked at her.

"You don't think she'll shoot a cop, do you? It's the middle of the day, in plain sight."

Parkman was beside her now. "Maybe we should go. Staring out the window like this, we're attracting attention. And we need to head north."

"You're right. This isn't our business. We can't save everybody." But even as she said it, she had an urge to head over and ameliorate the circumstances.

They turned away from the window and strode through the coffee shop, out the door, and around the building.

That's when Sarah heard a gun go off.

Chapter 15

JULIE FINISHED HER BURGER, grabbed her Coke and fries, and headed back out to her car. Once she was situated, she got back on the road, drove through town, and headed toward the Tim Horton's by the highway. It would allow her to eat the rest of her fries and drink most of her Coke before buying a coffee.

She hadn't gone one kilometer when she noticed the OPP cruiser behind her. She had to stop eating and place her hands on the wheel at ten and two. But the rearview mirror kept pulling her eyes. At any second, the cop would flash his lights, and she'd have to pull over. Running wasn't an option. He'd radio ahead, and a hundred cops'd stop her before she ever got to the Toronto area and executed her plans, whatever they were.

She maintained her speed through twists and turns and

kept the vehicle in the center of the lane.

Maybe Ron was right. As soon as she got away from the cop, she should dump the weapons and drive to Ottawa for the weekend. This wasn't her. She had no idea what to do or how to get Sarah's attention. This was an alcohol-induced psycho plan that was going to get her into trouble.

"Don't give him a reason, don't give him a reason," she whispered over and over to herself.

As a private citizen going about their private routine, didn't the cop have to have a valid reason to pull her over? He could make one up, but still. And if he did make one up, would she argue it in court? Highly unlikely, considering what she was up to.

Although, what was she up to, exactly? Granted, killing that man in her garage was self-defense, and that could be argued, but where was she going with a car full of heavy artillery? Would she actually pretend to use it? Deep down inside, she knew she couldn't. This idea was a dead end.

It had to be some stupid fantasy to win Ron back, to show him the extent of her love.

That made her an idiot. No man was worth risking her freedom.

"Idiot, idiot, idiot," she whispered repeatedly as she stared at the mirror.

Having a cop behind her made everything real and brought it all into focus. Maybe she'd discard the weapons, wipe everything down, and go back to Annemarie's.

"What the hell was I thinking—"

A loud horn snapped her eyes from the mirror. She slammed the brakes with both feet. The weapons in the back seat shot forward and onto the floor.

She almost drove right through a red light. A school bus had stopped partway into the intersection, and the driver gestured at her. She could've sworn he mouthed the words, *What the hell*, as he eased forward through the intersection.

The cruiser had stopped behind her.

"Oh, shit, shit, shit."

She stared at the red light, willing it to turn green as she was parked over the crosswalk and slightly into the intersection.

Should she drive back the five feet or wait? The cruiser had left ample room for her to ease back, but the light would change by the time she had it in reverse. That's the way it always worked, didn't it? The second her hand touched the knob to shift into reverse, the light would change.

Decision made. She'd wait.

The light changed. She started forward, ensured she got through the intersection safely, then checked her mirror.

No red and blue lights. Yet.

He wasn't going to pull her over.

Good. It was an oversight. An easy mistake. Cops had to get used to seeing drivers a little paranoid when they were following them.

Although he was staying pretty close to her bumper. From the quick glances she was catching, it appeared as if he was tapping on something to his right. Oh shit, he's speaking now. Probably on the radio. Talking to his dispatcher.

About her? Or was he getting called to a crime scene?

The coffee shop turn was only seconds away now.

The single whoop from the cruiser's siren jerked her eyes

back to the mirror. His red and blues were on, and they were bright, even in the afternoon sunlight.

She smacked the steering wheel with her hand and then scrunched up her face because that hurt.

"Ouch," she whispered, shaking her hand several times.

The turn to the coffee shop passed on the right as she slowed to a stop on the shoulder. Just over the hill was Highway 11 and her continued journey to Toronto. But that was all over now. What if he wanted to search the car?

The urge to vomit came back—she was so nervous. Being caught with all the weapons she had in her car would be a couple of years in jail for sure.

This was one of those moments where the next few decisions left lasting life-long consequences—or rewards.

As she watched the cop tapping away at something to his right inside the cruiser, the lights still rolling on his roof, she came to understand something.

Getting caught with the weapons was serious trouble. Getting caught later after running from the cops wouldn't be as bad. The lesser of two evils.

So, whatever happened, she would listen to him, comply, and be nice. Apologize and admit that seeing him so close had befuddled her, but she wouldn't let him search her car. And if it got serious, she would simply drive away. Find somewhere secluded and dump the weapons. Then, turn herself in and say she was afraid for her life. Make up a story about Ron and his time in the war and how a man—the cop —was at her car door, and he had a gun on his hip. And she would cry. A lot.

That might work because she couldn't afford a weapon's

charge of this magnitude.

The cop finally got out of his cruiser. She rubbed her palms back and forth on her thighs in an attempt to dry the dampness accumulating there.

Looking all authoritative in his uniform, the officer strolled up behind her vehicle, touched the back for some reason, then continued up the driver's side and stopped at the back window.

And her heart leaped out of her chest.

She'd totally forgotten to check the weapons back there after jamming on the brakes. Did the blanket still cover them all? She thought she'd heard them fall onto the floor.

The car was still running, so she could power down the window. She did that now, lifted her head slightly, and smiled at the man.

"I'm sorry," she said. "I was watching you and didn't see that red light." She shook her head and laughed in a way that was supposed to be laughing at her own stupidity, but it came out as a nervous laugh.

"Ma'am, could you please step out of the car?"

"Excuse me?" She twisted farther in her seat to look directly up at him. "Don't you want my driver's license, registration, and insurance slips?"

"We'll get to that, ma'am, but first, I need you out of the vehicle."

"Officer, come on. I'm not drunk or anything." She swung back to the mirror and looked at the sclera of her eyes. Bloodshot. She turned back to him. "Okay, sure, my eyes look bad, but that was last night."

"Ma'am, this isn't open for discussion. Please exit the

vehicle. I've asked politely, ma'am. It's a lawful order."

"Then tell me why you've stopped me. I'm a private citizen and don't get out of my car when any man asks me to."

"I understand that, but I'm not any man." The cop moved away from the back window and glanced inside the front. She specifically caught him looking at her hands for some reason. "I'm an officer of the law, and it is my lawful right to have you exit your vehicle at a lawful traffic stop. Please do so now."

"Okay, I will. No problem." She focused on his legs for a moment as a car whooshed by their position, then another one. Each time a car went by, the officer edged closer and then backed up.

"Ma'am? I don't want to have to ask you again."

She snuck a glance behind her waist.

And it all came clear to her.

The OPP officer had pulled her over for distracted driving or some other minor shit. But when he approached the vehicle, he saw half of the stashed weapons in the back seat because they had been shoved forward, and the blanket wasn't covering them anymore. In her one quick glance, the assault rifle's barrel was exposed.

"Turn off the vehicle and step out, now." His voice was stronger, reaching a more serious tone.

She nodded. It was over, and she was doomed. There was no winning Ron back or finding Sarah Roberts. There was just jail and years of court dates and expensive lawyers. The regret made her even sicker. She could've stayed at home or even stayed with Annemarie.

What a dumb bitch I am, she thought.

But since she'd come this far …

Julie clutched the car keys gently. "Okay, Officer, I'll get out. If you insist."

She turned off the car, pulled the keys, and made to pocket them.

The cop stepped back to allow room for her door to open.

With her right hand slightly hidden by her waist, she lowered it, felt around for a grip, found one, and then opened the door with her left hand.

When she placed one foot on the concrete, she raised the weapon and pointed it at the cop.

"Step away from my vehicle," she said, her voice strong and serious. Her eyes caught the safety catch on the side and flicked it with her thumb.

"Hey, hey, take it easy now." The cop stepped away, walking backward toward his cruiser. "You don't want to do this, ma'am."

"How's that? With all those weapons in there?" She didn't mean to, but she gestured toward her car. "No, I don't think so. Here's what we're going to do."

The officer stumbled and almost tripped into the hood of his car. When his hands lowered to break the fall, she could've sworn he was going for his gun.

The urge to stay alive blinded her to reason, and she pulled the trigger.

She truly didn't mean to and didn't even know if the weapon in her hand was loaded.

But it fired, and the report was so loud it frightened her.

"Oh shit," she whispered out loud but couldn't hear it

with her own ears.

Chapter 16

RONALD HARRIS WATCHED THE schoolyard, then glanced at his watch. Not long now. His sons would come out, another day of learning finished, and he'd get them in his vehicle and out of the city where they'd be safe.

It was the only way.

Since his work truck was wrapped with his company name and phone number, he decided to park it and rent a Jeep. It was as high off the ground as his pickup and could easily shield his sons from prying eyes.

Little Jason was only six, and his older brother Michael was eight now. The pain they'd been through in such a short time was something he couldn't fix. He had a say in their future, and as far as the law was concerned, he'd done nothing wrong. But yet, CAS said his boys belonged to them until they *allowed* his sons to see him.

What about living with him? That's a totally different conversation, yet they were allowed to live with him before he walked out on his abusive ex-wife.

No one ever thought men could be abused—ever—and they were wrong.

Ron would never hit a woman. Sure, he'd lose his temper and even defend himself by warding off Bridgette's punches, but he never hit her once. Even when she sucker-punched him and gave him a black eye. Angry, clenching his fists, aching for retribution, Ron walked away to nurse his wounds with whiskey.

He didn't hit her then, and he wouldn't hit her now.

Cops even came to their home once. He'd wanted to leave, and Bridgette had called them on him because he had wine with dinner. Nothing came of it, and he didn't drive, but he'd chatted with the officer about his black eye.

The cop told him he shouldn't defend himself. To this day, over two years later, he still remembered that conversation like it was last night.

"What?" he'd asked. "You've got to be kidding."

They were standing in front of the open garage door on his driveway.

"Look, here's how it works," the cop said. "Let's say you block a punch, grab her wrist so she doesn't keep hitting you, and push her away, you know, to stop the barrage of flailing hands."

"Which is exactly what I did."

"Right, but she falls to the carpet and gets a carpet burn."

"Okay, so what? Shouldn't be attacking me, then."

The cop's patience grew thin. "I get that, and at this

point, you haven't lashed out in violence in the sense that you're hitting back, right?"

"Right."

"We show up, and she's crying on the front porch, saying you beat her up. She shows us the carpet burn mark or the redness around her wrists. What do you think happens next?"

"You come inside and speak with me. I'll show you my fat lip, black eye, or whatever. Get the story straight."

The cop shook his head. "That's not how it works. If she's got a carpet burn, bruising on her wrists, and maybe even a cut from some self-induced injury, you're the one getting arrested."

"That's ridiculous. What would the charge be, liar assault and emotional battery?"

The cop shrugged. "Hey, I'm just trying to help a guy out. Man to man, don't touch her. Don't even defend yourself. Today, it's not good enough to be blocking her punches. If she gets hurt, you're in trouble."

Ron recalled registering how wrong that was somewhere in his mind.

"Are you saying allow her to pummel me?"

The cop nodded. "Doesn't seem fair, but yeah. If you want to stay out of jail."

"Even if I'm missing a tooth, she's broken my nose and kicked me in the balls?"

He nodded again. "You can run, can't you?"

"And if I lost my shit one night and broke her nose, you know, to say, enough is enough. What then?"

"You know what then, Mr. Harris."

"Then arrest her. Look at my eye."

"You really want me to go in there and arrest your wife with her children clinging to her lap, crying that their father has been drinking and wants to drive somewhere?" The cop shook his head. "Look, I hate domestics. I hate coming to these calls. We're wrapping this up and leaving. Don't drive, Mr. Harris. Stay home, and don't fight with your wife." The cop started toward his cruiser. "I've given that advice for free. Don't make me come back."

Ron clenched his fists as he stared at the school. It was a sunny afternoon in September, and he still felt the rage of those horrible nights in the last six months of living with Bridgette.

And now it had been the third time a teacher had complained about bruises on Jason. So, CAS seized his kids on the same day CRA seized his bank account for back taxes, and the Family Responsibility Office, or FRO as everyone called them, was threatening to take his driver's license for non-payment of child support.

It was all coming down to him going bankrupt and losing everything—although he couldn't bankrupt child support—and nobody cared that the genesis of all of this was a relationship gone sour. He just didn't want to be with her anymore. It wasn't healthy to stay with Bridgette. Emotionally, physically, or otherwise. He had suffered, his boys had suffered, and it was bound to get worse.

But now, two years later, he was suffering in ways that drove people to suicide.

Julie cared, but he couldn't drag her down with all this.

The weapons collection was his out. The men he'd been dealing with were ex-military, which he appreciated. They were his platoon from their time in Afghanistan. Their original plan had been put into play, and he couldn't allow that.

So he stole their stash of weapons, and they wanted them back.

He'd made a huge mistake to add to his long list of mistakes, and here he was today, waiting to steal his kids from some CAS woman in a rented Jeep, with ample weapons in the back of the Jeep, along with a credit card he'd saved untouched for such an outing if it was ever needed.

The school bell rang. Moments later, the school's doors opened, and little kids poured out in droves. He almost cried seeing the tiny children, so innocent, so wonderful. Why did he get a raw deal? All he ever wanted was that white picket fence, the wife, the kids.

Had they stayed together and remained healthy, business would've been thriving, and there'd be no child support payments, no family law lawyer swindling over twenty-thousand from him, which he couldn't afford. And so far, the only result of the supposed equalization was more payments he needed to make.

With a quick shake of his head, he was back in the Jeep. He had to stay focused. Mikey and Jay were about to exit the building at any moment, and he needed to see which car they got into.

Thoughts of Julie and what she might be doing raced through his mind, but he pushed them away. Julie had supposedly killed a man at their home. They were getting close and would discover where his kids went to school. Soon, they would take the kids and kill the CAS woman.

They didn't care. He knew his old friend Hamilton well, and Hamilton would do anything to fulfill their plans.

So Ron had to take his own kids. It was the right thing to do. He would keep them safe as any father would. But more importantly, it was the noble thing to do. Once they were gone, out of the CAS's hands, their handler would also be out of harm's way.

He turned on the Jeep.

Tapping his thumb on the steering wheel, he watched hundreds of kids fill the field and the sidewalk, and some on the road as they ran or walked to waiting cars. Kids were passing his Jeep now, laughing, spinning, talking about a movie and where to meet later.

He heard all this and wished that for his boys. A normal life. A normal childhood. Dreams, memories, and freedom to be young and have a good time. Even break a few rules and get in trouble once in a while.

But he feared a lot of that innocence was gone for his boys. The divorce was hurting them, their caregiver—Bridgette—was hurting them, and now strangers were taking care of them.

Jason came into view. Followed by Michael.

His heartbeat shot up as a spike of adrenaline filled his stomach with an acid mix.

This was it. His one time to get his kids.

Which car were they headed toward?

He followed them as they walked along the sidewalk, passing a red Volvo, then a Camaro, a later model station wagon.

They stopped by a Ford Escort and opened the door.

The act of watching his kids, his boys, his own flesh and blood, enter someone else's car, someone he didn't know, drove him insane.

Once they were both inside, he was close enough to see the woman in the driver's seat helping Michael with his seatbelt.

Like a studious driver, she checked her blind spot, turned on her blinker, and eased away from the sidewalk carefully and cautiously.

So far, that was the only thing he appreciated.

A moment later, they passed the front of his Jeep. He put it in gear and turned out into the road to follow them. Up ahead, at a four-way stop sign, the CAS vehicle was already going through.

Ron slowed at the stop sign but had to wait while a black SUV was already there.

It turned in behind the Ford Escort with his kids in it, and Ron motored the Jeep through the intersection, falling in behind the black SUV. He eased left to see the Escort, then settled back into the center of the lane.

He'd make his move as soon as the SUV was out of the way. It had to be a quiet residential area. Someplace where the cops would take at least five minutes to arrive. Someone would call them, he had no doubt. By the time they were called, Ron would have already absconded with his boys.

The Escort turned onto Algonquin Road. The SUV followed, and so did Ron.

The Escort got on Highway 11 and turned south. So did the SUV.

That was starting to worry him. The woman in the Escort

took her time with the boys. She was tasked with keeping them safe.

So why didn't the SUV pass her when they had the chance?

Ron followed them both at a distance as they drove by the O'Brien intersection and all the way around to the North Gate Mall. Finally, the Escort exited the North Bay area entirely and continued south on the highway toward Powassan.

With that stupid SUV right behind them.

That couldn't be Hamilton's men, could it? There had been some kind of small war on the streets of Toronto that morning. It was all over the news. Emergency task forces had been mobilized after a dozen cruisers had responded to the sounds of guns. The media was having a heyday talking about the *war* that went down on Toronto's streets. Even with all the gun laws, blah, blah, blah.

Sarah Roberts's name came up in connection with the group of vehicles that had been destroyed. Then, the flow of information hitting the media stopped, and now, no one knew the truth.

But Ron Harris suspected what had happened.

Sarah Roberts was named in the news after last night's MATADOR misfire, although Ron never aimed at the plane. One of Sarah's bullets buzzed by his ear. She could've killed him, which wasn't his plan at all.

After that connection, Hamilton's team would've gone after her. And if she had protection, well, a gunfight on Toronto's streets made sense.

So if they thought Sarah had their stuff, why come after

him? Why go after his kids?

Staying far enough back to remain undetected, Ron withdrew his sidearm and ensured it was loaded and ready. He leaned over, opened the glove box, and withdrew another gun. It, too, was loaded and ready.

If it were Hamilton's men, he'd have a hard time getting his kids from them without being killed.

Although, would they kill him since he was the only one who knew where their stash was?

He couldn't allow them to snatch his kids for leverage.

About a dozen kilometers short of Powassan, the Ford Escort signaled to turn off the highway.

The SUV followed.

"Dammit." He smacked the steering wheel. "Now what?"

He couldn't risk driving to another exit. It was too far. He'd lose them. He had to follow, but these guys were highly trained. They probably already made him.

"Fuck it."

Ron slowed the Jeep and turned as the SUV took another corner ahead.

Five minutes later, the three vehicles were driving on a back country road surrounded by thick trees. Ron had pulled back a fair distance. It was a perfect spot to get his kids—if he had been alone with that Ford Escort driver.

What if he didn't come today? Where would his boys end up then?

Anger warmed his collar, and he tightened his grip on the steering wheel.

The SUV's brake lights lit up. Ahead, the Escort angled left onto a long driveway.

Ron slowed the Jeep, unsure what to do, waiting to see what the SUV would do.

Without a signal, the SUV followed the Escort down the driveway. He hoped and prayed it wasn't Hamilton's men. Instead, let it be the authorities driving with the old woman to ensure the kids safely made it to their foster house.

Ron drove by the entrance to the house and continued on. Mentally, he logged about fifty meters, then pulled over and cut the engine.

Always good with a distance shot, he exited the Jeep, opened the trunk, and grabbed a rifle.

Without closing the back hatch, he ran into the woods about ten feet and followed it back toward the house where the SUV and the Escort had gone. The leaves hadn't started falling yet, so other than random twigs, he was only making light footfall sounds. But as he drew closer, he slowed and moved with a lighter step.

Someone shouted something. It was a woman's voice.

He raised the rifle and used the scope to look in the direction of the house. Close enough to hear her yell but still too far to see anything yet.

No longer mindful of the noise, he sprinted through the trees, ducking branches and shouldering through others until the house came into view.

There were days like this back in Afghanistan. The terrain was different, but women screaming and men running to their aid with weapons were the same.

He'd killed over there, too. Not by choice, as he never had wanted to take a life, but by necessity.

For some reason, it all came back to him at that moment.

Running, someone screaming, the rifle in his hand.

He zeroed in on what he needed to do. He wasn't saving just anybody this time. He was saving his own flesh and blood.

The house came into view, and what he saw horrified him and would haunt his dreams for the rest of his life.

He counted two men. One held his boys, and the other held the driver of the Escort. His boys were crying. The Escort driver was whimpering and saying *No* over and over.

"Tell us where Ronald Harris is, and you live," the man holding the Escort driver said.

"I don't know where he is," she screamed. "We've been forbidden contact for several weeks."

The man placed the barrel of a handgun against her forehead, and her *No* turned to, *Please don't*.

"One last time," the man said.

Michael screamed and looked away, holding his little brother.

Ron rested his shoulder against a tree, prepared the weapon to fire, popped off the scope cover, and aimed it at the man holding the woman. He estimated the distance with hardly any wind. After a couple of adjustments, he placed his finger inside the trigger guard, peering through the scope, holding the weapon steady.

"Last chance, bitch," the man yelled.

"I swear, I don't know where—"

The rifle spit and the man's head jerked back violently. He was already falling when Ron spun toward the other man holding his kids.

Instinctively, that man ducked and dropped behind

Michael and Jason while he searched the woods, looking for his partner's shooter.

The woman lay on the gravel driveway screaming, no doubt covered in blood.

His boys shouted and cried, but Ron had a job to do. Focus on the man who is trying to abduct his boys.

Even though he was able to see the man's forehead in his scope, he couldn't take the shot. It was too close to his kids.

The man backed the kids up to the SUV and opened the back door on the passenger side. He dropped to his knees and pushed Michael inside, then Jason. The door slammed shut with his boys inside the vehicle.

Sweat eased down Ron's forehead, threatening to go in his eye. His muscles were showing signs of strain. The guy had to show himself now, or Ron would lose his chance. He held the gun another moment.

But the man was gone.

Ron lowered the weapon and stared at the SUV. Both boys were still inside, but the man had disappeared—

The driver's side door opened. How did he get over there?

Ron jumped ahead five feet to lean against another tree, understanding the man must've laid down and rolled under the vehicle to reach the other side undetected.

The SUV began to back out of the driveway. The screaming woman was calming down, only muttering to herself now as she crawled toward the house.

Ron raised the weapon, took aim, and locked his finger on the trigger. At the end of the driveway, as the driver turned the back end to the left, Ron took the shot through the passenger window.

The vehicle stopped turning and slowly drifted across the road to the shoulder, where it came to a rest after bumping into a tree.

Ron was already running through the bush before the SUV came to a complete stop.

As he neared it, he could hear his boys screaming in the back seat, and his heart stuttered in fear.

Gun up, ready to fire again, Ron ran around the front of the vehicle, giving it a wide berth. The man in the front seat rested sideways against the window, his face a bloody mess. The bullet had traveled through the passenger window and hit the man in the temple. A perfect shot.

He couldn't believe he still had those skills since it had been so long since he was last deployed.

At the side door, he ripped it open.

"Come on, guys. Daddy's got you." They fell into his arms. "No one's going to hurt you now. The bad guys are dead."

They hugged him fiercely, screaming *Daddy* as they clung to his waist.

He let them hold him for a moment, then said, "We have to leave now, guys."

With one step and then another, Ron led his sons to the rented Jeep. He tossed the rifle in the back and got them strapped in. Then he ran around to the driver's side, hopped in, and had them heading back the way they had come minutes before.

When he passed the foster house, the woman was no longer outside. Probably inside now, calling the police. There were dead men outside her home, and some other guy had kidnapped the two kids she was in charge of.

Maybe it was a good thing she was inside when he drove by. She would've never seen his Jeep if she hadn't noticed the SUV following her. And he had parked down the road.

There was a chance he could keep the rental for a little longer.

Until he had a plan for the next step.

In the mirror, his boys sobbed in each other's arms. He would calm them down at the cabin and explain things as best he could. It probably wasn't the best place to take them, but at least no one would know where they were.

The cabin was remote and something he financed over a year ago. Julie knew nothing about it. No one knew about it. The man he bought it from died six months ago. Rundown and left to rot, he got it for next to nothing. Fixing it up in his spare time kept him busy. Extra work days for six months was all it took. Eventually, they could connect him to the cabin, but that wouldn't happen in the next few days.

That little cabin housed all the extra weapons.

The ones he took from Hamilton's mercenaries.

The weapons that started all the trouble.

Chapter 17

Sarah ducked in response to the gunfire. She'd heard it so often that she knew exactly what it was.

"Parkman, get the car." She handed him her nearly full coffee cup. "Meet me over there."

The traffic cop was just getting back to his feet. He had stumbled when the woman fired her weapon. She still held it low at her waist, almost out of sight to passing cars.

They were talking. The officer was by the hood of his car now, his hands raised to his shoulders.

Sarah reached the edge of the parking lot. Thick grass and a low ditch separated her from the parked vehicles at the side of the road. She was close enough that they would hear her if she yelled, but she didn't want to startle the woman.

"Keys," the woman shouted.

She wanted the cop to hand over his keys so he couldn't

follow her. That was a short-term fix. There would be a BOLO on her vehicle seconds after she pulled away from the curb. Sarah expected to hear sirens at any moment. Like Parkman said, dispatch would have all of the woman's information. This wasn't going to end well for her.

Although Sarah had to stop her from shooting a cop.

"Give them to me," the woman shouted, her free hand held out, palm up.

All the cop had to do was grab her wrist and yank her off balance enough to dislodge the weapon. Sure, it was risky, but there was a high chance of success for a woman who appeared to be an amateur at this.

Sarah slowed at the small incline near the shoulder of the road. Fifteen feet away, she caught Parkman in the rental, easing up behind the cop car. He stopped twenty feet back.

She raised her hands out to the side and cleared her throat. The woman's head snapped her way, saw her, then snapped back at the cop. She retreated a couple of steps from the officer.

"Are you okay, Officer?" Sarah asked.

He nodded three rapid times. Probably was shitting his pants and couldn't find his voice, which was understandable.

"Not your problem," the woman shouted at her.

"That's where you're wrong," Sarah said, advancing closer, slow step by slow step.

"How's that?" The woman asked, her eyes not leaving the OPP officer.

Two pickup trucks drove by, followed by a small hatchback. Sarah waited for them to pass, then stepped within ten feet of the woman's car.

"See that man in the parked car behind the cruiser?"

The woman edged to the right to glance around the officer.

"Yeah. So?"

"He's called every law enforcement agency this side of Toronto. We watched you get pulled over from the coffee shop window."

"That was you?" This time, the woman glanced at her, paused, then turned back to the cop. "Holy shit," she muttered under her breath.

"Holy shit what?"

"You're …"

"I'm what?" She figured stalling was a good tactic, but it had several problems. Parkman hadn't called anyone. And this officer's colleagues would be coming soon. Sarah didn't want to be detained again. Also, the woman's gun hand was shaking so much that Sarah worried she might shoot the cop by accident.

The woman took another look at Sarah, then refocused on the cop.

"You're Sarah."

The cop was staring at her now. Even he shook his head. "Holy shit," he muttered as another car raced by. "You're working together, aren't you?"

"No, sir, we are not. This is your traffic stop, and I was having a coffee." Sarah addressed the woman. "Lower that weapon before it goes off and hurts somebody. And trust me, you shoot a cop, and you won't see the outside again for a long time."

"You've shot cops. You're outside."

Sarah and the officer exchanged a glance. "Yeah, well, that's different. They deserved it. And hey, wait a second," she advanced closer, "don't use me as an example for anything."

"I need help," the woman said.

"I imagine you do." Sarah moved to spitting distance from the rear of the woman's vehicle. "You can start with a good lawyer."

"No. I need your help."

"That probably isn't what you need."

The woman took two steps closer to the cop. "Place your hands on the hood of the car where I can see them."

The cop did.

Sarah glanced back at Parkman. He raised his hands and shoulders through the windshield in a what-gives gesture. She held up one finger to give her a moment.

"Okay, you win," Sarah said. "Everyone's doing what you want. Jump in your car and take off."

The cop glared at her. She narrowed her eyes back. *Fuck you, I'm trying to stop this nervous bitch from killing you by accident.*

The woman fumbled in her pocket for something as a black van drove around them.

That's when the first sirens could be heard in the distance. The officer probably hadn't responded to his radio, or he was able to send a distress signal of some sort. More cops were coming. This woman had all of one minute before she was surrounded by an army in blue, and Sarah wanted nothing to do with it.

The woman yanked out a fob. The car's trunk popped.

The woman leaned down without taking her eyes off the cop and lifted it up all the way.

"I said I need help," the woman repeated. "Your help, Sarah Roberts."

Sarah's eyes widened when she saw the weapons in the trunk.

"Where the fuck did you get your hands on that?" she asked, stepping around the trunk without regard for the woman holding the gun. She wanted Sarah's help. She wasn't about to shoot her.

"My boyfriend, the man you almost met last night near the airport, needs your help."

Sarah slowly faced the woman. Sometimes, things still surprised her.

Without looking at Parkman, she waved him forward. The gravel crunching under the rental's tires told her he saw the gesture.

"That's why I couldn't let this policeman stop me, take me in." The woman looked at Sarah as Parkman pulled up and stopped beside them. "A lot of people are at risk," the woman added. "People I care about. Will you help?"

"Ma'am, you're one crazy lady." Sarah strode in front of her and opened the passenger door to their rental. The sirens were no more than one more arc in the road away. "Get in your car and drive away, but give me the gun first."

"Really? You'll help?"

Sarah nodded and held out her hand. The woman hesitated.

"What next? Where will we meet?"

"Use the ramp on the other side of the bridge over there."

She pointed, then leaned in closer. "Head south on Highway 11, then pull over five kilometers down. Wait for us. We'll be a minute behind you."

The woman's eyes watered. Was she going to cry?

"Oh fuck me, don't start crying." Sarah shook her hand violently. "Give me the gun and go. Now!"

She slapped the gun in Sarah's hand, dove in her car, and squealed away.

"You shouldn't have done that," the cop said, straightening up.

"What? Save your life?"

The cop reached for his lapel mic.

Sarah pointed the weapon at him. "Don't."

He stopped with his mouth open, about to speak.

"Let go of the mic."

He did, frowning, his hand falling to his side.

Sarah aimed the weapon low and fired. The cruiser's front tire deflated instantly with the new hole in it.

The cop jumped back several feet when the gun fired, almost losing his balance.

"What the fuck?" he shouted, his face turning red. "I thought you were one of the good guys."

"Sorry to disappoint."

She dropped into the front seat of the rental.

"Hit it. Follow that woman."

Parkman slammed the accelerator down in pursuit without a single word.

Chapter 18

ANNEMARIE WILLARD TRIED EVERY number she had for Julie Perkins and then started in on Ronald Harris's phone numbers. She called his construction company line, personal, and house number but got no one.

Last night was fun. She drank, but not as much as Julie. Although, it took her until midday to feel somewhat better. And now she couldn't get ahold of Julie. She'd lost her friend and needed to find her before she did something stupid, like trying to get back with Ron.

He kicked her out. That was the problem with women, Annemarie thought; they went back every time. It looked weak, pitiful. When you're with a man, be with him all the way. *Need* him in your life, fine. But if he fucks around, lies to you, and then kicks you out, never crawl back—ever.

"If there's any crawling or groveling or begging, that's

on him, babe," Annemarie said, heading for the door.

The car keys were on the hook tacked to the wall. She snatched them up and half ran, half walked to her car. She had promised Ron she'd keep Julie safe, and now she'd lost her.

Getting across town to Ron and Julie's place would take twenty minutes. And if she found Julie there, she'd have to lay out the realities of life. It was time to grow up and learn a few things about relationships, about her man, Ronald Harris, ex-Canadian military, ex-sniper, still on a mission.

Annemarie had known Ron for over a decade, since before he was with Bridgette. She'd watched their marriage crumble and even had Ron over for a couple of nights while he decompressed from one of their big fights. Nothing ever happened between them, and nothing ever would. Their relationship was forged during their time overseas when they served side by side. They had always kept it professional.

Taking Julie in last night was prearranged. Ron had called and said he had to fix things. Annemarie understood what he meant. He'd asked if Julie could come over, then explained the rest.

Annemarie was getting used to helping Ron out. But this time, he may have problems he couldn't resolve, which would haunt him for the rest of his days, and he'd wanted to distance himself from her and Julie.

These were things she couldn't help him with. As far as she was concerned, Ron had lost his mind with what the news was reporting all day. Although it was lucky for him, they weren't using his name. So far, other people were being blamed in the media for all the trouble Ron was causing.

First, it was the airliner missile attack that sources said Sarah Roberts was responsible for.

Then, some military gunfight took place in the fashion district of downtown Toronto, a block off Spadina. Some say Sarah was there, too.

Police were apparently responding to an altercation near a school on Brant Street and Adelaide. Witnesses claim a group of men in SUVs kidnapped another man. Apparently, two or three men got away and were now speaking with the authorities. It hit the news so fast because these three men were directly connected to Sarah Roberts.

A breaking news piece in Annemarie's area made her want to go find Julie immediately. Someone had shot and killed two people near Powassan, about a twenty-minute drive from North Bay, which was quite close to Ron and Julie's place. The breaking news piece said it was a developing story, but they had a source claiming it was a case of parental kidnapping. More details were still coming in.

Parental kidnapping? Could Julie have gone after Ron's kids? Did she have the balls to pull off something like that?

Annemarie didn't think so.

Then who? Or was it even connected to Ron's kids? It could have nothing to do with them at all.

But Annemarie had grown increasingly worried since last night's attack on that airliner and Ron's message to Julie about an attempt to garner Sarah Roberts's attention.

She made it to Ron's house in under twenty minutes. She passed the house slowly, looking for any signs of cops, but saw nothing that spooked her. A vehicle was parked on the road out front, but that was it. She suspected she knew who was driving that car.

Which probably meant Julie hadn't returned to the house, and neither had Ron.

She turned around six houses away, then drove back to Ron's house, where she parked in the driveway.

The not knowing, the indecision, was nerve-racking. The way Ron was acting lately, one false move, and he could kill her. She didn't want to spook whoever was in the house, but she needed answers.

Like, where was Julie Perkins?

She turned off the car and exited the vehicle. The highway was too far away to hear any vehicles. A few birds flitted in a nearby tree, but other than that, the area was quiet.

A quick survey of the front windows told her she'd attracted no attention inside the house yet.

If that vehicle parked out front was who she thought it was, they already knew she was there and wouldn't be standing in the bay window.

Without a care in the world, she strode up the driveway and over to the front door, where she knocked. A legitimate friend of the family—someone who made sense and was supposed to be there, wouldn't check over her shoulder and act all suspicious-like, so Annemarie didn't. She just walked up to the door and knocked.

No one answered. She knocked again, then twisted around nonchalantly to check the road as if waiting for the door to be opened.

The street was empty of nosy members of the public.

She thanked her lucky stars that Ron and Julie lived off of 654, which was far enough south of North Bay that their community wasn't piled in close, house after house, cookie-cutter-like. There were yards, trees, and land separating each property.

In a final effort to let whoever was inside know that she was there and not leaving, she rang the doorbell.

Still no answer.

"What the hell?" she muttered under her breath.

After a backward glance at the parked car in front of the house, she was sure she knew who should be inside Ron's place.

One last look along the road both ways and then she tried the door handle.

It turned in her hand.

She slipped inside and closed the door.

The idiot had ransacked the living room. She wondered if she should announce her presence or roam freely.

What if he was on the toilet? If so, he'd come out blasting at her.

"It's me, Annemarie Willard," she said, loud enough to be heard. Then added, "Belleville." She used her code name, too, so her team would know her. Getting shot by accident would suck.

There was no response, which spooked her. Horrible ideas assailed her thoughts. She'd feel better with a weapon of her own. She chastised herself for not bringing her gun.

The first stop had to be the kitchen.

She moved forward, carefully watching the hallway, listening for anything.

At the alcove to the kitchen, a fast food bag from a local burger joint was on the table with a half-eaten burger left on the wrapper. Fries had been spilled onto the wrapper as well, and a dollop of ketchup made a circle on some napkins.

Someone hadn't finished their lunch.

She placed a hand on the burger, then lifted a French fry from the center of the pile. Room temperature cold.

Whoever it was didn't walk away when she knocked on the front door—too cold.

A short scream escaped her when the central air kicked on. She ducked so fast that she bumped one of the chairs with her knee.

"Motherfucker," she grunted, holding her knee.

The house was so quiet that when the air clicked on, it sounded much louder to her frayed nerves than it should have.

Relying on the table for support, she stood straight and put her weight on her good leg. It stung for a minute, then was better.

She scanned the living room and the kitchen, waiting for someone, but no one came out of hiding. No toilet flushed. And with the air going now, she wouldn't even hear a creaking sound behind her.

"Dammit," she whispered.

She retrieved a steak knife from the drawer beside the fridge and held it in her clenched fist, the blade aimed along her forearm.

Then, tentative step after tentative step, Annemarie searched the main floor of Ron and Julie's house, finding nothing and no one, her nerves buzzing. The hair on her neck still stood out from being spooked by the air conditioner, but it stayed up because the house was too cold.

In the hallway that led to the garage, she clicked the off button on the digital display, and the central air clicked off.

The house fell into blessed silence again.

She glanced at the access door to the garage. That's where Julie said Ron kept his weapons. Where they'd had their fight last night before Julie came over to her place.

That had to be it. Someone was in the garage. Either that or the basement, and she really didn't feel like going in the basement.

She placed a hand on the doorknob, then said in a loud, easygoing voice, giving her goosebumps. "Hey guys, it's Annemarie. Where is everyone?"

She opened the access door to the garage. Immediately, her hand released the knob, and the door swung shut on the horror lying on the ground inside Ron's garage.

"Holy ass," she whispered.

She grabbed the door and tore it open, then stepped in over the body. The garage was empty. No car and no weapons adorned any shelves.

She leaned down to inspect the body.

Gunshot victim. Multiple gunshots to the chest. Blood ran down his cheek from his mouth. The man would've died within a minute as several bullets entered near his heart. His Israeli-made Uzi lay beside him, untouched. And she didn't recognize him, so it wasn't Hamilton or any of his close team members. This was someone else.

Would Ron leave the weapon behind? There was no way Julie could have done this. It had to be Ron. But why would he return to the house?

Annemarie got to her feet and pulled out her cell phone.

Then she saw the vomit.

"Oh no …" she whispered. "Julie."

Ronald Harris wouldn't vomit. Ronald Harris had seen combat. This would rattle anyone, but Ron would hold his own.

Julie would vomit.

Annemarie glanced back at the body. That many bullets were overkill, amateur. Julie emptied her weapon in fear. And she caught him in the middle of lunch.

This smelled of Julie, but Annemarie couldn't figure out how she had the guts.

On her cell, she dialed out. After two rings, it was answered.

"Ham here. Go ahead."

"It's Belleville."

"Wait a moment, Belle."

She waited, rubbing her knee. It was already feeling better.

"Go ahead, we're encrypted."

"One of ours is down. Shot in the target's garage. I suspect the target's female companion did the shooting, but I can't confirm."

"Are you saying our contact at the target's house is dead? Repeat."

"Affirmative. Cleanup crew needed."

"And where is the target's woman? We need her, too."

"Understood. Will reacquire her immediately."

There was a dangerous pause on the other end of the line. Annemarie dreaded the next words, hoping her life wasn't forfeit.

"Remain on site and make sure no one enters the premises. Cleanup crew ETA is twenty minutes. Locate the woman and bring her to us before midnight. That is your new directive."

The line died.

Without Julie, Annemarie wouldn't see the sunrise tomorrow. These people weren't the forgiving type.

But she had another plan, something Hamilton did not know of. She was working her own angles, and soon, everyone would know where her loyalties stood.

Julie was supposed to be her charge, her responsibility. Letting her go, and now one of theirs was dead, was unforgivable. Bringing Julie in was her only chance at surviving this with Hamilton.

Unless her own plan came together first.

But where the hell was Julie? And how could she find her in—she checked the time on her phone—eight hours?

Annemarie Willard almost puked where Julie did, but she held it together long enough to make it back to the living room, where she sat by the bay window to watch the road. Her alternative plan had to work, or she was dead. After getting involved with these people, a death certificate was the only way out.

The second the cleanup crew arrived, she would leave. Then, she would drive aimlessly around town, calling Julie's number in a desperate attempt to save her own life.

A life for a life.

It had been done before and would be done again long after Annemarie's flesh was part of the soil—wherever they chose to bury her body.

Chapter 19

HAMILTON SET THE PHONE down and studied the faces of the
team watching him.

"Someone's down?" Ajax asked.

Hamilton moved around the table where the phone sat
and took a seat on a metal chair.

"It appears our friend has a formidable accomplice."

Tor cleared his throat. "The woman? Julie?"

Hamilton nodded. "Belle thinks it was her."

"Thinks?" Tor asked. "How does she not know? Isn't
Julie with her?"

"She said she suspected the target's female companion
did the shooting, but Belle couldn't confirm. That would lead
me to believe Julie is no longer with her. I gave her till
midnight to produce her. Belle said she would reacquire the
woman."

"How did she lose her?" Ajax asked. "And because of that, our house watcher is dead. That's another one." Ajax smacked the couch beside him and got to his feet. "How many more, Ham? Tell me, how many more of us have to die?"

Hamilton glanced over at their captive, then back to Ajax. "Your tone, Ajax."

"You know," Aaron said. "You guys all sound so ridiculous using city names. I'm really trying not to laugh."

Hamilton reached for his gun. He'd lost so many men. Maybe it was time to even the score.

Scarborough grabbed his wrist and held it firm. He shook his head and pointed at the knives clipped to his waist.

"You want the job done right," Scar said, "you use a knife. Leave scars, allow the man the pain of leaving one life and entering another." He released Ham's wrist and got to his feet. "We scream and cry entering this world. Who knows what's killing us and sending us here? I like to return the favor for those fortunate enough to leave this plane at the tip of my knife."

"Sit down, Scar," Tor blurted. "No one's killing him yet. We need him."

Hamilton got himself under control and tugged at Scar's arm.

Scar retook his seat.

"Watch your mouth, punk," Tor said to Aaron. "You're on borrowed time."

"Sure, okay." Aaron nodded. "Got it. And that coming from a guy named Toronto. Smart."

"Okay, Scar, chop him up."

Scar jumped to his feet, but Hamilton yanked him back once again.

"Guys, fuck off with this shit. We have to think."

"Yeah, well," Ajax mumbled. "We've been thinking, and so far, we've lost a lot of our team. Two men at that foster bitch's place an hour ago, a few men this morning fighting Sutton's team, the watcher at Markham's house, a few men are incarcerated after visiting his apartment"—he pointed at Aaron—"and more men to this punk's skinny friend off of Brant Street. We should've killed him." Ajax glared at Aaron. "Your little punk friend can fight, but I'm coming for him when this is all over. Gonna blow up his family, his house, his life."

Aaron vibrated his shoulders. "Ohh, you're scary. My little punk friend is ten times the man you are."

Ajax charged him and landed two solid punches before Tor shoved him off the prisoner. Ajax lost his balance and dropped to the floor.

"Ajax," Tor shouted. "Ham runs this gig, and Ham said to leave him alone. This isn't your fucking show."

Ajax rolled over and propped himself up on his elbow. "A couple of punches never hurt nobody."

"My name is Tor for a reason."

"Yeah, Toronto," Aaron whispered. "Big city, big man. You the whole GTA, or just the downtown?"

Tor faced him. "Sure, make jokes. You're only half right. I'm Toronto, but call me Tor, short for torture. He's our best cleaner, so he's Ajax. Hamilton is Ham because he is the best at communications, you know, like a ham radio. Mark is Markham, but it's really because the man we're hunting is an expert sniper. He hits the mark."

"Stop with the introductions," Ham shouted.

Tor spun around and glared at Ham. "Does it matter? This punk won't live through the day. Like he's going to tell shit to anyone."

Ham got to his feet. "It matters because I say it matters."

Tor stared him down for half a minute, their eyes locked on each other. Tor blinked, then looked away.

"As I was saying, Belle is for Belleville," Tor continued. "She's the only woman in our crew, so we named her Belle. Windsor over there is quiet. He comes and goes like the wind, hence his nickname, Wind. No one ever hears that fucker. And Peterborough is Peter because his—"

A weapon fired, cutting the descriptions short. Tor dropped at an angle, bounced off Aaron's legs, then hit the floor in a clump. On the way down, arterial blood had spurted from his neck, covering Aaron's face and chest. The captive shouted something unintelligible and drew his head back to keep blood from pumping into his mouth.

Then Tor's body was overcome with seizures. Aaron gagged, spit out blood, breathing hard like he had been running.

Ajax was putting a weapon away in his belt line when Hamilton charged him. Before Ajax could get his hands up, Hamilton drove three heavy punches to the man's face.

Ajax dropped to escape the attack and rolled away.

"What the fuck did you do that for?" Hamilton raged, already reaching for his own weapon.

"What?" Ajax said, touching the bloody lip Hamilton just gave him. "He defied your direct order in front of us all. He pushed me and deserved a big fuck you for that." Ajax spit on the ground beside him. "So I sent him home. No harm, right? I mean, he's always talking about the other side like it's some lovely hangout."

Hamilton fought every urge to shoot Ajax, but they couldn't fall apart at the seams and start killing one another. They were too close to their objective and too close to the end. The amount of men he had left was just enough to complete the planned executions.

Now that Tor was dead, he needed Mark—his sniper—more than ever. Locate the man, get their goods back, remind him of his commitment, and persuade him to finish the mission.

They'd be done quickly, and the world would know their name.

It had been Mark's plan from the start. And he was the only man with a wife and kids.

So, the leadership of the group fell to Ham. And now everything was falling apart. They'd even resorted to killing each other.

Ham checked Tor's pulse. His body had stopped vibrating, and his chest wasn't moving. Tor's eyes were wide open, staring at nothing.

There was no pulse. However, there was the stark smell of urine. Both the dead man and the man strapped to a metal chair beside him had pissed their pants.

Aaron gasped in breath after breath.

Ham holstered his weapon as Ajax got to his feet and moved away. In his fit of rage, Ham stared down at their pathetic prisoner, the boyfriend of that psychic bitch that had caused them so much shit. He didn't know how Sarah got her hands on their MATADOR, the one that was lost forever, seized by the authorities. Under intense questioning, Aaron didn't know where Sarah was at the moment either. The fucking bitch wasn't answering her cell phone, and that ex-cop Parkman wasn't answering his. Ever since Mark stole their shit, everything had gone wrong, and now they were down to the five team members in the room. If he still included Mark and Belle, they'd be at seven. But Mark had gone rogue, and Belle was a lost cause. She couldn't even control her target, a female civilian. Julie was supposed to be leverage if Mark couldn't complete the final stage.

All of this was Ronald Harris's idea from day one. That was the ironic part. The man planned the entire thing. He even took on the name Markham, or Mark, because of his intense sniper skills. And they all agreed to take on names from Ontario cities to show their support for the cause.

And now it was Mark—or Ron as he knew him overseas years ago—who had fucked it all up.

They should all walk away and go back to their lives. Let the authorities clean this shit up. Hamilton and the remaining crew to his left could blend in, disappear, and move away from the area. They'd done it before and could do it again.

He withdrew his weapon and aimed it at Aaron's forehead.

"Hey, Ham, what are you doing?" Scarborough asked. "If he has to die, let me do it. I want some fun, too."

Aaron glared up at Ham, then leaned forward, the skin of his forehead pressing on the tip of the weapon, edging Hamilton's hand back several inches under the pressure.

The bastard wants me to do it. He's defying me, challenging me.

They held each other's gaze momentarily, then Aaron broke off and leaned back, breathing rapidly again. Ham let the gun drop to his waist where he held it, studying the pathetic man in his chair.

"You think you're so tough," Ham whispered. "Let's see you go overseas and fight for your country." Ham spit on him. The chunk of saliva went high and landed in Aaron's hair. "I swear," Ham tried to say, but it came out as a hissing sound through his teeth. "You die tonight or tomorrow. I will not allow you to breathe the same air as this man here." Ham pointed at Tor. Then he leaned closer to Aaron. "You fucking hear me? Dead, motherfucker. Underground, buried, ants and worms, beetles in your fucking eye sockets, dead."

Aaron's hands and feet were bound to the chair with loads of duct tape, so there was no way he could block the elbow that Ham shot out. It connected with his cheek and knocked his head sideways.

But the defiant prick yanked his head back quickly as if nothing affected him. Aaron's eyes were wild, his face still covered in Tor's blood. It was enough to drive Ham to kill him, but somewhere deep in the back of his mind, he gathered the strength not to kill him. He would even leave his mouth alone so the man could talk. Heaven forbid they get the psychic bitch on the line, and their leverage had swallowed all his teeth, and she couldn't recognize his voice, his plea for help.

Hamilton reminded himself of that as he swung back and drove Aaron in the same cheek his elbow just hit. Then a left to the other cheek. Four or five more blows to the upper head area, and then Ham struck him hard in the rib cage, and Aaron screamed in pain. One more solid kick to the man's jawline might shut him up.

"Hey, Ham." Scar was behind him now. "Fuck man, you're killing him. We might need him alive."

"Leave me alone," Ham shouted, spinning to glare at the assembled team. "I know what I'm doing, do you? Call that Sarah bitch. Call someone else. Find Mark. Call Belle and learn more details from her. Fucking do something." He was screaming at them now, something he rarely resorted to with his men, abroad or at home. "Get me results because that's what I'm doing right now. I'm getting results." He turned back to Aaron, who was whimpering in the chair, his head hung down, chin to chest. "Tor is dead because of this fucking guy. His *humor*, his taunting us. Everyone could use a good beating once in a while."

He bent over to get closer and shot a fist into Aaron's ribcage again.

The man bound to the chair screamed like someone was twisting a knife in his kidney.

"That's right, scream baby," Ham shouted, getting his voice louder than Aaron's. "No one will hear you in this place."

One more jab to the ribs, then an uppercut that missed its mark. Ham's knuckles grazed off Aaron's jawline, and he ended up punching him in the eye socket.

Aaron blinked rapidly, trying to clear his eye. Without hands, he seemed to be struggling with the beating.

Ham tried to control his rage, recalling a thought about

avoiding Aaron's mouth. Maybe it was good the uppercut didn't connect. If he'd cut the man's tongue off or severed a chunk of it with Aaron's teeth clamping down, his ability to talk would be thwarted.

When Hamilton pivoted back to the team, only Windsor was still sitting in his chair. That man was always quiet, so Ham didn't care. He could watch all he wanted.

He glanced down at Tor's body, then back to Aaron.

The man's left eye was swelling fast. He glared defiantly up at him with his good right eye, his mouth shut now.

"You got nothing to say, punk? You ready to keep that mouth of yours shut now?"

Aaron's mouth twitched, then opened slightly. "You're a spineless child, beating on a man who's tied up," Aaron whispered. "If I make it out of this chair, I will kill you with my thumbs to show you how small you are in my world." He lifted his chin higher. "Fuck you, cunt."

A fury so unlike Hamilton raged through his body, and he punched Aaron again. Then again. And another ten times without stopping. He forgot about his pledge to himself to keep Aaron alive. He forgot about needing the man as leverage.

And then Wind was beside him, holding his arm, plying him back a foot. He wouldn't hit Wind. He was spent, all angered out.

And Aaron was done. The man's face was a mass of blood, torn flesh, and more blood.

Hamilton blinked, and the world refocused.

He saw Tor on the ground and looked at Wind.

"I don't …" he started, "know what that was."

Wind nodded and eased him back. He pointed at the sinks along the wall. They were in the basement bathroom of an empty sports stadium. Plenty of toilets, plenty of sinks.

Wind wanted him to wash up.

"Is he alive?" he asked.

Wind shrugged.

"Okay," Ham said and moved to the sinks. The skin had split over his knuckles, and they were already swelling. He hadn't lost his temper like that in ages. Sure, he'd fought hard before, but something about this piece of shit drove him mad. He would have to stay away from him. Otherwise, he'd kill him.

When he glanced over his shoulder at Wind, the man had a finger under Aaron's jaw, checking for a pulse.

Wind met his gaze and nodded. He held up his other hand and pressed two fingers close together.

Aaron had a weak pulse, and he was still breathing.

Ham nodded, dried his hands, and left the room, his hand on the butt of his weapon.

The urge to fire several bullets into Aaron's swelling eye sockets drove him from the room.

He needed air. He needed to calm down.

Killing the one piece of leverage they still had too early was reckless.

They'd lost Julie, the girlfriend. They'd just lost the man's kids. All they had left was that psychic bitch's connection to Ronald Harris, which was tenuous at best. And the man in the other room would lead them to her.

It would have to be today, or he'd just kill him and go hunt for her on his own.

"Today, you fuck," he said to himself.

He checked his watch, clenching his hand tighter on his weapon, enjoying the tingle of pain in his hand.

"You've got a couple of hours to wake up, then one more call to Sarah." He continued walking through the stadium. "Then you die."

Chapter 20

"There she is," Sarah said, pointing.

Parkman was already slowing down. As they pulled to a stop on the shoulder, Sarah jumped out.

"Who are you?" she asked.

The woman had exited her car and was just shutting her door. "My name is Julie Perkins. I know the man who tried to shoot down that airliner last night. That's why I was trying to get your—"

"What does he do for a living?"

Julie frowned. "Odd question at a time like this, but he's in construction. Owns the business."

Sarah moved closer as a truck drove by them. "Name?"

"Ronald Harris."

She nodded. That was all she needed. "Get in," she gestured to their car and started back. No cops in view yet, but they were less than a minute behind.

"Not without this."

Julie popped her trunk and leaned inside. When she righted herself, her arms were wrapped around a large automatic weapon. She ran along the side of her car and ran by Sarah toward the rental.

"Where the hell did you get that?"

"My boyfriend collects weapons." She carried it to the rear of their car. Parkman popped the trunk from the inside. "I can't leave the weapons. I think they're the reason he's in trouble."

"Your boyfriend is in trouble because of what he tried to do last night with weapons like that."

"Help," Julie pleaded. "They'll impound my car. If these are found inside, later on, when they catch me, I'll never see the outside of a prison cell."

There was nothing about illegal arms that Sarah wanted any part of, but she didn't want to leave them behind in an abandoned car on the side of the highway, either. Since Julie was determined to take them, she helped speed things up.

From the back seat, Sarah carried another large weapon. Both of them fit in the rental's trunk without an issue. Once all the weapons were stowed safely out of view, both women sat in the back seat to talk.

Parkman got them back on the highway.

"At the next exit," Sarah said, leaning forward to speak to Parkman, "get off this highway and head into town. We need another car."

"Thought so," he said, getting them to a hundred kilometers an hour quickly. "But they'll be looking for us in town."

"Not right away. They'll be on the highways initially. Once they find Julie's car, they'll put out a BOLO for ours —"

"And it'll be parked somewhere obscure in Huntsville," Parkman finished.

"Exactly." Sarah turned to Julie. "Tell us everything."

Julie nodded. "Can we change cars first? Let me get my shit together. I mean, I almost shot a cop by accident. I didn't mean to have the gun go off. And I need coffee. Then, uninterrupted, as we head north, I will tell you what I know."

Sarah watched the woman, studied her a moment, then nodded. "Fair enough. You just went through quite the ordeal. Parkman, hand me back my coffee." He did, and Sarah sipped from it. "Find a shopping mall or a large grocery store. We'll park in the middle somewhere, then start walking. We'll get you a coffee on the way to rent a car."

"What about the weapons?" Julie asked. "We need those."

"We'll get them once we have a new vehicle."

Julie nodded and glanced out the window as they wound through the tree-lined streets of Huntsville.

"There's a bridge up ahead. When we get to the end of the older part of town, on the other side of that bridge, there's a mall to the left."

"That'll do."

Twenty minutes later, they were jumping in a new four-door Kia with tinted back windows. Parkman drove them to the mall and waited until no one was nearby to transfer the weapons safely and out of sight into the rear of the Kia. After

Parkman grabbed their meager belongings from the first car, they were finished and back on the road again. They hit a drive-thru, loaded up on coffee, and got on the road going north. Sarah saw seven cruisers so far, two racing by with their lights on but no sirens.

She breathed a sigh of relief as they headed north on Hwy 11 because no roadblock had been erected yet. They were free to leave the area.

Julie held a large cup in her hands, staring down at it.

"Something happened to Ron when he was overseas," she started.

Over the next twenty minutes, while Parkman drove watching their mirrors, Julie told them everything she knew about Ron. The divorce court, his slow decline in finances, the back taxes taking its toll, children's aid snatching his kids, and even the courts threatening to take his driver's license, effectively strangling the man into nothingness. Julie said what he did last night was in desperation, in a crazy hope to get Sarah Roberts's attention.

"Well, it worked," she said.

Julie went on about staying at Annemarie's, then taking Ron's call and realizing that the job fell into her lap to get Sarah's attention. While collecting the weapons to plan some stupid stunt, she shot an intruder in her garage.

"And that's it," Julie said. "Huntsville was a stopover for lunch when I got spooked by that cop following me, and he pulled me over. Then you showed up."

Sarah listened and waited for anything from Vivian but couldn't detect a thing. She hadn't heard from Vivian in twenty-four hours, and they were smack dab in the thick of things.

I'd love to know what to do next, sis.

"Well, it sounds like you're onto something, Julie. Although, I can tell you this isn't about the ex-wife. None of this concerns CAS or CRA or impending bankruptcy."

"How can you be so sure—oh, right." Her eyes widened, and her mouth stayed open a moment. It was like she just realized Sarah was sitting there. "You're psychic. Holy shit, I forgot."

Sarah and Parkman exchanged a glance in the rearview mirror.

"I don't have to be psychic to know this is much bigger than Ron's personal problems."

"How so?" Julie asked, frowning. "Then what's this all about?"

"I'm not sure, exactly. Contrary to the idea that I'm psychic, I'm actually not. I can hear my sister whispering sometimes. I'm sure we all have had some psychic moments in our lives. People call it intuition. Some don't recognize it for what it is, and they ignore it."

"And you know it's your sister?" Julie asked.

Sarah shrugged. "I think so. I've questioned it in the past, but when I met her in Denmark when I died, I'd have to go with it's my sister."

Julie shook her head briefly, her hair flying up and settling down in her face. "What? When you died?"

"I had a near-death experience. When I went over to the other side, she was there. We chatted. Resolved to continue doing what we're doing for years to come."

"Wow, Sarah, you are one fascinating woman."

A short laugh escaped her lips. "I've been called a lot of names in my life. Can't say that one's come up yet."

She looked behind them, then settled back in her seat. No one following them. No cops around whatsoever. They were all focusing their efforts in and around the Huntsville area, and the last sign they passed showed a turn-off for a place called Sunridge.

"Do you have any idea why Ron would want my attention?" Sarah asked.

"No." She shook her head. "I mean, I didn't even know your name until he called last night. Annemarie and I researched you online, and there are a couple of small connections, but I'm grasping at straws."

"Grasp away. You might hit on something."

"But I don't want to say something that'll offend or hurt you."

"I'm a big girl. Hit me with it. I'm unoffendable."

"Well, when CAS took his kids, it seemed like that was the last straw. Ron lost it. And with what happened to you, you know, with what happened earlier this year ..."

Sarah nodded her understanding. How could something so personal be searchable online? How could anybody with a question about her get that answered on their home computer? That was one of the reasons she'd avoided social media. Sure, she was behind the times as everyone and their dog had an Instagram account, Facebook profile, and Twitter. And she'd even considered opening those kinds of accounts to talk about some of the things she'd done or even tidbits Vivian shared, but it hadn't happened yet, and evidently, it didn't matter. Her private life was already out there, just waiting for anyone to read it.

She momentarily watched the road out front, staring at the small strips of paint separating the lanes.

"I'm sorry," Julie whispered. "See, I didn't want to say anything—"

"No, it's fine." Sarah met Julie's gaze. "What else is there? Give me another reason."

"As crazy as this sounds, I think Ron wanted your empathy and then your help to get his kids because he's a good father, and he couldn't stand them being with some foster parents when he could take care of them."

"So you're saying he wanted to convince me to care about his kids and then help him kidnap them?"

"Well, when you put it that way, it does sound stupid."

"And that's why I'm telling you there's another angle. There's another reason." Mentally, she kept going back to the weapons in the trunk, some of what Sutton had said, and the team of soldiers who attacked them that morning. "Tell us, where does he get these weapons?"

"I don't know. He was a sniper in some combat battle group of the Canadian Forces. He was one of, like, forty-thousand Canadians who served over there, and he was one of the last to come home. I think it was March of 2014 when he arrived back. I didn't know him then, but I knew Annemarie, and she had known Ron for over a decade, even longer than his wife. Anyway, after Ron and Bridgette split up, Annemarie arranged a dinner for us, and it's been a great few years until about six months ago as things got worse around the house."

"And you don't know where the weapons come from?"

Julie shook her head. "He's been collecting them since the day he returned. It drove Bridgette bonkers, so I heard, and I didn't care for it, but I didn't mind. Until he came home with that HK-33 thing." She shook her head again. "Highly illegal and made to murder a lot of people at once."

"That and the MATADOR he took to Toronto to aim at a plane filled with innocent people."

"Yeah, but he wasn't going to shoot it down. He told me that himself."

"Did he tell you we"—she gestured with her hand pointing at Parkman and herself—"shot at him and almost hit him? He could've been killed. That was a stupid move."

"On the phone, he said it was stupid because it got your attention, but he failed to meet with you."

"He could've just called me. You know, I'm sure my number's online somewhere. Everything else seems to be." She tapped Parkman on the shoulder. "Speaking of phones, where's Sutton's?"

"Right here." He retrieved it from the center console.

The battery was getting low when she turned it on—under twenty percent—but she wouldn't need it much. There were seven new messages in voicemail. Probably, General Whyte or his representatives were attempting to reach her. She turned it off again.

"Who's Sutton?" Julie asked.

"Long story, and probably the connection that we're looking for." She looked up at Parkman. "I'll call Whyte once we track Ron."

Parkman nodded.

"Since my phone still has that fake sim card that Sutton

put in it, mine's as good as dead. Where's yours?"

Parkman handed her his phone.

She tapped the screen and saw over twenty missed calls.

"Holy shit, Parkman, you haven't been answering your phone."

"When you fell asleep this morning on the way out of Toronto, I turned it to silent. Didn't want to wake you." He shrugged one shoulder. "Just forgot to turn it back on."

Sarah scrolled through the missed calls. "You've had multiple calls from a PRIVATE CALLER and several from the Toronto Western Hospital." She glanced up at Parkman, a knot of worry forming in her gut. "Who's in the hospital? Do you know anyone?"

"I don't know anyone recently admitted." He shook his head.

Sarah tapped the number, and it started dialing immediately.

"Toronto Western, how may I direct your call?"

"Someone has been trying to call us on this number, but we aren't sure who?"

"Your name, ma'am?"

"Sarah Roberts, but this is Parkman's phone."

"His full name, please?"

"I don't know." She glared at him in the mirror. He still hadn't told her his name.

Julie gave her a funny look.

"I'm sorry, I can't really help you. Maybe have this Parkman fellow call us back when we can speak to him—"

The phone beeped an incoming call. Sarah pulled it from her ear and stared at call display. The Toronto Western

Hospital again. She tapped the button to switch lines.

"Hello?"

"Sarah!" Daniel almost shouted. "Thank God."

Her stomach tightened. Did something happen to Aaron?

"Why are you in the hospital?"

"It's not me, it's Alex." At the mention of Alex's name, she bent over and rested her head on the back of the front seat.

"What happened to him?"

"Sarah, you're not going to like this."

"Try me."

She pushed the phone into her ear while Daniel explained what happened after they left them that morning on Adelaide.

"They were tracking the phone," she whispered. "They were sitting around, waiting in that area. They must've just missed us but saw you guys talking to us."

"There wasn't much we could do for Alex. He'll be in the hospital for a couple of days. I'd go over the list of injuries as the little fucker put up a harsh fight, but there were just too many men. I'm pretty sure he killed one or two of the other guys."

"If it's the same team who hit Sutton's team hours before that, I'm surprised Alex isn't dead."

"They didn't kill him for a reason. They want you."

"Me?" She swallowed.

"Yeah, and since Alex wasn't your boyfriend …"

"So they waited until Aaron came along."

"I'm sorry, Sarah."

"Is Aaron … dead?"

"No, but they took him with them."

The PRIVATE CALLER number had to be Aaron's kidnappers.

"Benjamin?" she asked, trying to hold it together, but tears never listened.

"He's okay. He didn't get shot this time."

She wanted to laugh but couldn't.

"I'm sorry, bad timing. It's just, he's sitting right beside me and told me to say that. Listen, Sarah, it'll be okay. We're all fine. We'll get Aaron back. He's lived through worse."

She nodded, turning away from Julie and Parkman to stare out the window and wipe her eyes.

"I know," she whispered, her voice breaking. "He'll be okay. You guys stay safe and watch over Alex. We need him."

"Doctors said he'll fully recover, but it'll take a while."

"He's a fighter. He'll be kicking ass inside of a few days."

"Sarah?"

"Yeah?"

"I'm sorry."

"I know."

"There were six or seven of them. Heavily armed. Fully strapped and loaded with advanced Kevlar of some kind. There was nothing we could do. Aaron practically volunteered to go."

"I understand, and, of course, he would. Look, I have to go"—before I break down on the phone—"but please, call with updates."

"Thanks for answering. We were getting worried."

"Phone was on silent. Talk soon. Send Alex our love."

The line died.

And Sarah sobbed for what these people had done to her friends. Ronald Harris had illegal weapons. These men who attacked Sutton's group were well armed with shit that was in no way legal. Ron had a military history, and these men were looking for him. Somehow, they associated her with Ron because the news covered the MATADOR weapon and pasted Sarah's name everywhere in connection with it.

And that led to Aaron being kidnapped.

But why?

Leverage to make a deal with you, Vivian whispered.

"Oh, there you are," Sarah said out loud.

She felt Julie's eyes on her. Parkman looked at her in the mirror.

"Sorry, having a chat with my sister."

Shit, this still feels weird sometimes, Vivian.

Take the next phone call, and just know I'm sorry.

What's that supposed to mean? Sorry about what?

I wish it were different.

"Yeah, well, fuck you," she said out loud. "Tell me what to do if you want it to be different!"

Bloodshed and heartache ... because of that, I'm restricted in what I can tell you.

Julie seemed uncomfortable now. She leaned against her door, trying to get away from Sarah.

Sarah raised a hand to let her know everything was okay.

"Sometimes, my sister and I fight." She glanced at Julie. "Don't sisters fight?"

"I guess so."

The phone rang.

Call display said, PRIVATE CALLER.

"Here we go. The people who kidnapped Aaron and put Alex in the hospital are calling."

"Alex is in the hospital?" Parkman blurted. "How's that possible? Did they run him over with a bus?"

"I'll explain everything after this call."

She hit the answer button.

"Start talking," she whispered to the people whom she would hunt down and kill, one by one, for what they did to her family and her men.

Nobody fucks with mama bear.

Chapter 21

Hamilton came back to the bathroom staging area, where Aaron sat strapped to the chair. His head still hung low, body slouched forward.

Wind sat tapping on his phone. Probably playing Tetris again. The man was obsessed with it.

"Still breathing?" Hamilton asked, pointing at Aaron.

Wind nodded.

"Smelling salts?"

Wind set his phone down and headed over to a case in the corner.

Hamilton had a chance to calm down in the half hour he'd been out of the room. At least now, when he killed Aaron, it wouldn't be in a fit of rage. He could do it calmly, even enjoy it.

Later, they'd round up the other three assholes they let go

by Brant Street. Let's see how Sarah liked it when all her friends were dead. Hamilton only authorized their release because they were too much trouble to contain. It could've been handled. But it was more trouble than they wanted, and he'd figured Aaron was the only one they really needed.

Tor's body had been taken away. A blood stain was all that remained of the man Hamilton had fought alongside in Afghanistan.

The world had changed since they'd all returned to Canada, and not in a good way. No one cared about what happened to them overseas or what it took to stay alive, the men they lost along the way.

When Ron came up with his nickname Markham as a way to remember where he was born, but also to be called Mark, it made a lot of sense to Hamilton. They'd all taken on city names, and then one night, Markham—or Mark as he preferred, but it was still hard for Hamilton to think of him by any name other than Ron—told them his idea about executing Canadian officials, one by one.

Step one was to collect the weapons and vehicles. That was all done now, but Ron fucked up step two, which was supposed to launch two days ago.

He'd taken their stash of weapons and hid it somewhere. Some of these boys had sold everything for this final mission. They couldn't take it here, back in civilization, where no one cared or understood them. Sure, any of them could move on, grin and bear it, and try to stay off the streets, but this plan gave them purpose, and they all thanked Ron for that.

Did they ever imagine that they'd actually start executing

important people? No, not really. Did any of them want to break the law? Absolutely not. But when it came time to stop collecting weapons and walk away or go forward with the plan, they all said fuck it, and prepared a list of potential targets.

Wind was pivotal in creating a long list of names and researching their routines. Several other members were brought in to help, and when Ron seemed strangely absent as he was dealing with his divorce issues, Annemarie, or Belleville—Belle for short—was brought in to monitor him.

Ron's woman, Julie, didn't suspect anything, which was fine with them. She was collateral and didn't need in on it. At a point, Hamilton wanted her removed from the picture as Ron was proving difficult, and the team suspected she was the cause. But Belle stressed that Julie had nothing to do with it. So she was tasked to watch Julie.

Everything was screwed up now because Ron took their stash, Julie was gone, and quite a few of his men were dead with a couple in custody, and Ron's plan had gone to shit.

All Hamilton wanted to do now was execute everyone involved in fucking him and his team over, get the weapons back from Ron, kill him and everyone helping him, then regroup and fight another day.

They'd move to Saskatchewan and live on a farm in the prairies or some shit. Just to stay off the radar for six months or a year. Then, one by one, they'd plan hits and take down elected officials who weren't sympathetic to the men and women who served their good country.

Ron had a solid plan, one they all fell in line with. But now that plan was going to get him killed.

Wind returned with smelling salts and handed them to Hamilton. He retook his seat and started tapping on his phone again.

Hamilton didn't ask where the rest of the team was, as it didn't matter what he would do next.

On his cell phone, he opened the camera app and snapped a picture of Aaron the way he was sitting. Next, he grabbed a fist full of Aaron's hair and lifted his head. The man was still unconscious and probably would remain so for another day or more if Hamilton didn't use the smelling salts.

He snapped a few more pictures from each side of Aaron's ruined face. Then he let go of the man's hair, and his head dropped like dead weight, bobbing once.

The kind of damage would probably last for quite some time if Aaron were to live more than the next ten minutes. His entire left side had ballooned out with swelling, sealing his left eye with puffed-up flesh. The purple and jaundiced-looking bruising all over the man's face and neck was horrific. Blood oozed from several places where Aaron's skin had split. He had to have a broken cheekbone or an orbital bone or something with the way his face appeared lopsided now. That kind of swelling wasn't something someone saw after a knockout in a twelve-round boxing match. No, this man's face was ruined and would probably need some kind of corrective surgery to put it back together again.

Hamilton's knuckles ached from the thrashing, but that was okay. That kind of ache made him feel good. He wanted to smash Aaron again and again at that very moment, but he didn't. The man had a purpose as leverage. After that, his purpose ended.

Hamilton was prepared to make one more phone call to Sarah or Parkman or whoever answered, and if they didn't, he would execute Aaron, and they would vacate the premises. As a team, they would decide what to do next. Go after Aaron's three friends or stop kidnapping people for leverage, as it wasn't working, and just head north to help Belle search for Julie and Ron.

He checked his weapon. It was ready to fire. Once he got Sarah on the line, if he did, executing Aaron and sending her the before and after picture would give him great pleasure.

He dialed the number.

It rang once, then again.

Hamilton raised the weapon.

If two more rings went unanswered, he would put a bullet in Aaron's forehead.

The third ring came and went.

He applied pressure to the trigger.

Something clicked on the phone.

"Start talking," a woman said.

Hamilton lowered his weapon and stared at Wind.

"Who's this?" Hamilton asked.

"You know, I thought you would've been better at this," the woman said. "You beat up Alex, then absconded with my man. There isn't a hiding place on this planet that'll keep you safe."

She sounded like she was talking through her teeth, and it made him feel good. Her anger meant he was getting to her. It also meant she loved this man, Aaron, and killing him would incite her further, cause her more anger, and she'd make a mistake.

Perhaps before leaving for the prairies, the team would have to meet up with Sarah Roberts and show her what men did in wartime. He'd seen her picture and that morning in Sutton's SUV. He knew how hot she was. The woman could easily take a *hard* beating by a real man.

"Sarah Roberts," he whispered. "You may want to watch your mouth, you little bitch."

"You must have kids, talking to me like you're a parent. Grow up. Just explain the terms or fuck off."

"All business. I like that."

"Your team hit Sutton this morning."

She didn't ask a question. This woman was matter-of-fact with everything she said, and Hamilton found that seriously attractive.

"Yes, but it seems acquiring you has become a tedious chore."

"Sit back, relax. I'll come to you. You don't even have to lift a finger."

Oh wow, this woman was turning him on. He needed a woman like this in his life. One with balls and zero fear.

"Good, then I don't need my leverage."

"No, you don't. Drop Aaron on a street corner somewhere and tell me when and where the meet-up will be."

"How do I know you'll come?"

"If you think I'd miss a chance to stare into your eyes as the life fades from them, you're sadly mistaken."

"Man, you are turning me on. I love a strong woman. Maybe when we meet up before we try to kill each other, we could go a couple of rounds in the grass. I could show that vagina a thing or two."

Sarah didn't respond.

"I'm sorry, did the tough little girl hear something offensive? Did I say something to bother you?" He laughed. "Not so tough after all, eh bitch?"

She started talking again, but he pulled the phone from his ear and opened the text option. He texted the three pictures of Aaron he'd just taken to the number he was talking to Sarah on, then put the phone back to his ear.

"Just to be sure," he broke in on her rant of threats, "I wanted you to see we're taking good care of your boyfriend. I sent you three pictures."

The sound of rustling and a car engine in the background filtered through to him. Sarah was looking at the pictures now. There was a gasp, then another one.

"Your life just ended," she whispered.

"I think I'll just put a bullet in Aaron's face right now. That sounds like it'll incite you to come after me. I mean, I really want to meet you."

Sarah was quiet again.

"Did that bother you?" he asked. "You're quiet all of a sudden."

"Shut up. I'm listening to something."

He frowned. "I tell you I'm about to kill your boyfriend, and you're *listening* to something?"

"Yeah. Hold the fuck on."

Hamilton turned to Wind and shrugged. He pulled the phone away from his ear and whispered, "She's absolutely fucked in the head."

When the phone was back to his ear, he said, "Enough

fucking around. Aaron's dead." He raised the hand, holding his gun to place the barrel on Aaron's forehead. He wouldn't need the smelling salts after all. "Come find me. Then we'll talk. And you can tell me all about Ron and how you got my MATADOR."

"Wait," Sarah said.

Hamilton paused.

"Stop the car," Sarah shouted. "Now!"

Hamilton heard the engine slow in the background.

"Hamilton, that's your name, right?"

How the hell did she know that?

"For some reason, I'm hearing Wind is with you, but that doesn't make sense … wait, I know where you are. A stadium of some kind. Okay, hold on …"

Hamilton couldn't stop the chills running down his back and arms. Even his legs burst out in goosebumps. Listening to Sarah tell him some psychic bullshit freaked him out in a strange new way. But how could she know? Psychic phenomena were a joke, something to swindle money out of unsuspecting idiots. Wasn't it just another business?

The phone he used was encrypted. There's no way Sarah could trace the call, and even if she had the technology readily available, she couldn't be doing it from a moving vehicle, could she?

The car's engine in the background had stopped.

"I'm going to send you a picture now," Sarah said. "Something of importance to you. Something of great value."

He frowned. What the hell could she have that was important to him?

Peter, Scar, and Ajax entered the room. They all

exchanged looks, and Wind motioned for them to wait.

"Something's telling me your team just arrived," Sarah said. "Shit, why didn't you tell me you picked city names. Wind would've made sense then. He's Windsor."

Hamilton had never heard anything so amazing and scary in his entire life. Consumed by involuntary shaking, his hands wouldn't stop. Goosebumps rose on his arms. He didn't want to speak for fear his voice would betray him.

"There," Sarah said. "I've taken my pictures and sent them back."

Hamilton heard the ding.

"Hold," he said, maintaining the integrity of his voice for that one word.

He opened the photo in the text when he pulled the phone away from his ear.

Several of their weapons were piled in a trunk. The HK-33, the Belgian FN, and a couple of compact Galils were there.

With the phone back at his ear, he asked, "How the fuck did you get my shit?"

"I've got the rest, too. Come and get it. But I warn you, if Aaron dies, you get nothing from me. All this shit disappears. Then you disappear."

"I don't get threatened by a stupid bitch." He'd found his voice and had no problem getting all the anger into it. "Fuck you. Keep them. I'll buy more weapons. Consider hunting season officially open. My team is now hunting a female animal, a bitch, and when we find you, I will personally slice your fucking head off, then fuck your corpse. We don't need Aaron anymore. Say goodbye."

Hamilton raised his weapon and fired several times in Aaron's direction, then ended the call.

Chapter 22

Sarah bent over by the open trunk and vomited in the bush along the shoulder. She stepped back a couple of feet, dropped to her knees, and wept, her anger overwhelming her.

Aaron was alive. She knew that. Vivian told her. Those bullets were aimed at Aaron, but each one missed him. Vivian had to tell her, or Sarah was done. End Aaron, end it all.

Vivian showed up after Sarah gave her an ultimatum. Either help or they were finished. Parkman would turn the car around, drop off Julie, empty the guns, call General Whyte, and get taken in. They'd explain everything and walk away. It was either help save Aaron or never contact her again.

Vivian said there was a way and started talking. It felt good to have her back in her head, close enough to almost feel her.

But those pictures of Aaron were grotesque. What had they done to his face?

Her stomach roiled at her role in this, and she couldn't handle it. She retched, her recent coffee taste filtering into her nose as she gagged.

"Sarah." Parkman was beside her, his hands on her shoulders now.

She wiped her mouth and allowed herself to be rolled into his embrace. Parkman held her so tight she didn't want to leave his warm, comforting arms. It reminded her of when she was young, and her father would hold her. Like he couldn't let go. Which made sense because her parents had lived through Vivian's murder and grieved her passing. Sarah was their second chance, their only chance. Of course, her parents would cling to her in such a way.

She eased back out of Parkman's grasp and handed him the phone. Without a word, he opened the text and stared at Aaron's face. Julie glanced over his shoulder, and both of them placed a hand over their mouths.

Sarah fought the urge to puke again. Why was she so weak when it came to Aaron? Was that what love was? By opening herself and becoming vulnerable, she had become weak. He was the only one—well, Parkman, too—that she would fight and die for. They deserved her sacrifice, her vulnerability, and her love.

And dammit, she deserved theirs.

Same goes for you, Vivian. Stick around now. You've been warned.

I'm here. Always have been.

Yeah, right, Sarah thought.

There are restrictions ...

"We have to go," Sarah said. "I'm going to kill every one of them." In moments like this, with the rage seething through her, her voice came out raspy, masculine sounding. It had a gravelly note like she was speaking through a sore throat. "They didn't have to go so far."

"These kinds of people don't have limits." Parkman shook his head and held out her phone. "What they did this morning to Sutton and his men ... do you know if Aaron's alive?"

"Yes, Aaron's alive." She took the phone back. "I have assurances."

"You can trust these guys?"

"Not them. Vivian told me."

"Oh, she's back?"

"I'm as surprised as you. I had to threaten her."

"How do you threaten something you can't touch?"

Julie stood off to the side, listening in, her expression one of surprise and fear.

"An ultimatum. I told her we were finished if she didn't step up and help. The butterfly effect has brought us here because we went to the airport last night." She paused to let a large semi-pass them. When it was gone, she said, "So, what happened to Aaron is on her. Fix it, or fuck off. That's sort of the gist of it."

"Damn." Parkman stood back and leaned on the rear of the car.

"Let's go. We can talk on the way."

Once in the car, Sarah said, "There's a motel at the corner

of this highway and a street called O'Brien in North Bay. Go there for the night. Vivian said this would all be over by tomorrow morning."

"What are we going to do in the meantime?" Parkman asked, and he got them back on the highway.

"Make a couple of phone calls."

She turned on Sutton's phone. Enough battery for at least two phone calls. She dialed Darwin's number in Italy by memory. Sarah motioned for quiet by lifting a finger.

On the third ring, something clicked, and Darwin picked up.

"It's Sarah."

"Okay, didn't get a number. You blocked it?"

"Not my phone."

"Oh." He paused. "You need me?"

"There's no time. Unless you have Bruno available."

"He's out."

"Out?"

"One year off."

"Why?"

"Too recognizable. After Texas, you know."

"Right."

"He's sleeping in my basement right now. Enjoying the Italian countryside, drinking and eating too much."

"He deserves it."

"He does. New paperwork is coming for him, too. You'll know him as Bruno when you see him again, but in a year, he'll be a brand new man."

Sarah understood that probably meant some plastic surgery, too. If Bruno ever planned to return to North

America, he would have to return as a John Doe.

"You got anyone else sitting around?"

"What's going on, Sarah? The line's safe. Talk freely."

"Too much to say, too little time."

"Summarize. I've read the news already. I know about that attack last night. And the one in the fashion district. That was all you?"

Sarah talked him through the high points leading them to the search for Ronald Harris Construction and how Julie was with them. She finished with Alex in the hospital and Aaron, a hostage.

"Vivian says we meet them tomorrow. This exchange will get bloody. Could use your help."

"Twelve to fifteen hours isn't enough notice. And you're four hours' drive north of Toronto. I'll make some calls, but I can't promise anything."

"If I give you a number, can you trace it?"

"Sure, if it isn't military. That would take longer, even if I could."

"It's civilian."

"Shoot."

Sarah turned to Julie. "Give me Ron's phone number."

Julie recited it from memory, and Sarah repeated it slowly.

"Got it," Darwin said. "I'll set it up and program it so it's a constant trace."

"Constant?"

"Just means the second he uses the phone, my system will triangulate his location to within meters of where he is. After that, I can track him in real-time like the Find My

Phone app would do. My system will log the second he turns it off and where he is when it powers up again, hence constant."

"One sec." Sarah turned back to Julie. "What's your cell number?" Julie told her, and she told Darwin. "Text or call with whatever you have to that number after we hang up."

"Got it."

"Now, we're going to try calling Ron. How long should we wait until you're set up?"

"Call anytime. It's set now. Once he picks up, I don't need much to affix a location. I can stay on him from then on."

"Okay, stay with me while we call." She turned back to Julie. "Call Ron. Tell him we're together. And tell him we need to meet so I can help him."

Julie nodded.

Sarah snuck a glance at Parkman as he drove. They were entering North Bay's city limits. Her stomach ached from emptying, and her nerves were rattled, coming down from the adrenaline high. She needed to eat and sleep for a bit. And she needed to hear more from Vivian. Then get Aaron and be done with these people.

What really worried her was the prophecy of bloodshed and heartache. Vivian hadn't talked about the heartache stuff yet.

When Sarah turned back to Julie, she shrugged. "He's not answering."

"Did it go to voicemail?"

Julie shook her head.

"Then it's probably on and ringing."

Julie jerked, shooting up a hand.

"Ron?" she said. "Is that you?" Then, "Oh, Ron, are you okay?"

Sarah whispered into her phone, "Getting anything?"

"Working on it," Darwin said. "Less than a minute. Probably sooner."

Sarah watched Julie again. The woman wiped her tears.

"I know, baby," she whispered. "But I have a surprise." She glanced up at Sarah. "I am in a car with Sarah Roberts." After a pause, she said, "I'm not lying."

"Give me the phone," Sarah said, waving her free hand at Julie.

"Here she is," Julie said and handed Sarah the phone.

"Ron, I can help."

"Too dangerous now," the man said. It sounded like he'd been crying. "They came after my kids."

"Let me help you. Where are you?"

"Go home, Sarah."

The line died.

"Tell me you got a fix on the location," Sarah blurted into Sutton's phone.

The line beeped as someone was trying to call Sutton.

"Sarah," Darwin said, caution in his voice.

"What?" she stammered, unable to hold back her urgency.

"I needed at least ten more seconds."

"Can't you see where he is just by his phone being on?"

"That's the issue. He ended the call and killed the phone. Either turned it off or pulled the battery, depending on the style and make. I'm sorry."

"*Fuck*," she screamed at the roof of the car. "Were you able to narrow it down to a five- or ten-mile radius?"

"Sure, I could see that his phone is located within a forty-mile radius of North Bay, but that's it. Ten, maybe twenty more seconds would've given us the address and street number."

"You think he knew that?"

"No idea. My system has him in the queue, though. Get that phone on again and make it last a notch longer, and we'll locate him."

"Okay, thanks, Darwin. Send my love to your wife and tell Bruno he's in our thoughts."

"Will do. I'll reach out to Julie's number if something comes up with Ron's phone."

"Deal. Gotta run."

Sarah clicked off as the phone rang again.

"What?" she snapped into Sutton's phone.

"Hold for General Whyte, please," a woman said.

There was a clicking sound, then the general was there.

"Sarah Roberts?" he said.

"What do you want?"

"You need to come in, Sarah."

"Come in where? And do what?"

"Let us bring you in, debrief you. End this mess. It seems we have a common goal."

"Don't presume you have any idea what goals I may have."

"Running around recklessly as you are will only get you killed. Work with us instead of against us. There are things at work behind the scenes that you are not apprised of. I have men that will protect you—"

"Protect me? Like what happened this morning when Sutton's men were attacked?"

"We were woefully unaware of our enemy and their newfound abilities. That mistake won't happen again."

"You're fucking right it won't. Because Sutton's murderers will be dead this time tomorrow."

She hung up, killed the power to Sutton's phone, then tossed it in the back seat. She may need it later. She hadn't given Julie's phone back yet. She dialed Ron's number again, and it went straight to voicemail.

"Where would he go?" she asked Julie.

"I have no idea. He could be anywhere."

Sarah looked at Parkman. "Darwin said Ron is somewhere in North Bay and the surrounding area."

"Then we're close."

"Not close enough. We need him for the meet."

"Because of the weapons?"

"Yes, but also because of Markham."

"Markham? The city northeast of Toronto?"

Sarah nodded. "That's his code name for the little operation they were doing. He's called Mark for short. Stands for marksman as he's the sniper of the group."

"All that from Vivian?" he asked.

Sarah nodded.

"And she can't tell you where Ron is?"

Sarah laughed. "Yeah, that might be asking too much. She really pisses me off sometimes."

Sarah clenched her fists and stared outside, watching North Bay in a new light. It had been years since she had been there, but she remembered it well. Men from the Sophia Project had burrowed deep in the bowels of a decommissioned underground fortress to draw psychic information from her. It had lured Rod Howley from hiding just before he was killed. Hank Frommer died, too, which was good because the man had no honor.

It was a long time ago, and there have been many funerals since then.

Although, things would be slightly different. She was back in North Bay willingly this time, but the funerals were still coming.

Every single man Ron—Markham—worked with or conspired with to kill Sutton's men, hurt Alex, and kidnap and torture Aaron was coming to a brutal end.

Sure, revenge called for digging two graves, but that wouldn't be enough.

Sarah had the plan to dig a dozen.

Chapter 23

"Was that Mommy?" Michael asked.

Ron shook his head. "No, that was Julie."

He set the phone on the coffee table and lifted Michael off the couch.

"Time for bed, buddy."

His younger brother was already asleep. They'd been watching a show on their iPads when Jason nodded off. Out here, there was no internet and no WiFi ability on their iPads. Ron didn't have to worry that his boys would stumble onto Facebook or some news channel and see that half the province was looking for him for parental kidnapping. They probably already posted an Amber Alert, too, especially after finding two dead mercenaries on the property of the Children's Aid worker's foster care house. And if she saw him take his boys, Ron's name would be on an arrest warrant.

All because of the plan they forged in Afghanistan. It was a brilliant plan at the time, and it felt right. They called it "War Pigs" after that Black Sabbath song.

Fate could be cruel, with karma coming in at a close second. Within days, if not weeks, Ron would be torn from his boys and imprisoned unless everything he had planned for tomorrow worked out. Other than a visit at some maximum security facility, he wouldn't see his boys until they were young men, or worse, fully grown men.

Forget back taxes and frozen bank accounts. Forget all about taking his driver's license and passport. None of that mattered if he lost his boys.

And everything about Hamilton's plan screamed of Ron losing his boys. He tried to plead with the man, but he wouldn't listen. He drove to Toronto to meet the team, fellow soldiers, and platoon. But Hamilton refused to change the plan. Canada had lost soldiers overseas in the many years Canadians were acting as peacekeepers. They distributed medical and relief supplies, helped rebuild schools, and dug wells, but most importantly, they helped stabilize the region after Taliban rule. Hamilton wanted payback for the losses, but Ron knew it was more than that. It was personal. Hamilton wanted payback for the pain and suffering they had all endured, but the Canadian government couldn't give two shits about individual soldiers.

The problem for Hamilton Sand Markham, John Cormier and Ronald Harris, was that they personally lost twenty souls, people they had known, and it made them angry.

The plan to execute government officials was immature, naïve, and reckless. By the time they all came home and years had gone by, Ron figured it was a dream, a thing of the past. But to Hamilton and the platoon, it was still a reality.

When they wouldn't listen to reason, he stole ninety percent of their weapons and absconded with them in the middle of the night several days ago.

Knowing it was a death wish and having nothing left to live for anyway, he did it in a final act of bravery for his country.

He wanted to cripple Hamilton and his fellow soldiers and release a statement of their plan so men like Sutton could be better prepared for what was coming, but that was too late.

He'd even entertained the idea that Sarah Roberts could help. Her recent celebrity inspired him. He recalled her name from years ago, and now she was in the papers again for something she'd done in Texas.

With no idea how to reach her, he staged the MATADOR attack and almost got her. But that put her on Hamilton's radar.

And got Sutton killed.

Then they came after his kids.

The time to deal was over. This was his last night with his boys. He would return them in the morning, say his goodbyes, and take every weapon he's got to Hamilton, or rather, Hamilton would come to him.

Then he would kill them all.

There was no other way out of this.

Absolutely none.

Once he had Michael tucked in, Ron returned to the shack's small living room and scooped up Jason. He kissed his boy's forehead and took him to the room as well. The building was more of a shack than a cottage. Thin walls, no electricity, with a small door and two windows. There was no bathroom and no running water. The outhouse was behind the building, and if it was raining, he always pissed in an empty milk jug. That piss-jug episode of *Trailer Park Boys* always made him laugh because it wasn't just the truckers who used them. It was hardened Canadian boys roughing it near the wetlands of North Bay.

They couldn't stay here long. Well, Ron could, but his boys were used to a way of life. They needed to charge their iPads tomorrow. They needed a bathtub. And they needed a fridge, a stove.

But for one night, they needed their dad, and for the love of all that's fucked in this world, no one was going to deny him this one night with the boys that were his own. His flesh, his blood.

Once they were both nestled in the small bed in the shack's one room, Ron opened a beer and laid on the couch. This was his one night where no one knew where he was.

Tomorrow was another day, one where the pain stopped for him. Sure, it would start for his boys, but thousands of others grew up without dads. And even if some miracle took place, and Ron made it through to the end of the day, he might still lose his kids and head straight to jail.

No, it would be better if it all ended tomorrow.

In one big blaze of glory, he ended the pact he started with Hamilton all those years ago in a faraway land where so many people died.

War was Hell, and he was still living it.

Every day.

Chapter 24

"Pack everything," Hamilton ordered. "We leave nothing behind."

"Where are we going?" Ajax asked.

"North." Hamilton moved over to stand beside Aaron. "Clean him up. Find him another pair of pants. I don't want his piss all over my Hummer."

"What are you going to be doing?" Scar asked.

"Disposing of Tor's body." He glanced back at Ajax briefly, then stared at Wind. "You coming?"

Wind nodded.

"This is a simple operation, men. We're in, and we're out. One hour. Hose this place down. When Wind and I return, we'll load up and head north."

"Why north?" Ajax asked.

Hamilton was tempted to just respond by telling

everyone it was an order. Questioning his authority was insubordination. But these were different times, and these men were here willingly.

"Because Ronald Harris lives in North Bay. His wife and kids are there. His girlfriend, Julie, and our woman, Belle, are there." He moved closer to Ajax, staring him down. "Ron is the likely killer of our two men at that foster woman's house, and Julie likely killed our man in her garage. There is a fuck load of activity in and around North Bay, and if a deal or a meet is to take place for our stolen weapons, it'll happen there. That good enough for you?"

Ajax shrugged and turned away. "Guess so."

Hamilton fought the urge to shoot the man. They'd grown lazy and less disciplined in the six years since returning to Canada.

The wind seemed to have an inner compass for Hamilton because he placed a calming hand on his shoulder and pulled gently to turn him away from Ajax. He nodded toward the door.

"Let's go," Hamilton said.

They'd already loaded Tor's body in a bag and zipped it closed. At the back of the Hummer, Peter was shutting the hatch.

"All good," Peter said. "Ready for disposal."

"We'll be back in an hour. We leave for North Bay at midnight. It's about a four-hour drive with stops for food, coffee, and probably gas. Make sure Aaron's ready and bring a rope."

"Rope?"

"Yeah, I need a rope for Aaron. I have a plan."

"To hang him?"

"Something like that."

Peter smiled. "You're the boss."

Hamilton got in the driver's seat, and Wind got in opposite him.

"How did this fall apart so fast?" Hamilton asked.

Wind shrugged.

They stared out the windshield at the lights of the city in silence. Then Wind cleared his throat and pointed.

"I know we have to go. We have a job to do."

Hamilton started the Hummer, dropped it in drive, and pulled away.

"We have to kill Ron, you know." He looked over at Wind. "There's no going back now."

"That Sarah girl, too," Wind whispered.

Hamilton almost stopped the vehicle. Wind rarely spoke, and when he did, it was always something worth talking about, something meaningful, important.

"Agreed. Sarah will die as well. And Aaron."

Wind nodded.

"Those other three that we let go when we took the boyfriend should probably be taken care of, too."

Wind nodded again.

"We'll just kill them all. Then we can end this."

Wind was still nodding as they pulled off the main road and started down a dirt path en route to Tor's final resting place.

"Tomorrow will be like we're back at war," Hamilton said, wondering why he was still talking. Possibly to calm the nerves. "The only difference is we're on Canadian soil killing enemy combatants."

Wind nodded. "I kill Ron."

Hamilton glanced over at him. "He's yours."

Wind stopped nodding.

This time, he smiled.

Chapter 25

"SARAH," A WOMAN WHISPERED. "Sarah, wake up."

It took a second to hear the voice, register it, then snap awake and bolt upward.

She grabbed the woman, found her neck, and yanked her close, still blinking rapidly to focus her vision.

"Sarah, it's me, Julie."

She relaxed her grip, then laid back on the bed.

"What? Why are you talking? What time …?"

"It's almost four in the morning. I've got Mikey on the phone."

"Who the hell is Mikey?" she asked, rubbing her eyes.

"Ron's son."

Ron? His son?

Sarah shot up again and swung her legs over the side of the bed. The room spun momentarily, and there wasn't enough light to see the whole room. Parkman had taken the pullout couch, and each woman had a queen bed to themselves. He was still sound asleep.

"How did he call you?" Sarah asked.

"One second," Julie whispered into the phone. She lowered it with her palm on the mouthpiece. "He's using Ron's cell phone."

"How long have you been talking?" Sarah was wide awake now.

"About five minutes."

"Darwin should have traced it by now. If it's four in the morning here, then it's ten in the morning in Italy." She nodded. "He's probably got a location by now, but keep him talking. Ask where he is. Learn whatever you can."

She headed for the bathroom, jumped in the shower, toweled off, and dressed in the same clothes. It would be over today, and she could go home for fresh jeans then.

When she stepped out of the bathroom, Julie was off the phone.

"Well? Anything from Darwin?"

Julie nodded. "Darwin wants you to call him."

She frowned. That was strange. Why couldn't he text the address?

Parkman was sitting up on the couch, a toothpick in his mouth, his hair standing straight up. If they traveled under any other circumstances, she would fluff it higher, have fun with him, and joke about his age. He had to be hitting forty now, and this life was taking its toll on him. The man couldn't do this forever.

And I won't do it without him.

As she walked by him, she tapped his head once and then grabbed the phone from Julie.

She dialed Darwin's number, waited for the clicking sounds, then moved toward the motel room's window and stared out at the dark streets. The clock said it was ten minutes after four. It had been days since she'd had a good night's sleep.

Darwin answered.

"You got it?" Sarah asked.

"I got it, but the location seems strange."

"Strange how?" Sarah turned around to face Parkman, a hand over her stomach.

When they'd checked into the hotel, Parkman left them alone to buy food. He'd returned from the restaurant across the street, a greasy spoon, which was situated beside a sex store that sold adult toys. Who knew that could be such a big business in North Bay? The food wasn't so bad, but her stomach was turning.

Without Darwin's help on Ron's location, she'd have to rely on Vivian, who had promised to stick around and see this through, but she'd taken off again last night. Restrictions had been her reason for fleeing, whatever the hell that meant. They would be having a conversation about those restrictions sooner rather than later.

"The phone is out toward Mattawa, south of Hwy 17, off Maple Road. The signal ended on a road called Palangio Road."

"What's strange about that?"

"You know how Google mapped the world with street view."

"Yeah, that little guy you can drop on maps."

"Exactly. Only a small section of Palangio Road seems accessible with this street view thing."

"So, that means what? They forgot a section?"

"Not sure, but I'm scrolling along it, and I can see how narrow this road gets. This swamp area has thick trees and foliage right at the road. Very backwoods like. I don't know what he's doing back there, but I can't even see who owns the land in the few minutes it took you to call me back. There are no houses in the area this signal took me to. Sarah, without a contingent of men to back you up, I recommend you don't go."

"Darwin, you know me, and you know I need that location. Otherwise, I'll find this Maple Road off Hwy 17, and then I'll find Palangio Road and start walking, shouting Ron's name."

"Not a good idea, Sarah."

"Then text me a GPS lock on your location for Ron's cell signal, and we'll do it that way. But Darwin, I'm going in. I have no choice."

"Thought so. Texting everything now."

Parkman got to his feet and gestured toward the shower. Sarah nodded. He padded off to the bathroom.

"Okay, I've sent everything to the phone you're speaking to me with." Sarah heard the beeps as texts came through. "Just promise me you'll be careful."

"When am I not?"

"Yeah, not a question I'm willing to answer. Shit, I wish I was there."

"You found anyone who can help me?"

"I've made a few calls. Waiting to hear back. There is one lead, but it's remote."

"Okay, don't worry about it. Vivian told me this all ends later today. Even if your lead panned out, they'd probably have to come from Toronto, and it would be too late."

"I won't give up, though."

"You never do, Darwin. Gotta run. We're heading out."

The line clicked off. Darwin was no doubt reaching out to his contacts again. The man proved invaluable time and time again.

But this time, they were on their own. No Bruno, no band of highly trained mercenaries on Sarah's side. They were a group of three.

Parkman came out of the bathroom while Sarah was putting on her shoes.

"Are we all going?" Julie asked.

"That would be the plan," Sarah said. "If I can't talk to Ron, reason with him. Maybe you can. And if he shoots first, I need Parkman there."

"Gee, thanks."

She glared at him in a friendly way, then resumed tying her shoes.

When she sat up, she stopped to take a breath.

"Listen, Julie, there's a reason Ron has had his cell phone off all this time. Now that my friend has traced it, Hamilton and Wind, or whatever their names are, can trace him, too. We need to get to Ron and get him out of there before the bad guys get there."

Julie nodded, her lower lip quivering.

"It'll be okay," Parkman said. "We can be there within

the next half an hour and have them all safely out by five or five-thirty. We understand the other guys are still in the Toronto area somewhere."

Julie sniffled and wiped her nose. "I just, I just couldn't live with it if something happened to him or his boys. He's had such a rough go of it."

Sarah got up and hugged her. Julie held on tight.

"Why did Mikey call you?" she asked.

"He said he couldn't sleep with his brother kicking him and wanted me to read him a story. It's something I've done off and on for the past year."

Sarah pulled back and stared into Julie's eyes. "That story thing you do might have just saved everyone's life."

She released Julie and headed for the door.

"Let's go. We have to get there before they do. I have a bad feeling those bad guys we spoke of are close."

Sarah stepped out of the room and headed for the exit at the side.

Her sister was back, following her close.

Today's the day, Vivian whispered. *There will be bloodshed. I'm sorry. And heartache.*

"I know," Sarah muttered. "We've covered that. Anything else you're withholding?"

Restrictions forbid me from revealing more.

"We'll be talking about those restrictions later," Sarah whispered. "You don't get to pull out. Not when we need you the most."

"What's that?" Parkman asked from behind her.

"Nothing, just telling my sister we need to talk. But that's later, providing we make it to the end of the day."

"Sounds grim."

"It is."

"You okay?"

"No."

"Okay, that's not good."

"My heart's still beating. Aaron's still alive. We have hope." She turned to face him. "Right now, that's all I can ask for."

Parkman nodded and put a comforting hand on her shoulder. How could it get so fucked up in such a short time?

Outside, they ran for their rental with Julie in tow, the whole time Sarah worrying about the *heartache* part.

What did that mean?

What was coming?

Chapter 26

"Got something," Hamilton said, staring at his mobile tracker. "Ron's phone was on, and it's still on."

"Then it's a trap," Scar said. "No way he'd leave his phone on. He knows we'd be tracking him."

Wind glanced over from the driver's seat and then back at the road.

Hamilton spun around in his seat and looked back at Scar and Aaron. Their prisoner's hands were bound extra tight with rope, the flesh of his hands a deep red. Even in the dim light in the back, he saw just how red because it contrasted with the white of his forearms.

Scar guarded Aaron with a knife in each hand. Hamilton knew what Scar could do to Aaron if the prisoner tried anything stupid.

Through the back window, the second Hummer's

headlights were about a hundred yards back, staying close.

He angled the light from the monitor of his tracker to get a better look at Aaron's face. It had been a while since the big mouth took his beating, and he was still somewhat conscious but not alert. The pain had to be intense. The left side of his face—after falling victim to Hamilton's right hook—was a bloody mess. Definite bone break or fracture in the cheek and orbital bone. No way that much swelling came just from a batch of hits without a break. He looked like he had a cantaloupe growing out of his cheek and eye socket. The swelling was so intense that his left eye, lid, and lashes had disappeared under it.

"Shit, this kid might need a doctor soon."

Scar shook his head. "Why? He'll be dead soon." He leaned close to Aaron, then touched him on the forearm gently with the tip of a blade, drawing blood. "See, he doesn't feel a thing. The guy's fucked."

Hamilton watched the small line of blood as it rolled over the man's forearm and into his lap.

Scar laughed. "I think this time you *actually* beat someone's brains in. This guy's been acting like a vegetable ever since."

Hamilton tried to *feel* something for Aaron, but nothing came. No emotion came to the surface, no empathy, no sympathy, no care in the world for the man in his back seat. He fought the urge to have Scar throw him out of the moving Hummer. This prisoner and hostage business wasn't what they did. They killed people. That was it, plain and simple.

"I want him dead," Hamilton said. "But we've brought him this far, so he stays alive a couple more hours until we find Ron, kill that meddling whore, Sarah, and get our shit back. Then we go back to our mission."

Scar bounced in his seat twice, showing his excitement. "Can I cut one of them?"

"You can cut them all if you want, but I can't guarantee they'll be alive when you start cutting."

"Come on, Ham, leave me one. I need to scar someone. I need screams."

"Yeah, those screams raise the hair on my arms. I've heard your work."

"And isn't it a work of art when you can *hear* it?"

"Sure, Scar."

Hamilton turned back around. "How far to North Bay?"

"Forty minutes," Wind whispered.

"Take a right on Highway 17. Head toward Ottawa."

Wind nodded.

"You don't think it's a trap of some kind?" Scar asked.

"It may be, and we'll account for that. Either way, this is our only link to where Ron might be. We have to investigate it."

Hamilton brought up Google Maps and found the road leading into North Bay.

"Looks like the sign will say, Highway 17 East to Ottawa, and it comes before we enter North Bay."

"We're going to Ottawa?" Scar asked.

"No, we're just taking the highway a few minutes to …" he paused as he widened the picture and then zoomed in on the turn-off, "Maple Road. We're taking a right on Maple." Hamilton looked up at the highway, staring straight ahead. "I'll navigate as we go. We'll be at Ron's place in thirty minutes, and then we'll end this."

"Exciting times," Scar said. "So exciting."

The sound of blades sliding the length of each other came from the back seat.

Scar was eager to cut something, to make a name for himself, and Hamilton couldn't wait to watch.

There will be blood, he thought. Rivers of the shit.

Chapter 27

Parkman turned onto Palangio Road and hit the high beams.

"Low beams," Sarah said. "He'll see us coming for miles."

Parkman dropped the headlights back to low.

"He'll still see us."

"I know, but we'll kill the lights half a kilometer from where the signal is."

"Kill the lights?" Parkman glanced at her, then back to the road. After another look at her, he said, "Sarah, it's midnight black out here. We're surrounded by thick woods. There's no moon. No headlights means I can't drive."

"Sure you can. I'll show you a way."

He exhaled a sigh. She knew the man and understood him. That sigh wasn't exasperation. It was nerves. He didn't like driving a road where you couldn't turn around. The branches of the trees were so close that they were smacking the windshield and sliding along the side windows. There was no way they could turn around. Two feet to the left or right would put his wheels into a slight depression where the ditch was, or the grill would smack a tree. The road was better suited for a golf cart than a car, but still, they forged on with Sarah staring down at the exact location Darwin sent them.

The road turned left, then right, rose upward on a small hill, dipped, and moved to the right again. It reminded her of an old hunting trail that had been widened enough for four men to walk shoulder to shoulder. Unless they found somewhere to turn around or the road fed out onto another road, Parkman would have to back out all the way, and that probably wasn't going to happen until daylight, which was over an hour yet.

"There's got to be another way out, right?" Parkman said.

"I was just thinking that." Sarah scrolled along the map on Julie's phone and saw that Palangio Road eventually turned into Quae Quae Road.

"Looks like it does turn into another road and feeds out to civilization."

"Phew," he whispered.

Julie leaned forward in the back seat, her hand on the shoulder of Sarah's seat. "Ron wouldn't have his boys out here in the bush. They're in a cabin or something. And, he would've driven here in his pickup. We're close, I know it."

Sarah went back to the coordinates, scrolling through them. It had taken twenty minutes to get there from the turnoff on Highway 11. Every minute counted, and it felt like they were going agonizingly slow, but it couldn't be helped.

"And you've never been out here?" Sarah asked.

"No, never. I have no idea where Ron is. If there's a cottage or something here, he never told me about it."

"Okay, Parkman, cut the lights."

"You kidding?"

"Stop the car."

They only went twenty kilometers an hour, so stopping was easy and quiet.

"Kill the lights."

Parkman did. The darkness enveloped them absolutely.

"We're close. About a hundred yards to Darwin's red dot here. Turn on your parking lights only, and then dim the dash."

Parkman did as he was told.

"The orange light should be enough to see the edges of the road to stay in the middle. Ease forward without applying gas and get me to within fifty yards. You good with that?"

Parkman nodded and took his foot off the brake. The Kia eased forward. Gravel crunched under the tires as the vehicle moved along the dirt road, edging closer by the second.

Sarah pocketed the phone and grabbed her weapon. She made sure it was loaded and ready—not that she wanted to wound or kill Ron, but a girl needed protection—and grabbed the phone again.

"Okay, this is good."

Parkman turned off all the lights and stopped the car.

Sarah opened the door, then yanked it closed when the interior light came on. "Can you kill that?"

Parkman fumbled with dials on the left of the steering wheel, then sat up. "Got it."

Sarah opened the door. The interior remained dark.

"Sarah," Parkman said. "You shouldn't go alone."

She leaned back down into the open window. "We can't spook a man like this."

"Like what?"

"A former military man on the run from, well, everyone. And he's got his kids in there, wherever there is. He will kill anything that moves. If he detects three people advancing on his shack, cottage, or whatever's out there in this swamp-infested area, he might mow us all down. And I understand he's got the firepower to do it, not to mention he was an accomplished sniper in the Canadian military."

"Hey, wait, did I tell you he was a sniper?" Julie asked.

Sarah smiled. There was no time to get into it.

"Parkman, drive on until you reach where the road widens some. Find a quiet spot to park. Stay hidden. I'll come for you soon."

"What if something happens to you?"

Sarah glanced down at the road, shuffled her feet, then looked back up and stared at Parkman's face. There wasn't enough light to see his eyes.

"If something happens to me, go home. There will be no more of this life for you, me, Aaron, or the boys. If something happens to me, it's the way it's supposed to be, and I don't like it any more than you, but we can't keep doing this. Too many people hurt, too much death."

"Sarah, I don't like this any more than you do, but stopping is not the answer. Hundreds of people would be dead without what we've done—*you've* done—over the past decade. Sometimes, our side takes a hit, and I'm sorry for Alex and Aaron. There's no question—you have to keep going. This isn't a death-wish scenario."

"Okay, no death-wish scenario, but I have to go. The others are coming. I feel it."

"I know what you're doing, and it doesn't work for me. You're not my boss, my leader, or just a confidante. You're my friend. I won't let you walk into a trap."

Sarah smiled. "Parkman, this isn't a trap. Ron doesn't even know we tracked his phone. I just want you safe if this goes south. Is that too much to ask?"

"Yes, it is. I decide my future, my safety."

"Parkman, you're right, but I have to go."

She detected a slight nod in the dark. The door shut softly, and then Parkman started the car forward, the parking lights back on.

Sarah watched the vehicle until it rounded a corner and was swallowed by the darkness. He was right. She was being protective. But dammit, too many people had been hurt, and she couldn't bear it anymore. Good people, fighting on the right side, lost because Vivian didn't save them.

Restrictions ...

Is that what she meant by restrictions? She wasn't a god, after all. She was just Sarah's sister. Involving anyone else was at their own risk.

That made sense, but since Sarah broke the rules on this side of the universe or whatever the hell it was, Vivian would have to break the rules on the other side.

"Bring Aaron home to me, sis," she whispered. "Or I

fucking swear I will get killed on purpose, jump to the other side, and kick your spiritual ass."

Sarah had to wipe both eyes to see better as she turned and entered the bush on the side of the road.

Chapter 28

Ron rolled over and slipped off the couch. When his butt hit the floor, he snapped awake, his hands flying up in a defensive posture.

It all came back to him. They were in his cabin, safe and sound, his boys sleeping in the other room. That's why he was on the couch.

He relaxed his hands and let them fall to his side as he rested his head on the wooden floor. As much as exhaustion begged him to sleep, his mind ran with possibilities and paranoid theories. What if they found him with his boys? What would happen to Jason and Michael? Ron would be killed, there was no question. Probably by Scar or Tor, or both. Scar would leave scars, and Tor would torture him. Hamilton would love that. But Jason and Michael couldn't be around for that. Snatching his kids was the right thing to do because Hamilton sent two idiots after them, but he needed to drop off his boys somewhere today. He couldn't be caught with them. And, if an Amber Alert had been sent out, he was too visible. A man with two boys was harder to locate than him on his own.

But where? Who would take care of his boys? A foster family? Yeah right. They were just in it for the paycheck. Or because they liked little boys and girls in devious ways. Sure, there were legitimate foster parents out there, but Ron had a hard time trusting anybody with his kids. They were his flesh and blood, and he would kill for them. He'd kill Hamilton and his whole damn team to remove this threat, but they were all too highly trained for him to get them by himself.

Although he was willing to try.

The old gravel pit wasn't far from town. Later this morning, he'd drop his kids a block from school, call the authorities and tell them where they were, then call Hamilton and tell him to meet at the gravel pit for his weapons. This needed to end, and Ron would take as many of them as possible before being killed.

Maybe his boys would grow into men hearing about his kills in the Afghanistan conflict and how, even after coming home, he died in a blaze of glory executing other ex-soldiers who brought the war home with them.

He sat up and reached for his phone.

The table was empty.

His stomach dropped. Did he knock it off the table? Could he have forgotten and placed it somewhere else? Or had someone been in the cabin?

Still on the floor, he inched around the couch and

scanned the kitchen in the dark. As far as he could tell, no one was there.

Unless they were in the other room with his boys.

On his knees, he pushed off the couch and stood in his small living room, fully awake, all senses firing, listening for anything. There was no breathing in the dark corner, no creak of wood. It was almost fully black without a single sound coming from anywhere.

He could only hope no one had entered the cabin.

Knowing the cabin intimately and with the minute amount of light filtering in from the outside, Ron moved softly toward the bedroom.

He edged around the door and peered inside. It was so dark he couldn't make out much, but no one had tried to jump him yet. His breathing was calming, but his heart still raced.

Hands forward, he moved into the room, feeling for the bed. Then, he moved along the bed's edge until he got to the pillows. He got close enough to see both his boys sleeping deep, their chests rising and falling easily. A huge relief swept over him. He ran his hands gently upward to hover near their noses. He needed to feel their breath, their life source coming and going.

His boys, his pride and joy, his life.

They were the reason he abandoned the entire agreement, the pledge to come back to Canada in 2014 and plan an attack on the war pigs who sent so many young men and women to their deaths over the years.

Even though it was six years later, and Hamilton was ready to start the executions, it was a suicide mission, and

Ron couldn't leave his boys without a father.

Although, pulling out of Hamilton's crew would probably leave them fatherless anyway.

When he pulled his hand away from Michael's face, his finger bumped something hard.

Ron leaned back and touched it.

His phone was slightly under Michael's face like he'd fallen asleep while talking to someone.

A panic like he'd never felt before rose in him.

He eased the phone out from under his son's face. Michael stirred awake enough to roll over.

Ron brought it to his own face and touched the volume button.

The phone was on.

Ron pivoted and ran from the room, scrolling through to see if anyone called him. There was one call made slightly before four in the morning.

Michael had called Julie.

He breathed a sigh of relief. At least it was just Julie.

But what did he tell her? What could they have talked about?

As he made his way out of the bedroom, Ron wondered the worst thought of all.

Was someone able to trace his phone? And if they did, how close were his enemies at that moment? Outside, watching? An hour away? Closer?

They needed to pack and leave this place. They were no longer safe here.

In case anyone was advancing on the property, he moved to the front window with stealth.

Outside, the small amount of light given off by a star-filled sky was enough to see where the trees stopped, and the sky started, but that was about all he could see.

In case someone was advancing with gear, a phone, a cigarette in their mouth, or anything that lit up, Ron continued to watch the blackness beyond his front window.

He stood there for at least three full minutes, absolutely still, watching nothing, until a small light blinked on briefly.

The movement caught his eye, and then it was gone.

This was no illusion, no trick his eyes were playing on him. Someone was outside, and they had a cell phone. The silhouette of the person's upper body had come into view briefly after the light was on, leaving an image in his mind.

Someone was approaching the cabin. To harm him and his boys. Possibly multiple someones.

There was no way he could allow that.

Ron moved away from the window and prepared his weapons for the assault on the cabin.

Then he eased outside through the back, one Glock in his waistband, the other aimed at the soft earth to the right of his feet, gripped in both hands. He stood there, scanning the area as best he could. After seeing or hearing nothing, he edged along the wall to the corner and moved along the side of the cabin. There, he hunkered down and waited for whoever was coming to show themselves. He assumed it was an entire assault team, so he waited at the side to kill whatever came from the back and whatever came from the front.

Only headshots, as Hamilton's men would be well-armed and covered in Kevlar. Neck shots if he could manage it.

They'd never see him where he was if they weren't

wearing night vision gear. He had to assume Hamilton's men were heavily armed and prepared, so he crouched lower, placing his body on the dirt up against the house.

They'd never see him. They would die without knowing where the shooter was, as it happens with snipers.

And that would be their second mistake.

Coming after him was their first.

Chapter 29

Sarah tried to find paths through the foliage but kept getting a branch in the face. One sharp branch cut her cheek. She touched the area, felt moisture, tapped her tongue on the tip of her finger, and tasted blood.

Vivian talked about bloodshed and heartache. In a fantasy world, that could be considered bloodshed.

A girl can hope.

She pressed onward, bringing the cell phone screen up every few minutes to ensure she was going the right way. One hand on the cell, the other shielding the light, with the screen on the lowest setting, she checked her location. And each time, she was off slightly because of having to traverse a small body of water or an extra thick area of trees and bush.

Nothing much moved out here at this early hour. She couldn't hear a single vehicle as they were far enough away from any road any normal human being would travel on.

Locating this man and his boys was taking too long, but she understood Ron's thinking. He was in the right place to thwart people like her.

And if he knew the woods or had some kind of security system in place, she was screwed. Although, she had Vivian to protect her, right?

"Sure," she mumbled under her breath.

In all the years they worked together, the time off Sarah took, even the pact they made in Denmark, she was starting to wonder if Vivian was keeping her end of the bargain. Yes, there had been casualties on Sarah's side, and yes, she wasn't some Marvel comic. The good guys lost in the real world sometimes. But if Vivian could foretell shit, why couldn't she simply mention some bad dudes were waiting around the corner, and they were going to hurt Alex and break Aaron's face. You know, a little heads-up would've been great.

Sarah could pass that little message along, and boom, no one gets hurt.

Restrictions were Vivian's excuse. What restrictions? And since when?

Without Vivian present to explain it, Sarah tried to block her thoughts and stop obsessing about what had happened. She couldn't do anything about the past, but she could bloody well change the future. That's something she had control over.

She kneeled, covered the phone's screen, then lit it up.

According to Darwin's data and where she was standing now, Ron's phone was no more than fifty feet directly in front of her.

She clicked the light off, slipped the phone away, and retrieved her weapon.

The sun was due in an hour or sooner. The eastern sky was already a shade lighter.

Gun in hand, Sarah stared forward at the line running along the tops of the trees. Slowly, as her eyes adjusted to the darkness, the lines of a building came into view on the other side of a small swampy area.

Ron's camp, his cottage or shed or whatever it was, stood in the full dark straight ahead.

She started forward, doing her best to test each footfall to ensure she didn't fall into the water. Several times, her feet sunk deep in the wet dirt, and once, her right shoe came off, but she was able to get it back on.

Waking Ron at five in the morning was going to be a surprise. On her way to the front of the building, she considered this and decided on surprise. She needed him startled, awake fast, and alert.

The boys needed to be readied and taken off the property before the sun rose over the trees.

She made it to the front yard and could easily see the building now. Her weapon would not be needed, so she stashed it in the back of her pants.

A branch cracked to the left somewhere.

Sarah dropped to her knees, had her weapon back out, and aimed that way before she lowered to her elbows. Eyes wide, she studied the line of trees and saw only darkness.

Another footstep crunched a leaf or something. Someone was in the trees, and even though she was prepared and armed, the hair on her arms still rose.

She needed Ron's help if that guy Hamilton was coming. She needed inside the cabin. Ron had to be woken up and

—

"Don't fucking move," a man said to her right.

Something applied pressure on the base of her neck. Her heart skipped a beat, and she almost shouted at being startled.

"How many are there?" the man asked, his breath tickling her ear.

How the hell did he get the jump on her? The fucking guy was a phantom.

"I'm alone," she whispered.

"Bullshit. The bullet will snap your spine, enter your head through the brain stem, and kill you." He leaned in closer, his body weight pressing down on her now. "You'll die fast without feeling a thing. So, one last time, how many are with you?"

Ron had watched her approach. Of course, he had. Sarah was trained in many things, from firing her weapon and hand to hand-to-hand combat. She even had a few martial arts skills, but she was nothing compared to highly trained military men like Ronald Harris. The fucking guy was a ghost.

"That's probably Hamilton's people. I'm Sarah Roberts. I came here to warn you. Your cell phone was on. I tracked it. So could they."

The man's body eased off her, but the gun stayed where it was, and his mouth remained an inch from her ear.

"You don't have a dog in this fight. Why are you here?"

"That's where you're wrong. I want Hamilton dead."

"Get in line. And shut up. No more talking. We wait.

They come out of those trees, they die."

His lips gently caressed her ear when he spoke, but she fought the urge to rub where it tickled. No way anyone five feet away heard anything, let alone thirty feet away in the bush.

More footsteps, another branch cracking.

The gun moved away from her spine. She angled slowly to the right and watched as Ron aimed at the trees where the person was walking.

She readjusted herself, locked her elbows on the ground, and stared down the end of her weapon at the trees, too.

If Hamilton's men were coming, Ron would need help.

Then, they could both leave.

Yeah, right. It sounded like Ron wanted to kill her, too. Which meant when the firing on the trees was done, she would have to subdue him somehow. Then she'd force him to listen to her and end this stupidity.

A body edged out of the darkness along the line of the trees. The sky had lightened enough in the east that Sarah could see where the person was. Another human stepped out from the trees.

Ron was holding his fire, so Sarah did, too. Probably to see how many there were.

In an odd twist, the first person to exit the trees stood stock still, their arms down at their side. They seemed to be staring right at Sarah and Ron.

Then, the figure pointed and whispered something to the other person.

Sarah couldn't hear what was said, but she caught that it was a woman.

And then it hit her.

It was Julie and Parkman.

"Ron?" Julie called. "I love you, baby."

Ron's gun clicked as he lowered it. "What the fuck?" he whispered. "Why did you bring her here?"

"You and I against the world, baby," Julie said. "Please don't shoot me. We're here to help."

Chapter 30

"Pull in here," Hamilton said.

They'd reached the turn-off to Palangio Road in good time. The sky was a notch lighter. That gave his team thirty minutes to get in and get Ron.

He jumped out and met with the other Hummer. Wind and Scar joined them from his vehicle, leaving Aaron alone, which was fine. The man was bound tight and secured to the vehicle. He couldn't release himself, and he couldn't run.

"Gather around." Hamilton waited until his team of five, including himself, got closer. Only Ron—he'd stopped referring to him as Mark or Markham because he went AWOL—and Belle were left, and Belle wasn't answering her phone. "Ron's signal is a few kilometers up this small road. Wind and I will track it, along with Scar. I want you two to turn around, drive this way"—he narrowed the screen of his iPad to show the route he'd highlighted—"up to Hwy 17, back to 94, then head south through a small place called Corbeil. See here, you'll hit a road called Quae Quae?"

Ajax nodded. "Looks like it connects with this road at the other end."

"It does. Palangio turns into Quae Quae. According to Google Maps, it'll take about fifteen minutes to be positioned at the mouth of Quae Quae on the other side." He glanced up to address his men. "Do it in ten."

Ajax and Peter both nodded.

"We'll take it slow, going in this way as we approach the area. We'll get him whether it's a cabin, a shack, or he's sleeping under the stars. If he runs, I want you two at the other end. We finish this now, in these thick woods. No one will hear us, and there are swamps around here. We'll dump Ron in one of them and be done with it. All clear?"

All four of his men whispered their acknowledgment.

"Okay, everyone, sync your watches to fifteen minutes from now. Nothing happens until then. You two, be in position and prepared to stop his pickup truck if that's what he's driving. Okay, go, let's finish this."

They dispersed without another word and got back in their respective vehicles.

Wind started along the tiny road, branches rubbing the sides of the Hummer. Hamilton tracked the cell phone as the dirt road led them deeper into the trees.

No one worried, no one spoke. There was nothing now but an impending battle. They knew Ron would defend himself. He was the one with the heavy artillery. He had stolen weapons that would destroy a civilian Hummer, so

Hamilton had to take it slow.

"Stop here," he said.

Wind slowed and stopped. He killed the lights without having to be told.

"While we wait for Peter and Ajax to get into position, I'll be in the back. In just over five minutes, I'll go on foot the rest of the way. You drive as close as you can without any lights on." He checked the iPad. "About two hundred yards. Wait for me there."

Wind nodded.

Hamilton hopped out, then turned back to Scar. "Stay with Aaron. When I come out with Ron, slice him up. They both go in the swamp."

Scar smiled and bounced a couple of times in his seat. At the prospect of slicing someone, sometimes, he resembled a six-year-old boy getting a dozen lollipops.

Hamilton closed the door softly, moved to the back of the Hummer, opened it, and glanced in at his weapons. He chose two compact H&K VP9s. For Hamilton, the Heckler and Koch VP series rivaled the Glock in several ways. It even felt different when he shot it at the range. Surprising Ron this early in the morning required something in Hamilton's hands he was most comfortable with, and the H&K was it.

Once they were loaded and ready, he eased the back closed and moved up to the window to speak with Wind.

The man lowered it.

"It's almost time. I'll be on the tailgate for at least a hundred yards. Start crawling up the road now. Stop at two hundred yards to wait. If you see anything, headlights, a car, someone out walking a dog, honk the horn to let me know."

Wind nodded.

"Go get 'em, boss," Scar said from the back seat.

Hamilton ran to the back and clung to the spare tire as the Hummer started forward. With his free hand, he watched the red dot on his screen ease closer by the second. When he estimated a hundred yards, he hopped off and ran into the bush. It had been fifteen minutes since Ajax and Peter took off. They'd be in position by now, and Hamilton needed at least five minutes to approach the area on foot.

The sun was higher now, giving him enough light to scramble through the trees quickly.

He stopped to check the iPad.

Fifty meters ahead.

He started running.

"I got you, you son of a bitch."

Chapter 31

Inside the cabin was a flurry of activity. Without much explanation, Sarah told them they had to leave.

Julie and Parkman said they couldn't sit in the car and wait as they were too worried for Sarah.

"Something told me Ron would want to hear it from Julie," Parkman said.

Sarah nodded. "Well, you guys did the right thing."

Julie and Ron had hugged as both of them wept a few tears. Ron wiped his eyes fast in an attempt to cover his face.

"Ron, gather your things," Sarah said, breaking up the reunion. "We have to leave within five minutes or less. We really need to go."

"My boys are in there."

"Then go get them. We tracked you. That guy Hamilton will be able to, as well."

He frowned. "How did you come to know their names again?"

"Ron, we can talk on the way. We have to leave." She didn't hide the urgency in her voice. "If we aren't on the road in minutes, I feel our last stand will be here, in the bush, and something tells me it won't end well."

Julie pushed him toward the boys' room. "Go, bring them to me. I'll take the boys."

Ron wiped at his face once more, then sprang into action. He had the boys out of bed, dressed, and out the door in minutes. The entire time, Sarah and Parkman watched the perimeter.

"Where's your pickup truck?" Sarah asked.

"Behind the bushes over there." Ron pointed.

"We parked up that way, too," Parkman said.

Ron introduced his boys to Parkman and Sarah as they left the cabin as a unit.

"Parkman and Julie, you two go with the boys. I need to ride with Ron."

"Hey, I don't like that," Ron said.

"I wouldn't either, but your truck is recognizable, and I can't tell how close Hamilton is."

"Hamilton?" Michael asked. "That's over an hour outside of Toronto, isn't it, Dad? Pretty far from here."

"You're right," Julie jumped in. "I love that you excel at geography."

Michael giggled, his eyes still rimmed red with having to wake so fast.

Sarah slowed her step, and Ron did, too.

She touched his arm. "You can't be with the boys again

until this ends."

"Well, it'll be over in a couple of hours."

"How can you be so sure?"

"I left Hamilton a message."

"In the cabin?"

Ron nodded. "I turned off my cell phone, too."

"Good, I wouldn't want them seeing we're leaving or where we're going. What was the message?"

"Meet at ten in the morning at the old gravel pit ten minutes north of the city."

"And what are we going to do there?"

Ron shrugged. "End this, I guess. There's no way I'm going to live on the run."

"You can't give them back their weapons."

"I won't. I have another plan. And you're involved."

"Oh great. Sounds delightful. You want to tell me this plan?"

"Not until we're in the truck—"

Sarah slapped his arm. "Dammit, I just heard they're close and *closing in*, whatever that means."

"Closing in?" Ron said. "Shit."

"Exactly."

They broke into a run and caught up with Parkman and Julie. Sarah and Ron scooped up a boy each and ran with him toward the vehicles. Without a word, Parkman and Julie came in behind them.

Ron stopped at his truck and yanked off the bushes he'd used to cover it.

"We're twenty more yards that way," Parkman said. "We parked in a small, cleared area."

"They're here. Vivian said we may be out of time."

"Okay, that's not good." Parkman leaned against the pickup. "We couldn't've come this far just to …"

"We're fine. Everyone, just listen. I think this'll work. Parkman, Julie, you take the boys. Get the rental and pull onto the road heading west. We'll be ahead of you. If we pull over, you do, too."

Parkman nodded.

"Now go!" she whispered.

All four of them bolted from the pickup.

"You drive," she said.

Ron headed for the driver's seat without a word.

Sarah ran around and got in the passenger side. She withdrew her weapon and laid it on her lap.

"I've been in touch with a General Whyte," she said as Ron turned on the truck.

"And?"

He backed out and started up the road.

"He wants me to stand down. Why is that?"

Ron glanced over at her, then back to the road. "Probably because of what happened to that team in Toronto yesterday morning."

"I was there."

"And you escaped. Several news agencies are running a harebrained story about you."

"I stopped reading that shit years ago, but sometimes I can't help it."

"There they are." Ron pointed.

Parkman flashed his headlights once, then fell in behind them.

"Let me think a moment," Sarah said. "We're not home free yet. Something's not right."

Ron just drove. He didn't respond. The gravel road ended, and they were on pavement again. On the left, a red mailbox sat at the road, a driveway led to a house. They passed another one on the right.

"Turn into that driveway on the left," she shouted. "Do it now."

Ron jammed on the brakes and hung a hard left. They narrowly missed a tall tree as he hit the gas again, and they rocketed along a short gravel driveway.

"Around to the back of the house. Kill the lights."

She swung around in her seat and saw Parkman driving in behind them, then whispered a silent *thank you* to Vivian.

A boat sat on a trailer, and an older model RV was parked under a canopy of trees in the back, but that was it. No other vehicles were on the property.

When Ron stopped the truck, she jumped out. His door closed softly as he joined her, a weapon already in his hand.

"I'd keep that down and out of sight. Don't want you to scare your boys."

Parkman pulled up, his lights off. Sarah stopped at his window to pat his shoulder, then kept moving to the corner of the house, where she looked out at the road.

A low-growl engine noise approached from the way they had been headed. Something like a tractor.

Ron stood a foot beside her, both of them mostly concealed from the road. The dust had settled from Ron's emergency turn onto the property, which calmed Sarah. Unless someone drove in and behind the house, they would remain undetected.

The engine drew closer, louder.

They waited until it was right in front of the house.

The vehicle came into view, and Ron inhaled audibly as both of them pulled back into concealment again.

A Hummer had stopped in front of the driveway, its nose aimed toward Ron's cabin. Vivian had been right. Hamilton's team was attempting to box them in.

Sarah drew back and leaned against the house. She glanced at Parkman, then Ron, both men staring at her.

They waited.

The Hummer idled out front. Everyone could hear it.

When the engine revved, she couldn't tell whether they were moving on or coming up the driveway. The risk was huge, but she had to know, so she edged around the corner of the house to look.

They were leaving.

Moments later, the Hummer was gone, the engine already sounding farther away.

"Too fucking close," Ron whispered. "If you guys hadn't come—"

He lowered his head and leaned against the house, his shoulders hitching.

She put a comforting hand on his arm again. "It'll all work out now."

"No, I almost got my boys killed. Hamilton would've buried us out there. The team we built is filled with monsters."

"Well, it didn't happen. We have to move on from this. There's another fight brewing."

"Yeah, and I almost shot you this morning."

"And you didn't." She shoved him, and he bounced off the house, his long hair going in his face. "Got your attention? What didn't happen didn't happen. Make sense? Now, let's go make some shit happen."

He moved his hair out of his face.

"Good. Cry later. Moan later. You're a soldier. Let's go. We need to leave and make a plan for this gravel pit meeting."

He closed his mouth and wiped his face, nodding.

"All good?" Parkman asked from the driver's seat of the Kia.

"Yeah, follow us until we find a place for a take-out breakfast. The boys need to eat."

"I need to eat," Parkman said.

Jason and Michael snickered in the back seat. It drew Sarah's heart to a new place and made her feel tender all over again. Oh, how she wanted her own little boy or girl. Her miscarriage was tearing at her and Aaron, causing some kind of rift, and she had no idea how to mend it.

She blinked, and she was hopping back into the pickup.

"Go into town," she said. "We're safe now. Find a breakfast place, then drive us somewhere private to eat. We say goodbye to Jason, Michael, and Julie, then play out how you want to handle the gravel pit meeting."

"That works for me. I was there yesterday. Everything's all set up."

"Oh really?"

Ron drove around the house and back onto Quae Quae Road with Parkman close behind.

"Yeah," he said after a minute. "I think you'll be surprised, and I suspect you'll like what I have to say."

"I could sure use some good news right now."

"This is good news." Ron slammed the steering wheel once. "Really fucking good news."

"You aren't acting like it. That's an angry gesture."

He faced her, then focused his gaze back on the road.

"I am angry. I'm hostile right now. Hamilton came after my boys. He's trying to ruin me, kill me. We fucking served together, and because I don't want to kill the mayor, or some elected official in Ottawa, then I'm out. Well, fuck him. I've planned a monumental surprise." He looked at her again. "One that'll even shock you. And I'm going insane thinking about the look on his face when he realizes I won."

"You're not getting ahead of yourself?"

"No." He shook his head violently, both hands gripping the wheel. "No, I won. I will win. This is over. And his whole team goes down. Scar, Peter, Ajax, Tor, and even—"

"Tor's dead," Sarah said, breaking into his tirade.

"Tor's dead?"

Sarah nodded. "Ajax killed him."

They drove in silence for a moment.

Ron cleared his throat. "How would you know?"

"Really? That's the question you're asking?"

Ron nodded and blinked a couple of times. "Sorry, just weird to see that psychic shit in action."

"You didn't see that Hummer in front of the house we hid behind?"

"Yeah, yeah." He leaned back in his seat. "Still weird."

More silence.

Then Ron asked, "Hey, can you see the end game? Who wins, who loses?"

"Nope. Can't see shit."

"Oh. Okay. Well, then. Had to ask."

"I only know what my sister tells me, and sometimes she's a bit emotional."

"Ouch."

"I'd go so far as to say she's been a bit unstable lately." Sarah looked upward. "You hear me, sis?"

Ron didn't respond. He drove with his mouth shut until they pulled over at a highway diner just north of the city.

She liked Ronald Harris for that.

Her issues with Vivian were hers alone.

And a reckoning was coming.

Chapter 32

HAMILTON STARED OFF AT the trees, breathing slowly to calm his nerves. They had the fucker. He was in his shack. But then he was gone.

When he spun back around to face his team, they glanced down as a unit at his waist. He'd forgotten a VP9 was still gripped in his right hand. He loved the feel of it, allowing him to express himself if needed.

Since it unnerved his men, he slipped it away.

"None of you saw a thing?" He ran a hand through his hair, stopping near the back of his head to tug some and release some tension. "How could he slip past us? He was just here. It's impossible."

Peter moved closer to Hamilton. "We stopped in front of all the houses on the way here and didn't see a thing. There weren't that many, so he must've gone down some back road or something."

"How about behind the houses?" Hamilton glared at him, then angled his gaze to Ajax. "Did you check backyards?"

Peter and Ajax exchanged a glance between them, then shook their heads.

Hamilton cupped his fist with his other hand and went back to that breathing thing to calm himself.

On the inside of the cabin, Ron had left a pad of paper open on a table in the kitchen. Four spray-painted arrows were aimed at it.

The note gave Hamilton coordinates to a gravel pit. It also stated a time.

They had a little over four hours to prepare as Ron wanted to meet them at the pit for ten in the morning.

Hamilton glanced up at Ron's place. The sun crested the farthest hill and basked the shack in the morning light. It was a rundown, beat-up tin shack that hunters might use for one overnight in the woods. Long since left to ruin, Ron must've bought it and rebuilt it some, as there was an actual bedroom, a couch, a coffee table, and a kitchen table. Even a couple of cupboards held non-perishable foodstuffs. Empty beer bottles sat by the couch.

There was no driveway to speak of. Ron had to park elsewhere and walk to the shack. That was probably how they missed him. He would have covered his pickup truck, run off in the dark, driven away, and headed into town.

Hamilton even supposed Ron could've driven right by Ajax and Peter, and neither would have been the wiser.

"Okay, new plan." Hamilton started walking toward the Hummers.

"What's the new plan?" Ajax asked, on his heels.

"Burn that fucking shack to the ground because fuck Ronald Harris. Then we go eat."

"Hey," Scar shouted.

Hamilton stopped and turned toward the Hummer, where Aaron still sat slumped in the back seat.

"Can we kill him now?" Scar asked. "C'mon, let me cut him up and toss him in the shack before the bonfire. Think of him as marshmallows."

"Marshmallows?" Hamilton scowled. "That's gross."

"What?" Scar pushed his hands out at his side. Each palm cradled a knife.

"He stays alive until we meet Ron."

"Why?" Scar couldn't hide the dejected tone in his voice.

"Because I said so," Hamilton shouted at him. Then added, "And because I think Ron had help getting out of here alive. We may need Aaron for something Sarah Roberts-related." Hamilton started walking again.

"Let me kill him, and we'll just pretend we have him when we talk to the bitch."

Hamilton stopped walking, his hands clenching, in need of his weapon. He restrained himself from grabbing it because Scar's life would be in danger if he drew it. Hamilton wasn't sure he could control himself.

"The whole point is that bitch is supposedly psychic."

"What?" Scar said.

Now, he sounded like he had no idea what was going on, and Hamilton didn't want to waste time telling him the details and the finer points.

"Look, Ron probably got away because that Sarah whore

told him we were coming. If that's true, which I have my doubts, but if for some cosmic, fucking universal reason that's true, then we can't kill Aaron yet. She'll know. We can't *pretend* to have him and certainly can't joke our way through this. Meet Ron at ten. Get our weapons. Kill them all, and move on. Scar, you can kill Aaron then. Wind gets to take out Ron. This is over in four hours. You'll get all the knife play you want. Just don't touch Aaron yet. Got it?"

Scar hung his head and nodded subtly. He looked completely dejected.

To make it up to him, he'd give Scar that bitch Belle, too. She still wasn't returning their calls. She'd vanished since the cleanup crew met with her yesterday afternoon.

Scar loved slicing up women. Using his knives turned him on, but using them on a woman turned him into a raging hormone.

When this was over, he hoped Scar could cut Sarah, too.

Hamilton calmed even more and was able to smile at the thought of Sarah's screams as Scar used his knife in her crotch.

"Okay," he whispered to no one in particular. "Now I feel better." He turned back to his men. "Burn the shack, then let's get some grub. I'm hungry. At ten this morning, we have some people to kill. And Scar." He turned to face him. The man's head was still down. He glanced up and met Hamilton's gaze. "When this is all over, you can cut up Aaron in front of Sarah Roberts, then use your knives on her for as long as you want."

"Really?" There he was again, bouncing on the balls of his feet like a little boy with newfound candy.

Hamilton nodded slowly. "You can do whatever you want to her. Fuck her, then cut her up." He shrugged. "Or cut her open and fuck the holes. I don't care. Consider her yours for all the restraint you're showing right now with Aaron."

Scar shouted something unintelligible and hopped in the back seat beside Aaron.

Hamilton just made the man's day.

Wind and Ajax had found a gas can in the back and were now lighting the shack on fire.

They'd be gone in minutes, and soon, this stupidity would come to an end.

Along with a bunch of lives.

He'd probably even have to kill that girlfriend of Ron's, Julie something. And his ex-wife bitch, Bridgette.

Why did so many people have to die all the time? Why couldn't they just do what they were told?

He inhaled deeply, held it for several seconds, exhaled, and started toward his Hummer.

Today was a good day.

A killing day.

And as hungry for meat as Scar was, Hamilton was hungry for blood.

Today, he'd get his due. There was no question in his mind.

Because he had a plan.

A deadly plan.

Chapter 33

They'd all eaten at a roadside diner. Sated, Sarah watched as Julie got Ron's sons settled in the back seat of the rental. They'd transferred all the stolen weapons to the covered area behind Ron's pickup. Everything except for the MATADOR was there, as the Toronto authorities had that now.

Ron said his goodbyes to Jason and Michael, promising to see them later.

Parkman handed Julie the keys to the rental.

"You going to be okay?" Sarah asked her.

Julie nodded, but there was sadness in her eyes.

"Go ahead," Ron said. "You can say it. I brought this down on us all. It's my fault—"

"I wasn't going to say that."

"Then what?"

Sarah eased back. Gangsters, hitmen, and bad cops were

one thing. Domestic disputes or emotional moments between couples were something altogether different. She would only intervene in the face of violence.

"Just that," Julie started, interrupting herself with a sob, "after this is all over, are we going to be okay?"

"Okay? How?" Ron paused, then seemed to understand. "Oh, you're talking about what I said in the garage the other night." He leaned down to look into her face, then lightly touched her chin and lifted her head. "Julie, honey, we've always been okay. I knew Hamilton was gunning for me, so to speak, and I needed you out of there. Breaking up with you meant you'd be out of my life and far from danger. Honey, we're fine now." He wrapped his arms around her, and she sobbed in his embrace. "There, there, honey. Remember, it's you and me against the world. We got this, baby."

She nodded into his shoulder, then he eased her off him and kissed her forehead. "Baby, you've got to go. Take my boys. Keep them safe. When this business with Hamilton is over, we'll figure out the rest of our lives, but first, I must be alive to do that. Unless we make a stand, that ain't gonna happen."

"I know," she whispered.

"You got this. Take them to Sudbury for the day. The bookstore, lunch, then when we call, come on back. Cool?"

Julie pulled into him again, and Sarah missed Aaron more than she could express. She looked away and stared at the morning sky, wondering how hurt her man was. How extensive were his injuries? Those pictures Hamilton texted her were horrific.

She also thought about what Vivian had said. *Bloodshed*

and heartache were coming. Bloodshed, Sarah understood. But heartache?

If Aaron died because of something Sarah was working on, how could she live with herself? There had been close calls and injuries before, but this was making her nervous. Vivian had talked of things she could reveal and things she couldn't reveal in the past, but she never said there were *restrictions* until recently. Could those restrictions have anything to do with Aaron's death? What if Vivian told her everything? Would Sarah change the course of future events to save her man? If so, would that jeopardize others?

All that made sense, and it helped her understand those restrictions because what she always aspired to do was for the betterment of everyone and not just Sarah or Aaron. She'd never been selfish in her pursuit of what was right. But who would fault her if she made personal choices on who would stay alive and who wouldn't? Wasn't that just a human condition?

So then, restricting Vivian kept Sarah on the right path.

If her assumptions were correct, the heartache was something she couldn't bear. She'd crumble under that kind of despair. Hadn't there been enough heartache? Hadn't people suffered enough?

She blinked. They needed to stay on point. Work hard and see this through. Quite possibly, everyone could be saved and she wouldn't have to deal with losing anyone close to her.

Sarah edged toward Parkman. "We need to go."

He went to say something, but Ron had turned around and was heading their way.

Julie got in the rental and turned it on before they made it to the pickup truck. Then she pulled out of the parking lot and headed toward Sudbury.

"We've got an hour," Ron said. "I won't need much time to get set up." He tossed Sarah the keys. "Can you drive?"

"Sure. You'll navigate?"

He nodded, and they all jumped in, Parkman sitting between them.

"While I drive, explain it all again."

"Once we get there, I'll show you where to drop me off. I was there yesterday. I'm all set up."

"How did you know to set things up in advance?" Parkman asked. "What if Hamilton demanded a change of locations?"

"I had planned on calling him to arrange it all. Also, explaining that his weapons were there and that the location was away from the main road and hidden, not to mention abandoned, he'd like the spot. I know him. If he refused and wanted something more public, I would've just told him to go fuck himself. I'll be at the gravel pit at ten. If he didn't show, he'd never see or hear from me again."

Sarah merged onto the highway and headed north, away from the city. "Which meant he'd probably show. He couldn't let a chance like that get away from him."

"And leaving that message in the cabin doesn't give him an option to not show now."

"Why the gravel pit?" Sarah asked. "I mean, besides the obvious reasons of it being far away from the public."

"Because it's covered over in sand now."

"Sand?" Parkman asked.

Ron leaned forward and braced himself with a hand on the glove box to look at them. "Sand covers most of the terrain out there. That allowed me to plant the explosives."

"Explosives?" Parkman's voice rose a notch.

"Yeah, tell us about those," Sarah said, glancing over at Ron. "What the hell?"

"I've strategically placed explosives in a dozen spots. They're buried in the sand and brushed over. Impossible to tell they're there without a metal detector. When we arrive, I will show you the exact parking spot so we aren't near them."

"If no one can tell where they are, how will you know?"

He held up his phone. "I've locked their coordinates in here. Each one has a code connected to my phone."

"You type the code, and boom?" Sarah asked.

Ron nodded and leaned back into his seat. "Exactly."

"And if something happens to your phone?"

"Nothing will. But, if something happened to my phone, I guess we're out of luck."

"These things aren't like land mines, right?" Parkman asked. "I mean, I'd hate to walk on one or drive over one. Might be a tad unpleasant."

Ron laughed and shook his head. "Not land mines. Only a code from my phone could detonate them. That and tinkering with their wiring. The pressure from a foot or a vehicle's tire wouldn't do a thing. Even the weight of a Hummer is fine. They're encased and formidable."

"Glad to hear."

"And I've got another surprise."

"Another surprise?" Sarah muttered. "I don't like this

many surprises."

"It's a surprise for them. Belleville is coming."

"Belleville?"

"Well, the team calls her Belle. Her name is Annemarie Willard. She served with us overseas. I've known her for a long time. When our team formed, she was all in. When the shit went down, she played the fence as a contact for me, but last night, she broke all communication with Hamilton's side. She's with us and will be in position"—he checked his watch—"in thirty minutes."

"You trust this Belle?" Parkman asked.

"With my life. When this shit started the other night, she took Julie in and was supposed to protect her, but that went awry when Julie bolted from protection and went home. Julie almost got herself killed in the process. She would've been in trouble if you weren't there to protect her in Huntsville."

"We got her to North Bay, and she should be fine today, but she'll still have to deal with the authorities when this is over."

"I'm afraid when this is over, I'll be dealing with them as well."

They drove in silence for about ten more kilometers, and then Ron pointed out the road that would take them to the gravel pit.

Sarah turned and headed along the wide road.

"Okay, this is it," he said as they drove out of a thicket of trees.

The area was covered in sand, just as Ron had described. It looked like a beach in the middle of the woods and was the size of a football field. The sand had hardened over the years, so it was easy to drive on, but the pickup shifted slightly to the right and left.

Sarah stopped and waited for further instructions.

Ron turned on his phone and opened an app.

"See here, that's all the devices under the sand."

Sarah and Parkman leaned closer. Twelve red dots were laid out on his phone's screen, each with an exact GPS coordinate hovering beside them.

"I tap on one of the dots like this."

He touched one on the far side of the expanse, and a small window lit up, asking for a three-digit code.

"Then I type the code and boom."

He tapped the red dot again, and the little window disappeared. Then, he minimized the app.

Sarah glanced out the windshield. According to the map, there was an explosive device ten feet in front of them. She couldn't see a thing.

"Okay, cool, but don't lose that phone."

"I won't because you and Parkman are meeting Hamilton and his team."

"We are?"

"Yup. You're going to drop me off over there." Ron pointed at a small ridge where a line of trees started. "I'll be five feet inside those trees with my sniper rifle, watching everything go down. I can pick off two or three of them before they can get a shot at you two."

"Comforting," Parkman said.

"And if they shoot at you two, you'll be covered in Kevlar. Only your face will be exposed."

"Where might this protective gear you speak of happen

to be?" Parkman asked in a British accent.

He didn't have a toothpick. Maybe this shit was making him nervous.

"You do that well," Ron said, staring at Parkman. "Everything's in the back." He nodded toward the pickup truck's bed.

"And where will Belle be?" Sarah asked.

"She's going to be coming over that hill there." Ron pointed to the far right.

"Sounds like you've got this all figured out. Any chance you want to just arrest these guys? Maybe call the authorities? Or is this wholesale murder?"

"I only shoot to kill if they do." Ron stared out his window. "I hope they don't. Give them the weapons. They'll give you Aaron. They leave. It's over. Let the authorities grab them from there."

"There's something else, isn't there?" Sarah asked. "Something you're not telling us."

Ron waited a moment, then leaned forward to look at Sarah.

"They will pay for what they have done and tried to do to my kids. Also, for what they did to Aaron. This was never about becoming rogue and attacking the Canadian military. This was an assassination plot that was a pipe dream. We came home, we got over it, we grew up and dealt with it. Life happens, and life goes on. But Hamilton and his band of rogues didn't get over it, and when they took a shipment of illegal arms to prepare for their war, I took their weapons. If they want to live to see tomorrow, that's on them. They will trust Belle, and she's here to broker a deal."

"Then what about us?"

"You want Aaron back, right?"

Sarah didn't reply. The man knew the answer.

"Then take these weapons as my gift. They're yours to negotiate his release. Aaron's captors will be here soon. While we wait for the meetup, please drop me off at that tree line. I need to get settled."

Sarah and Parkman exchanged a glance. There was something he wasn't telling her, but at the same time, they did need Aaron back, and with this much firepower and bombs to explode if Hamilton's team tried to run, the odds were already in their favor—heavily.

She started the truck forward, drove over the first explosive, and then released a shuddering sigh.

"Happy you know what you're talking about with these bombs."

"I've been in the military too long. Today, I retire."

"I don't know if I like the sound of that."

"Just know, this isn't your fight. Get Aaron, and then get yourself to safety. I want you to park over there, close to the woods. When it's done, get into the woods with Aaron and wait. Let Hamilton take my truck and the weapons. If anything goes wrong, Belle and I will be your backup."

"Hope it goes that easy," Sarah mumbled, knowing it probably wouldn't.

Bloodshed and heartache.

She was so afraid of what was coming within the next hour that she couldn't control the shake in her hands.

That was unusual for Sarah. But she had a stake in the game—an emotional gambit.

They had hurt her Aaron. They had beat him to a bloody pulp.

Even though getting him back was all that mattered to her, finding a way to hurt Hamilton meant a lot to her as well.

She'd certainly be looking for an opportunity.

A lot of people were going to hurt.

And some might be killed.

How to control the nerves until the bloodshed was her biggest challenge.

Chapter 34

HAMILTON STARED AT THE entrance to the gravel pit as Ron's pickup approached. Three people sat in the front. The driver appeared to be a female.

She signaled, waited a moment, then turned into the closed gravel pit entrance.

He checked his watch. The meeting was supposed to happen in less than thirty minutes. This made sense. Ron would want to set up and get prepared.

And yet, that was his mistake. Ron gave them four hours from the shack to the meet. His team was on site within one hour, scoping out the sandy area. They'd already set up and were waiting for Ron and his two psychic friends.

He'd wait until ten, give Ron the illusion he was in control, then drive along the access road to the gravel pit several minutes late. It would make them nervous. With each second that eased by, they would be wondering if he was actually going to show. And when he did, they'd be surprised by his genius plan about a minute before he killed them all.

They'd already located the only elevated place for a sniper on a slight ridge. Wind said he'd cover that area while Ajax and Peter hung out in the other corners. They were all armed to the teeth and ready to kill anything that breathed and obtain their stolen weapons.

"You've got about a half-hour left to live," Hamilton said, turning in his seat to look at Aaron.

The man had regained consciousness. He moaned some, but he still wasn't talking.

"That face of yours is hideous. You should have someone look at that."

Scar waved a knife in the air. "I'll take a look," he said, smiling wide. "Gotta open him up first to look, though."

"You'll get your chance." Hamilton nodded toward the gravel pit. "Back there, no one will hear his screams. You'll have at least a half hour while we transfer the weapons."

"That's it? I want to do the girl, too."

"I know, so kill him fast, then take the bitch in the trees."

"I'm gonna slice her up good and fuck her like the whore she is."

Aaron grunted something.

"What's that?" Hamilton asked. "You don't like what my friend said?"

Aaron moaned.

"Not sure you have a say in this game anymore. Your bitch interfered in our work. She sent me pictures of my weapons, and she knows too much about us." Hamilton turned back in his seat. "At first, she got me. I'll admit it. I actually thought she was psychic. But now I know better. Ron told her everything. That's what the MATADOR was doing in her hands at the airport. He confided in her when he shouldn't have. Now she knows too much and has to die." He shrugged. "It's not my fault. And trust me, Aaron, if Sarah had gotten involved by accident, I'd just kill her fast. Just shoot her in the face. Be done with it. I'm not some kind of animal." He laughed under his breath a couple of times. "But Aaron, she taunted me, tried to fuck with me. He played that psychic card, and it actually freaked me out a little. I mean, if someone's *actually* psychic, they'd know where I was, what I was doing, any time they wanted." He glanced at Scar. "We'd be fucked." They both laughed now. "So, because she messed with us, Scar gets to play with her. He can use his knives, his tongue, his dick, I don't care, but Sarah dies right after you do. Then you two can meet in Heaven or wherever the hell assholes and whores go."

The energy coming off Scar was infectious. Hamilton wanted to get the party started, but they had to wait. Not much time left.

"And another thing. If your bitch were psychic, she'd know we were coming and what we have planned for her. She'd know she was as good as dead and would never have shown up. Yet, here she is. That proves she doesn't have a psychic bone in her body. Oh, and she's fucking stupid. What amateur goes up against people like us?" He shrugged. "Whatever, it's her funeral."

Aaron mumbled in an attempt to speak.

"What's that?" Hamilton asked. "Can't hear you."

His jaw tried to move, but he winced and lowered his head.

"That's okay," Hamilton said. "Don't try to talk. You've nothing to say that we'd want to hear anyway. Just sit there and moan. You'll be out of pain in less than twenty minutes."

Hamilton watched the access road for the remainder of the time. No one drove along it, and there was no sign of police presence.

Nothing seemed off to him, and everything seemed right.

It was time to kill stupid people.

Then they could get back on track and kill the war pigs who decide to send men and women to war from behind comfortable desks while wearing recently shined shoes and expensive suits. Those people were his mortal enemy.

Sarah and her boyfriend were a stepping stone to greatness.

He was going to enjoy this.

"Go," he said to Scar. "Head up that access road slowly. Then you know what to do."

Scar nodded and started the Hummer forward.

Today was going to be a good day.

Chapter 35

Sarah grabbed Sutton's phone and checked the time. It was a couple of minutes after ten.

"They'll come, right?" Parkman asked.

She nodded. "I'm certain they'll show, but they're late."

Sarah glanced over at the ridge where Ron was hiding. It seemed far away, but for a man of his talents, it probably wasn't difficult to fire an accurate shot from there. The wind factor was low. What breeze they did have was blocked by all the surrounding trees.

Above them, the cloudless sky offered all the sunshine they needed. Over her shoulder the other way, Sarah watched the area where Ron had said Belleville was positioned.

She adjusted the thin Kevlar she wore under her shirt. She'd worn a batch of vests over the previous decade, but this one seemed tight. Parkman spent years on the police force wearing these things. He appeared quite comfortable in his.

She placed a hand on the butt of each weapon at her side. She probably looked like something straight out of the Wild West. All she needed was a Stetson or some equivalent. Either that or this was a scene straight out of *Breaking Bad* with all the sand. Even though they were in northern Ontario, the sand below her feet made her think of that scene where the school teacher said he was the danger.

That wasn't too far from the truth in this same scenario. Hamilton and his team were trained military, but they were walking into a trap set by a hunter. Sarah just hoped Ron's shot was true if it was needed. Taking a bullet in the vest hurt bad, but it was fine. It meant you lived another day. However, she didn't want to go through that. She'd seen what it had done to Aaron in Texas. He was still in pain from that incident.

Thinking about Aaron, she wondered if he'd ever forgive her. Parkman hadn't talked much about it. Aaron was tough, though. He'd been through worse and endured.

An engine growled low as a vehicle approached.

"Here we go," Parkman said. "We're on."

A large Hummer appeared on the road leading into the gravel pit from the highway.

Only one vehicle approached.

It angled toward the pickup, then stopped aimed at it from over fifty yards.

"We're not walking over to meet them," Sarah said. "And where's the second Hummer? They attacked Sutton's team with two."

A man slipped out the side door and walked to the Hummer's back.

"I don't like this," Parkman said.

"I don't either."

It was so quiet this far into the woods the sound of the man opening the tailgate was easy to hear.

Sarah moved a few feet to the left to be behind the pickup. She glanced at Parkman.

"You might want to take cover if he's got another MATADOR thing."

"Yeah. Good thinking." He eased farther behind the pickup. "But if they've got another one of those things, not sure a pickup will save us."

Someone had gotten out of the rear of the Hummer. Now, two people were standing there.

The man who left the passenger seat strode back along the vehicle's side and hopped inside.

When he closed the door, the Hummer moved toward them again. It edged along at a snail's pace, making the trek across the sand agonizing.

"What the hell are they doing?" Sarah asked, staring at the windshield of the Hummer.

"I think someone's walking behind their vehicle."

"What, to cover their flank?"

Parkman moved around the tailgate of the pickup for a better look. "No, this person is tied up. There's a rope around his wrists—" The hand he slapped over his mouth cut off his words.

Sarah snapped left, craning her neck. "What?"

Parkman faced her, his eyes wide and glistening. He

removed his hand from his mouth. "It's Aaron."

Sarah fought the urge to pull both weapons and fire every bullet she had into that windshield. Both driver and passenger would be dead. But if a stray bullet hit Aaron, or someone was in the back of the Hummer with a gun aimed at Aaron, she'd never be able to live with that.

Suppressing every emotional tsunami she faced, Sarah composed herself for the transaction. This wasn't a regular deal. Merchandise for cash or a barter scenario. This was her man, tied up and being dragged behind a Hummer. He'd surely die if the driver hit the gas and bolted from the area, as she doubted they'd stop to reel him back in while under fire.

This was their insurance. Pull your weapons. They drive away. Fire on their vehicle, they drive away. And there was only one vehicle in case everything went to shit. Then, the other guys could swoop in, finish the transaction, and leave with the weapons. A lot of what they were doing made sense, but she didn't have to like it.

Hate was such a strong word, but in that moment, she'd use it for Ron's colleagues.

The Hummer stopped fifteen feet from the nose of the pickup truck.

But that was wrong.

The angle was all wrong. From Ron's position on the ridge, he'd only be able to see the back corner of the Hummer. There'd be no chance to get a bead on the driver.

They'd have to take out the driver if this went south.

Sarah lifted her hands and stepped out into the open. When there was no movement from inside the Hummer, she pointed at the back of the pickup.

"Your weapons are right there, assholes," she whispered. "Come out, untie Aaron, load up, and drive away." She waited another moment, then asked louder, "What are you waiting for?"

The passenger spoke into something in his hand, then smiled at Sarah.

She did not like that smile. It came across as if he had one-upped her.

Something was wrong. She could feel it.

The passenger door cracked open. The man pushed it all the way, slid out of the seat, and dropped to the sand.

He edged around the door, his hands raised, too.

"Don't shoot me," the man said, his tone high like he was mocking a teenager. "I come in peace."

"Yeah, right," Sarah whispered.

The man lowered his hands. "Where are my weapons?"

"Where's Aaron?"

The man gestured with a nod toward the rear of the Hummer. "Back there. I put him on display so you could see him right away. We get our weapons. I have no use for him anymore." He stared at Sarah. "And no use for you, either. This wasn't your fight. Why get involved?"

"Who knows? Who cares? Does it matter now?"

He shrugged. "Guess not." The man looked at Parkman. "Can I see my hardware?"

Parkman moved to open the back of the pickup. He lifted the canopy and eased it off to the right, away from the Hummer and the man watching him.

The man moved forward a couple of steps and lifted up on the balls of his feet to peek inside the bed of the pickup.

"Fascinating. I could never tell if it's all there without a full inventory, but it looks good enough to me."

"It's all there," Sarah said. "Release Aaron, load your weapons, and we conclude our business here."

The man guffawed. "Hold your horses there, pretty girl. What's the big hurry?"

Something had happened. There was a problem. Ron was holding back on them. There was no way it would go this smoothly, and she knew it. But what was going on was anybody's guess as Vivian was absent—again.

Seething anger warmed her collar, and she fought to keep it under control.

Movement from inside the Hummer caught her eye. The driver listened to something on his phone. He tapped the screen and set the phone down.

The man standing outside made eye contact with his driver, who then nodded. Whatever they were up to was done, and they were ready.

They were about to learn what was going on.

The Hummer started moving again.

"Hey, where's he going?" Sarah asked, taking a step forward. "Aaron's still tied to the back."

The man held up a hand. "Take it easy. He only getting into position to load the weapons."

Sarah held back as Aaron stumbled into view. His hands were bound, wrapped over and over with thick rope. When she saw his face and the grotesque swelling on the left side, she fought an urge to scream. They had ruined his cheek, and his jaw appeared broken.

Her man stumbled once, then dropped to the sand, trying

to get his hands up in front of him before landing face-first on the ground.

"Aaron," she yelled, unable to hold back her shout when he fell.

He rolled onto his back and was dragged behind the Hummer for three more feet before the driver stopped.

She didn't care about the authorities, criminal prosecution, or any justice system. They didn't rehabilitate the people who did things like this to other people. Only she could exact justice for Aaron.

Sometimes, actions weren't accompanied by thought. And sometimes actions just needed to happen.

Sarah put one foot in front of the other toward the man standing in front of the Hummer.

The driver's side door shot open, blocking her path.

She stopped when a man hopped out. An ugly man with a knife in each hand.

The urge to say something sarcastic about bringing a knife to a gunfight didn't make it past her lips. Partly because she wasn't going to pull her weapon.

Live by the knife, die by the knife.

She moved into the man's inner space.

He lunged with his right, which Sarah expected. She parried in a half twist and bumped the knife hand with her forearm, thereby pushing his hand outward. She shot her right hand up into the base of his nose. All her anger, all her emotion was in that one hit. After contact, while the man's head was snapped back, her hand continued skyward until her elbow straightened and bent inward again.

When training kicks in, you don't think. You just react.

Sarah was already squeezing the knife out of the man's left hand before his head was lowered back from the first hit to his nose.

Someone shouted behind them, but she was too far into the fight—and beyond pissed off at that point—to ever consider stopping.

The knife cleanly in her hand, she shot a final thrust and planted the blade just above his protruding Adam's apple. It went hilt deep before she released it and stepped back.

A deep breath brought the world back into focus. All of that couldn't have taken more than three seconds by the look of surprise on the man's face. His nose spurted blood from each nostril, and something was sticking out at the bridge of his nose between his eyes now.

Heavy blood seeped from the neck wound, too.

The driver of the Hummer dropped the other knife and clung to the one stuck in his neck. He jerked it out, and along with it came an enormous amount of blood.

He dropped to his knees then, staring at her, the look of surprise turning to one of dread.

The only problem with that entire fight was it did nothing to calm her anger. She seemed riled up and even angrier than before she attacked him.

"Drop it," Parkman said.

The man with the knife in his throat fell face-first into the dirt beside the Hummer. His passenger held a weapon pointed at Sarah. Parkman held a weapon pointed at him.

"Shoot," Sarah said. "And you'll die." She moved around the man's body at her feet and stepped up in front of the passenger. "You're Hamilton, right?"

He didn't answer, but his eyes told her everything. He glared at her in hatred, the weapon still in his hand.

"I know I should apologize for what I did to your friend there, but you should treat your guests better." Hamilton didn't waver, but he didn't fire his weapon either. Sarah moved closer, the fury inside her making her feel irrational. She pressed her forehead against Hamilton's weapon. From the corner of her eye, Parkman moved closer, his weapon touching Hamilton's temple now. "You want to do an exchange, no?" she said, her teeth tight together. "Aaron for weapons? And yet you bring him here looking like that? What the fuck is wrong with you? That's the same as if I damaged all those weapons, and you returned Aaron without a scratch. Wouldn't that anger you, too?"

Hamilton clicked something on his weapon, aimed it skyward, and stepped back. He slipped the gun away, and Parkman lowered his but kept it gripped in both hands, aimed at the ground.

"He had a mouth on him," Hamilton said.

"So it's his fault you beat him up?"

Hamilton looked at something over her shoulder. "You may want to turn around and look at that."

"Fuck you. You want to keep breathing, grab your shit and go."

"Sarah," Parkman said. "Shit man. You may want to turn around."

"This is where tables start to turn." Hamilton sounded like he was proud of himself.

Sarah stepped out of reach of Hamilton by several feet, then turned to see what they were looking at.

A man was walking Ron toward them, a gun held to Ron's head.

"Yes, I'm Hamilton. And that man escorting Ronald Harris is called Wind, short for Windsor. No one ever hears him, and he always gets the drop on his target, hence the name Wind."

"Stupid," Sarah said. "We can hear the wind. All it does is make noise. You guys are just a bunch of little boys playing in a sandbox and making up nicknames."

"You and your asshole boyfriend have the same obnoxious mouth. I'm going to enjoy watching that mouth of yours suck the end of my gun."

"You'll never get the chance, Ham. You'll be dead inside ten minutes."

"That a guess or a psychic prediction?"

Ron whispered, "Sorry," as he strode by her. "Didn't see him."

"Or hear him," Hamilton added. He turned to Parkman. "You can put that away. Wouldn't want you to get shot for no reason."

Sarah watched another man approach from the cover of trees, then another. It was the rest of Hamilton's men. The names came to her. Ajax, Peter, and the man she killed was called Scar.

Now what? They were still armed. If everyone started shooting, there'd definitely be a bloodbath. Could that be Hamilton's plan? She doubted it. No one here was suicidal, and yet each person knew the body count would be high if the guns started firing wildly.

In under a minute, Sarah and Parkman were completely

outnumbered and outgunned.

"Who did that to Scar?" the man she thought was Ajax asked.

Before anyone could answer, Sarah stepped forward. Several guns rose to aim at her.

"We're going to unhook Aaron now, then walk out of here with Ron." She gestured at the pickup. "No need to unload. Just take the truck. Here are the keys." She eased them out of her pocket.

"Who put you in charge?" Hamilton asked. "What's to stop me from killing you, your friend here, Ron and Aaron? Huh? Answer me that?"

"Nothing, I guess." She shrugged. "I mean, you could certainly try—"

A woman was walking toward them now. She had to be Belleville. She had a rather large rifle-like unit held high on her shoulder. It was aimed at the group.

"What is she doing?" Sarah asked no one in particular.

"Oh, don't worry about her," Hamilton said. "She's with us."

"You may want to rethink that," Ron said. "I'd listen to Sarah and scramble. This is your only chance."

Hamilton laughed. He bent down, slapped his knee, straightened, and glared at Ron.

"We had a pact, man. Why'd you go and fuck all that up?"

"Our pact was shit, and it was stupid."

"No, we were supposed to come back here and fuck up all the people who ruined our lives. Payback, baby. That was our deal. Kill the war pigs."

"Yeah, sure, a deal made in anger and fear. We were afraid over there and wanted to have our revenge. It saw us through the hard times, but we were never supposed to follow through."

Belle was five feet behind them now. She lowered her weapon.

Ron faced her. "Thought you had my back."

"I did. In my crosshairs."

"Where's Julie and the boys?" Hamilton asked her.

"On their way to Sudbury for an outing," Belle said. "As soon as Ron calls her, they'll return to North Bay."

"You bitch," Ron spat, as he lunged for her. Wind held him back.

"Don't worry," Hamilton said. "We only want Julie. Your boys will end up in a foster home somewhere and be fine by us. We aren't animals. We won't touch your kids. C'mon, what do you take us for?"

Ron ignored Hamilton as he struggled with Wind. "I trusted you," he shouted at Belle.

Without warning, Hamilton sucker-punched Ron, and the man dropped to his knees, utterly dejected.

Sarah learned two things at that moment. One, Ron realized his life was over. He'd lost his kids, and he'd lost this fight. And two, it was Hamilton who beat Aaron. After he punched Ron, Hamilton backed away and shook his hand, wincing.

"Damn, that hurts," he claimed.

"You've got to let that heal some," Ajax said. "You can't keep punching people."

"You're all dead," Ron whispered from his knees.

"What?" Hamilton said, leaning closer to the man, still shaking his hand on the side. "Say again."

"You're all dead."

"Will someone please shoot him? I'm tired of listening to him, and my hand hurts like a bitch."

Ajax pulled out a weapon, walked up beside Ron, and placed it at his head.

"Any last words?" Ajax asked.

Hamilton spun around. "Just shoot him."

Sarah shrugged. "Okay."

She drew her weapon, aimed, and fired from four feet. Ajax's head jerked sideways violently with the impact of the bullet. His balance was lost, and he dropped to the ground. Even before he hit the sand, half a dozen weapons came up.

Before another shot was fired, something exploded twenty feet away, knocking anyone still standing off their feet. Several men body-checked the Hummer. Parkman bumped the pickup truck and dropped behind it.

Sarah landed hard in the sand and then rolled under the Hummer. She blinked sand out of her eye as she tried to see who to fire at next.

Another explosion rocked the vehicle above her.

Then another.

"What the hell?" she screamed.

Why was Ron blowing up his explosives? How was he doing it without his cell phone?

Sarah wiped her eyes clear and saw legs and arms moving around the wheels of the large SUV. People were crawling, some moaning. One of the Hummer's doors closed. Someone shifted it into gear.

Panicked, Sarah glanced down the length of her body.

Aaron was still hooked to the rope, which was attached to the rear of the Hummer.

It jerked forward, all four wheels spinning to grab purchase in the sand, kicking sand at least six feet behind it. In under a second, it was gone from above her, and Aaron was yanked so hard she could've sworn his shoulders would pop out of their sockets.

The rope was above her, and in the next instant, Aaron crashed into her.

She was already bringing the gun up in her right hand. Sarah clung to him and was dragged along for several feet while trying to apply the barrel to the rope.

Gunfire erupted around her. Another explosion happened somewhere farther away.

Aaron was slipping from her grasp as the sand was threatening to yank him from her, tugging at the neck of her shirt and the waist of her pants.

Then, the gun steadied for the briefest of a second on the center of the rope.

She fired as her left arm gave out, and Aaron was swept over her face.

His body stopped when his ankles were beside her ear.

It worked.

The rope had broken.

The Hummer's engine moved away from them as they lay on the sand.

Two more weapons were fired.

They were exposed now, out in the open. Yet, there was a part of her that didn't care. She had her Aaron back. They could leave. He could heal. She'd fix this. Everything could go back to the way it was.

Bloodshed and heartache.

"No," she screamed as she rolled over and got to her knees, raising her weapon to fire at anything that moved.

Hamilton was down, a large red hole in his forehead. Parkman was kneeling behind the pickup still, which had a batch of fresh bullet holes in the paint job on the side panel. Ajax was down from her bullet, and the other guy, Peter, was trying to hold back the blood escaping from his abdomen without much success. That left Belle and Wind.

She spun around in time to see Belle cradling Ron.

One more explosion knocked Sarah to her knees.

She twisted around in time to see the Hummer dropping back to the ground. Whoever was setting off the explosives had waited until it drove right over the one by the entrance. The Hummer drifted several more feet, then stopped, the entire front end engulfed in flames. The interior was a mess of smoke and orange fire. The driver hadn't gotten out and would not make it now. Wind was the only one unaccounted for, which meant he was in the Hummer, his flesh cooking.

She addressed Belle, her hand shaking from exhaustion and adrenaline.

"Whose side are you on?"

"Yours. Ron's."

"Then what was all that about?" Sarah's voice took on a crazed tone.

"I'm not a sniper like Ron. I had to get close to do any kind of shooting. You think Hamilton would've let me walk across that open expanse without thinking I was with him? I had to fool Ron at the last minute. Besides, I knew those bombs would help us. And you can check the bullets later. I shot Hamilton. Parkman nailed Peter."

Peter gasped his last breath beside her, then stopped moving. Parkman stood to his full height.

"You good?" she asked.

He nodded. "Not a scratch."

Aaron rolled onto his back and moaned.

He was alive, too. Sarah inhaled, relief sweeping through her.

She turned to Ron. "Where's your cell phone?"

"Wind took it when he caught me in the bush."

"Then who's blowing everything up?" Now, her voice really did sound like a lunatic raving.

"Actually, that's the one thing I was holding back," Ron said.

"Oh, my fuck. I'm going to kill you myself."

A convoy of military vehicles streamed in from the main road, dispersing men at the burning Hummer as the others headed toward the pickup truck and the carnage that lay near it.

Sarah counted eight Jeeps and Humvees as they parked in a semi-circle around them. All she wanted to do was run to Aaron, hold him, and whisper he'd be okay now.

"General Whyte?" Sarah asked.

"The one and only," Ron said.

"That's why he wanted me to come in, let it go? Because you two had a deal?"

"Yes, because Annemarie and I had already arranged everything."

Men were ejecting from their vehicles like a scene out of a war movie. They were fully armed and wearing camouflage. Once the second vehicle was surrounded, a back door opened, and a tall man in a suit stepped out. He adjusted his jacket, faced them, and then headed their way, escorted by six soldiers.

"Mr. Harris, Ms. Willard." Whyte glanced at Parkman for a brief moment, then turned to Sarah. "You've proven quite formidable, resilient, and difficult to manage."

Sarah shook her head. "Impossible."

"Excuse me?"

"Not difficult. I'm impossible to manage."

Whyte huffed. "Be that as it may, this wasn't your fight."

"Sure it was. Sutton came *to* me. Ron came *for* me. And look there"—Sarah pointed at Aaron—"that's my man, these monsters kidnapped and tortured. Whether you like it or not, it became my fight."

A man was removing the rope from Aaron's wrists while two other men with a stretcher waited nearby. Aaron was going to be okay. She could breathe again. They'd done it.

Whyte focused his attention on Ron and Annemarie. Maybe Ron's original plan was a good one, after all. General Whyte understood nothing when it came to a fight. All he saw was a win. According to him, Sarah—a woman—was to be controlled and managed. She lost all respect for him, his position, and his ability to lead in only a few seconds.

But that didn't need to be her focus, and she could give a flying fuck what the general thought of her. It was over, and now the healing could start.

They lifted Aaron into the back of a vehicle and closed

the doors. She turned to ask where they were taking him when the general spoke.

"Have you got it?" Whyte asked.

Ron nodded and unclasped his pants. He lowered the zipper, then slid a hand down to his crotch, tugged something, and pulled his hand back out.

A black device with wires attached dangled from his fingers.

One of Whyte's men took it from Ron and jogged back to a vehicle, where he disappeared inside.

"Well, then, that concludes our business for the day. Our deal remains intact. You're all free to go."

Whyte did an about-face and started back to the vehicle he came in.

"Where are they taking Aaron?" Sarah asked.

Whyte shouted over his shoulder. "North Bay civilian hospital. My men will drop him off."

"So that's it?" Sarah asked when she turned back around.

Ron nodded. "Annemarie and I have been granted amnesty."

"Amnesty?"

"On every point, all charges. There'll be no charges for either of you or Julie. Her name has been taken off the BOLO from Huntsville. You're free and clear to go."

"Then why does Whyte seem so pissed?"

The vehicles were easing backward and turning around, leaving the foursome alone with the bodies of Hamilton's team.

"He wanted Hamilton alive. He wanted to prosecute."

"And he was listening the whole time with that wire in

your crotch?" Sarah gazed at Parkman, then back to Ron, who was nodding. "He heard everything? Heard their plan to kill the war pigs, heard Hamilton talk about the origins of the plan, everything?" It all came to her in a rush. "And you struck a deal because there was no stopping Hamilton without killing him. But then you'd be up on murder charges —"

"By calling Whyte," Ron interrupted, "I was able to not only strike a deal to save my skin, but he also agreed to arrange for my boys to live with their father, a decorated military man. I served my country and did nothing wrong. Other than dreaming up a revenge plot that I never intended to put into action, I'm a good person. When I saw Hamilton had taken possession of those weapons, I had to stop him. So I called the cops, well, our version of the cops. And Whyte's pissed that Hamilton's team took out Sutton. Since I eliminated—with yours and Julie's help—the rest of Hamilton's team, Whyte's not really all that pissed. It's over. He knows that. I know that. And now we go back to our lives. I get my boys, and CAS and CRA will be off my back. We finally get to live and breathe again. As I said earlier, today I retire from the Canadian military."

"The bombs on your cell phone app," Parkman said. "Whyte had the same app, the same codes?"

"I couldn't risk being the only one. They were his bombs. We all planted them yesterday. Last night, Whyte gave their location to Annemarie here."

Annemarie nodded and produced her phone, holding it up. "All here."

"And when Whyte saw it was about to go down ..."

Ron and Annemarie were nodding.

Something else was bothering her. What had she missed

—

"Run," she said. "Everyone up. On your feet."

Parkman had been standing, leaning against the pickup, but Ron and Annemarie were still sitting on the sand.

Once they were all standing, they bolted from the pickup.

"Open that app," Sarah said to Annemarie. "Get us as far away from any unexploded devices as you can—"

The pickup detonated fifteen feet behind them.

All four adults were knocked at least five feet before smashing to the ground and rolling in a heap of limbs.

"Now I'm getting pissed off," Sarah screamed. "Can someone please stop blowing shit up!"

She crawled to Parkman, but he nodded he was okay before she got there.

Beside Annemarie now, she rolled her over. The woman blinked in surprise, then covered her eyes from the sun.

"What was that?" Annemarie asked.

"The rest of the weapons in Ron's pickup were just decommissioned," Sarah said. Ron was getting to his feet. Sarah continued. "When Whyte drove away without collecting them, I didn't think at first."

"But he knew we were sitting beside the pickup," Ron whispered.

"Does it matter to him? Really?" Sarah waved an arm. "I mean, look at the other bodies. He'll send a cleanup crew soon. No one will know this happened, and you're taken care of, too. There was no love for me, either."

Annemarie sat up and stared toward what was left of the

pickup.

"Are we sitting on a bomb?" Sarah asked. "There's at least six more that Whyte has control of."

Something exploded fifty feet in front of the pickup.

They all ducked at the same time but were too far to be knocked over again.

"If we survived the pickup blast, he's hitting those to kill anyone who is running for the road." She dropped beside Annemarie. "Open the fucking app and show us where the other devices are."

Annemarie felt around in the sand near her thighs and came up with her phone. The screen was cracked, and it wouldn't turn on.

"Shit," Sarah shouted. She got to her feet. "Ron, you helped plant them all. I count at least four more if there were a dozen, possibly five. Walk us out of here."

Ron glanced left, then right, confused about where he was.

Bloodshed and heartache kept going through her mind.

Parkman pointed at the tree line. "I say we make a break for the trees. None of the devices were in the trees."

"Ron?" Sarah yelled. "That work for you?"

The man looked utterly confused. He'd done everything Whyte had asked, and now Whyte was trying to kill him.

Ron's head bobbed like a lunatic as he nodded. The redness where Hamilton had punched him was widening. He seemed dazed and confused.

Sarah helped Annemarie to her feet, and they started running.

As the trees drew closer and another device exploded in

the distance, all Sarah could think about was Aaron.

Did they actually take him to the North Bay Hospital?

Would she ever see him again?

If something happened to Aaron, Ronald Harris's plan to execute top Canadian military officials was back on the table.

And Sarah would start hunting them.

A man named General Whyte would be first on her list.

Chapter 36

Sarah and Parkman entered the main lobby of the North Bay Hospital and strode up to the kiosk. Ten minutes later, they were waiting to speak with Dr. Hutton on the third floor.

"I'm just glad Aaron's here," Sarah muttered as they took seats in the waiting area.

"Why wouldn't he be?" Parkman adjusted the toothpick in his mouth from side to side.

"General Whyte didn't wait for us to leave the area when he started blowing shit up."

"Sure, because his weapons were in that pickup. An embarrassment. Ron was his mistake. One more bomb, and no one would know that any of this shit went down."

"Us too."

"Exactly. With us gone, Whyte returns to his job and life and doesn't need to lift a finger for Ron, Julie, or even

Annemarie."

"I guess I realize all that, but then why drop Aaron here? He was Hamilton's captive. He could talk."

"Whyte's probably the kind of man who doesn't want to get his hands dirty. Removing Aaron from the scene and having him in his military vehicle prevented him from outright murder. His men wouldn't comply with that sort of order. Same as a lieutenant ordering police officers to murder a man in the street. I'm sure some cops would, but most wouldn't follow that order."

Sarah jumped in. "And when his men returned to clean up the scene and pick up the weapons, they'd find that Ron killed himself by blowing everything, along with us, sky high."

"That's how he could play it, in my opinion," Parkman said.

They sat in silence for several moments, lost in their own thoughts.

"Sarah Roberts?" a man said.

She got to her feet. "You must be Dr. Hutton."

The tall man nodded but kept his hands in his lab coat pockets. His glasses were too large for his face, but he didn't seem to mind.

"Have you got a second?" he asked.

"Of course."

"Follow me to my office."

That didn't sound good. Sarah worried with each step what the doctor had to say. Anything else in life, she was strong and ready to fight. But she was worried about Aaron being lost somewhere in the labyrinthine halls of this hospital and his injuries unknown to her. The doctor could tell her he lost an eye or his face needed reconstructive surgery, and they weren't sure he'd live through it.

The urge to grab the doctor's arm and spin him around overwhelmed her, but she controlled it. And waited. With each step, she waited.

Is this the heartache, Vivian?

Sarah and Parkman took the two chairs opposite Hutton's desk inside the office. The man removed his glasses, placed them on the desk, then sat down. He clasped his hands together and stared at them.

It took all her willpower not to punch something, grab something to throw, or scream at him. In moments like this, she learned that being an adult was about having restraint. In her early twenties, she might have already yelled at him, railed at how they treated people in his stupid hospital, and made a fool of herself.

"We are doing all that we can at the moment—"

"Just tell us what's wrong," Sarah broke in. "How bad are his injuries?"

"He just came out of surgery for the broken orbital bone."

"The broken orbital bone!" Sarah shot out of her chair. She glanced down at Parkman, seething with rage. "If Hamilton weren't dead, I'd kill him. In fact, can I kill him again?"

Parkman tugged her sleeve. "Sarah, calm down. And sit."

The doctor had leaned back in his chair, the calm demeanor replaced with mild shock at her outburst.

"The man who did this to Aaron," the doctor started, "is

dead?" He hesitated. "You killed him?"

"Yeah, he's dead—"

"What Sarah means is," Parkman cut in. "There was an incident that took place, and a man died. An unfortunate situation. Now, please, carry on with Aaron. You were saying he just came out of surgery."

Parkman yanked her down to her seat. Sometimes, she needed him to remind her about adulting.

Dr. Hutton cleared his throat and placed his elbows back on the desk. "It's good he came in when he did. The swelling around the left eye indicated a cheekbone fracture, which he has."

"A cheekbone fracture—" Sarah blurted.

"Sarah," Parkman snapped and grabbed her arm again. "That's it. You're not allowed to speak right now. You're too emotional."

"I'm allowed to be emotional."

"Okay, then. Be emotional, but do it outside the office. I want to hear what Dr. Hutton has to say."

"Fine." Sarah lowered in her seat. Sometimes, she did need someone to tell her how it was, and as much as she hated it, she would only take it from the people in her life she trusted. If Parkman ordered her to do something, she could do it.

The doctor started talking again. "Aaron has an orbital bone fracture, and what complicates that is getting attention too late. As I was saying, we caught it in time."

"What happens if it's too late?" Parkman asked.

His hand gripped Sarah's arm tighter when he spoke as a reminder to control the outbursts.

"The bleeding around the eye due to the broken orbital bone is the major cause of swelling. An untreated orbital fracture can often lead to an infection in the eyeball itself. But I think we caught it in time."

"What else, Doctor?"

"His nose is broken, which is the most common thing to break on the face. The second most common is the jaw."

"Is Aaron's jaw broken, too?" Parkman asked.

How the hell can Parkman remain that calm? Sarah had to press her lips together to keep from saying anything. Her fingers dug into each thigh, the pain a reminder to just listen.

The doctor nodded. "It appears so. When he was in surgery, we considered orthodontic brackets on his teeth to —"

"Wire his jaw?" Sarah said, her mouth opening before she could stop it.

Parkman squeezed her arm. She nodded for the doctor to continue, her lips pressed together again.

"Yes, to wire his jaw, but the break isn't big enough to warrant that. Liquid diet for several days, then soups and Jell-O. He'll be fine with the jaw and nose."

"And what about the cheek and orbital bone?" Parkman asked.

"That should all heal within five to six weeks. We've set everything and will monitor him for the next week or so. We're hopeful the swelling around his eye will decrease in the next seven to ten days, and we'll be able to see some progress."

"Anything else we should know?" Parkman asked.

"At this point, our only concern is nerve damage. He

could walk away completely healed, and in months to come, this'll be nothing but a painful memory. But sometimes, with nerve damage, they only partially heal, and in some cases, they don't heal at all. We won't know that for some time."

"We understand," Parkman said, removing his hand from Sarah's arm. "When can we see him?"

"He's sleeping in the ICU right now. You can see him, but he won't wake up until tomorrow. Although, I should warn you. When he does wake up, he won't want to talk too much with that jaw the way it is. He's in considerable pain. It'll be several weeks before he talks without much pain."

Sarah fumbled with her fingers. She glanced down to avoid the doctor seeing the wetness springing to her eyes.

All those injuries because of her, the life she chose. Alex's injuries, too.

When they left the hospital, she'd have to call Daniel and get an update, then tell them about Aaron.

"For now, that's about it," Dr. Hutton said. "I'll advise you more as we move on, but when Aaron leaves here, no airplanes or deep-sea diving for him. Don't take him where he'll experience internal or external pressures. Also, no sneezing or coughing for quite some time. That could be an eye, cheek, nose, and jaw issue."

They stood, shook hands, and Sarah bolted for the door. Her stomach churned, and she wondered if she was going to throw up.

"You okay?" Parkman asked once he exited the office.

"No. I need to see Aaron, and then I need to get out of this place. I hate hospitals."

Parkman led her to the ICU by following the signs. Once

there, Sarah stared at her man's body covered up in sheets on the bed. His face was almost completely covered in white gauze and strips of bandages.

Parkman gave her a moment to be alone with him, then escorted her out of the building.

"I need a drink," she whispered, her voice breaking.

Ten minutes later, they were at a restaurant bar where Sarah ordered a whiskey, shot it back, then ordered another to sip.

"He'll be okay, Sarah," Parkman said when the waitress had left. He was trying to console her, and she loved him for it.

When she glanced up, he had a beer bottle in his hand.

"It's all my fault," she whispered.

"C'mon, Sarah. We all know the risks."

"Sure, going in. But I expect Vivian to help. To shoulder some of the load. She could've told me to warn the four of them on that street corner at Adelaide and Brant when you picked me up. They could've walked the other way, and Alex and Aaron would be fine."

"Fair enough," Parkman said. He glanced around, then leaned forward. "But Sarah, both sides take hits. That's how it works. They hate it, we hate it. And it's more personal for us because we all care about each other. I get it. I totally get it. There's no denying your pain and how you feel. But just don't take on all the blame. Aaron's a big boy and will walk away from this. He'll pull through."

The waitress brought her another whiskey. She sipped it, the drink burning her throat. Her stomach calmed with the first shot, so she took another sip.

Parkman drank from his beer, and they sat in companionable silence for several moments.

"Should I keep doing this?" Sarah asked.

Parkman stared at her for a few heartbeats. "My question to you is, how do you feel about it? I fear you're looking for an answer I can't give you."

"What do you mean?"

"I won't tell you to stop doing it, cling to Aaron, and go on to live your lives. But I won't say the opposite. If you stop, that's on you. If you keep going, that's on you, too. Whatever you decide, it has to come from you. I'll be fine with either choice."

"That's not fair."

He laughed. "How's that?"

"I wanted the decision taken from me."

"Ask Aaron what he thinks then."

"He'd say stop."

They stared at each other.

"Well, then do it for him if that's what you want. But you won't have me telling you what to do."

"But I don't want to stop."

"Then don't."

"Ooohhh, you," she said, her lips pressed close together. "Don't play with me." She drank the rest of the whiskey.

"Look, Sarah, I'm here to listen. Talk it out all you want. But I will never tell you what you should do. If you want my opinion, that's different. I'd tell you that."

"Well, fuck me sideways." She raised a hand, then dropped it to the table with a bang as the cutlery jostled. "Give me your opinion then."

"Don't quit. Vivian needs you, and you need her. In fact, after what I've seen over the years, the world needs you, too."

"Why didn't you say that the first time?" She tilted her head sideways to look at him, the drink already making her feel lighter and more playful, which made her feel guilty as Aaron was in a hospital bed at that same moment.

He shrugged. "You didn't ask for my opinion."

"Fucker," she whispered.

She waved for the waitress. "I need another drink. And we should order food. Then find a hotel. I'm exhausted."

"Sounds like a plan to me."

"Decisions another day," Sarah said, holding her glass high.

Parkman tapped it with his beer bottle.

"I'll drink to that."

Then he downed the rest of his beer.

"One more round?" the waitress asked.

Sarah fought tears when she nodded.

Bloodshed and heartache.

Oh, Vivian, this hurts. This really hurts. We've reached the heartache phase, and I don't think I can take it.

Help me, sis. *Please.*

Chapter 37

"SARAH?" SOMEONE CALLED.

She turned around and showed her boarding pass to security.

Parkman was running toward her. "Sarah, wait."

She took back her boarding pass and stepped aside to let others by on their way to the conveyor belts and metal detectors.

"Sarah," he said as he stopped before her, panting. "What the hell's … going on?"

"Catch your breath. It's okay. We've got time."

Parkman moved a few feet to the left and spun in a circle, breathing rapidly. "I haven't run … like that for …" He inhaled deeply, then exhaled. "I need to get in better shape."

Sarah averted her eyes. She glanced at airport security using a wand on someone, then turned and watched a family of four as they managed to yank six large suitcases toward the line at security.

"Sarah?" Parkman stepped into her line of vision. "I'm right here."

"I know. Sorry."

"What's going on?"

"Nothing."

"Then where are you going?" He snatched the boarding pass from her, and she lunged for it, but he held it high, away from her eager fingers. "Los Angeles?" He handed it back.

Sarah slipped it inside her passport pages. "For now."

"What's in Los Angeles?"

She shrugged. "The ocean. The coast. A nice drive up to Santa Rosa, see the parents."

"Wherever life takes you?"

"Something like that." She studied his face. "Why are you here?"

"Sarah, your plane doesn't leave for three hours. Come with me to that lounge over there. Have one drink. Come talk to me."

She owed him that. She owed Parkman a lot more than that. But how could she when she didn't want to talk about it?

Before she could answer in the negative, she nodded.

A large purse as a carry-on was all she had. A few cosmetics, her novel, a wallet, and spare panties. She didn't need much more for this trip.

Minutes later, they were seated in a generic airport lounge. They ordered wine and waited until it arrived, and then Parkman leaned forward to start.

"I heard from Darwin."

She gestured for him to go on.

"He said he was sorry he couldn't help more, but it sounded like everything worked out in the end."

She raised her right eyebrow. Everything had *not* worked out in the end. That part Vivian referred to as *heartache* was something she lived with daily.

"Well, you're not dead, right?"

She sipped her drink.

"Sarah, you have to come out of this funk you're in."

"I will, but like all wounds, this one will take time."

Parkman watched her over the rim of his glass while he sipped. He set it down and twirled the wine.

"Darwin said Bruno's doing well. Drinking a lot but working out all the time. Darwin set up a gym in the basement of his home in Italy. He'll return in eight months with a new name and look."

Sarah nodded and sipped some more.

"C'mon Sarah, talk to me. It's been two weeks since Aaron went into the hospital. You guys went home last week, and now you're leaving the country."

She stared at her wine.

"Aaron said you two are taking a break," Parkman added.

The pain burned her eyes, and she looked up at Parkman. She didn't mean to glare like she was angry, but her face couldn't hide her emotions.

"Is that the story? We're taking a break?"

He held up his hands. "Hey, take it easy. I'm just checking your pulse. We all love you, Sarah."

"Yeah, well." She moved her gaze back to her glass. "I

fucked up, and now I pay for it."

"What's that supposed to mean? You're not the self-pity type."

When she stared into Parkman's eyes this time, she saw his heart and warmth, and she wanted to tell him everything but knew she couldn't. Then her mouth opened, and she unloaded on him.

"We talked. Aaron wants out. He's wanted out since we met. He doesn't like what I do because he can't *protect* me. You've known him a long time. He complains about Vivian. Even when that cartel took his finger in Mexico, he fought on. But he's never liked what I do. And you know what hurts the most?" She wiped at her eyes. Parkman handed her a napkin. "This is who I am. Ever since I was eighteen, this is who I am. Vivian and I work together. I know there are drawbacks. I'm quite aware of them. *Serious* drawbacks. Restrictions are Vivian's term for it. But this is who I am. And if he doesn't want me doing it, he's asking me not to be me."

"So you left Aaron?"

"No," she blurted. "I wanted a compromise. Limit his exposure. Go back to the days when I worked with Darwin if needed. You too. Aaron was the one who asked me to move out. He doesn't want to see it anymore."

"Sarah, he doesn't mean that. This is killing him, too."

She wiped her eyes again, blew her nose, and attempted to compose herself.

"Parkman, I can be strong. No problem. I can even be strong for the two of us, Aaron and me. But sometimes, I need my man to be strong for me. So yeah, I'm hurting because he wants out. And yeah, I miss him. But what hurts the most is how I see him."

"What does that mean?"

"I've always seen him as a man who fought for his sister when she went missing all those years ago. He beat up a guy who was in his dojo because the man used what Aaron taught him to hurt his wife or something like that. Anyway, Aaron was charged criminally for that. He was shot multiple times, and all before he met me. I thought I'd found my rock, my Hercules."

"Okay, but you said something about how you see him."

"I see him as a soft baby boy right now, and that hurts. Nothing against soft men, but I didn't fall in love with one."

The tears came in a wave. She covered her face until they subsided enough to look at Parkman again. She had to blow her nose once more. Then, after a couple of calming breaths, she sipped more wine and met Parkman's gaze.

"I realize he was beat up," she whispered. "I know he was hurt badly. So was Alex. And for that, I'm deeply wounded. If he wanted out for a few months or for a year, no issue. If Aaron wanted out unless there was an emergency, even better." She was talking with her hands now. "I didn't want him to come to Texas where he was shot. I don't like him being involved in the first place. But telling me to move out? Telling me we're through? I mean, what the fuck is that, Parkman? Huh? Tell me. Why are we through?"

"Sarah, give him time. He'll come around."

"Some things are unforgivable. Sometimes, you have to man up—I hate saying that term—and do what's right, even if it's the hard things. Aaron's not doing that. He just wants out."

"So go." Parkman waved his hand. "Take a month, maybe two. He'll call you. It'll be okay. Aaron's just hurting right now."

"Parkman." Sarah leaned across the table, her stomach pushing against it. Their faces were a foot apart. "We were supposed to have a baby together. He was my life partner. For life. For good. Forever. There are no takebacks in that game. Then he gets beat up, and that's it?" She pulled back. "Fine, I have to move on, too. This is on me. It's what I do that caused this. I can live with that. I'm a big girl. These shoulders can handle it." She sipped the rest of her wine. "And don't get me wrong, I'm not downplaying how bad his injuries are. I know he could've lost an eye. We still don't know the extent of the nerve damage. Hamilton did a real number on Aaron's face. But overall, the double vision is going away. The swelling and bruising is almost gone. Another week, and he'll just be waiting for the bones to finish fusing. Sure, his nose will be crooked. Owen Wilson comes to mind, but that's a good thing. Owen's cute."

"It's a good thing?" Parkman asked as he watched her, his wine glass in front of his mouth.

"Sure. Aaron owns a martial arts gym. He has three teachers and classes all day, seven days a week. Everyone will give him more respect when the boss walks in, and his nose tells a story. Shit, I don't know."

"You done?"

She could only nod, the emotion choking her vocal cords. Parkman was always there for her, and she loved him for that. By taking off to LA, she was leaving him, too. She was leaving the three teachers, even though Daniel told her they didn't want her to go. Benjamin even said Aaron would come around. Give him a couple of weeks. Let them talk some sense into Aaron. If he didn't listen, they'd kick his ass.

Alex had made her cry the most. He'd pulled her aside and said he'd take another beating for her. Then another. And then he'd die for her. He'd never met a woman like her, and it was an honor to fight for her. Then he said she reminded him of his mother, and Sarah would always be in his heart no matter where she went. One phone call, and he'd stop the world for her.

Then he drove his point home by saying that Aaron felt the same. And one day, he would apologize, or Alex would kill him.

They cried, they laughed, and they all hugged.

But the result was the same.

Everyone loved and wanted her in their life, but the one man she loved on an intimate level didn't. The one man with whom she wanted a baby and a life.

Oh, the heartache, Vivian.

"You know what, Sarah," Parkman said. "You're right. Go take some time. Hit LA, rent a car and tour the coast. Go see your parents. Maybe you two need a little time away. From Texas to North Bay was only a couple of weeks. Give it time. Everything will come together."

"I believe that," she whispered. "It just hurts. A lot. Right now."

Parkman eased forward and placed a hand over hers.

It warmed her heart.

"Although, I don't know how long I'll get a break from

Vivian," she added.

"What does that mean?" Parkman withdrew his hand.

"She keeps going on about *The Delivery*."

"The Delivery?"

"Yeah, a few weeks from now." Sarah shrugged. "No idea what she's talking about." She sighed. "It'll probably be a good distraction from all this personal shit."

Parkman withdrew a twenty for the drinks and set it on the table. "C'mon, I'll walk you back to security."

They got up and headed out of the lounge. Parkman nabbed a couple of toothpicks off the bar as they strode back the way they'd come. She felt better if only a tiny bit. Parkman understood her, and that made a world of difference.

"You'll stay in touch, right?" he asked.

"Of course."

"And if you need me?"

"There's no one else I'd rather call." Which made her sad all over again. She should be able to call upon her man, her Aaron. But it seemed those days were over.

"Sarah?"

"What?" They'd stopped by the woman taking boarding passes.

"Did I ever tell you I'm psychic, too?"

She smiled and suppressed a small laugh. "No, Parkman, you didn't."

"Well, I can see the future. And in that future, I see you and Aaron back together, and he's being more understanding and less of a dick to you."

"Hmph, interesting future."

"You'd welcome it, right?"

She glanced at the floor, then back up at Parkman. "I'd welcome it over this pain, yes. But it would have to be genuine. I'm never going back to the way it was unless he's back a thousand percent. My life for his, his life for mine. Without a commitment like that, there's no baby either."

"I'd expect nothing less from the girl I know." He nudged her shoulder. "Go, get on that plane and enjoy your life a little. You deserve it."

She handed over her boarding pass. Parkman moved to the side. She glanced over her shoulder a couple of times as he watched her go.

"Sarah," he called from thirty feet away.

She stopped and stared at him.

"Stay out of trouble."

"Always," she shouted back. Then, "I still don't know your other name."

"One day you will."

Parkman turned around and walked away.

At the conveyor belt, the security officer smiled at her in a creepy way.

"Don't know his name, eh?"

"Don't start," she said. "Not you, too."

The man looked away and waved for her to walk through the detector.

Once she cleared security, she made it to the bathroom, where she sat on the closed toilet seat and allowed herself one more good cry. Ever since last February, it seemed all she did was cry now. Maybe she was softer, too. Maybe Aaron was on to something.

But she was alone now. Aaron was gone. Vivian was calling, yet everything she had done had led to people she cared about getting hurt.

No more.

She was on her own.

Well, she had her sister.

And *The Delivery* was supposed to hurt—bad.

Sarah had never been more ready.

She wiped her face, washed her hands, and exited the bathroom.

At the gate, in the waiting area, she brushed her shoulders and stared out at the planes on the tarmac.

"Bring it on, sis," she whispered. "Bring it on."

Afterword

DEAR READER,

Certain parts of *The Hunt* were hard for me to write. This isn't the place nor the time to delve too deep into my personal life, but I'd like to say a few things.

I am not aware of the numbers, but I'm pretty sure men suffer abuse at the hands of their spouses more often than we know. Whether it be emotional or physical abuse or both, it affects men and women alike.

The more we speak about these things, the more out in the open they become, and the more awareness we can have. It'll help others deal with it, and in some cases, it may even ease their suffering.

In 1996, I married the woman of my dreams, and we had two daughters. In the last half of the marriage, problems arose that I don't want to go into here, but that marriage dissolved in the spring of 2008. My ex-wife got custody of our daughters.

To make a long story short, she made several parenting errors, and Children's Aid got involved. I lost my mind with worry and did everything I could to get my daughters to come and live with me.

The—insert expletives here—CAS workers told me that if I flew to Ontario to pick up my daughters, I would be arrested.

What Ronald Harris dealt with in this story was written from the truth.

There are another hundred details regarding this case, and I'm not under any gag order, but I really just don't want to go into it all now.

I flew to Ontario anyway, and I sat in court to fight for my girls, and I ended up getting full custody of both of them. They came to live with me and escaped that abusive woman who left them emotionally scarred.

Since then, they're both well-adjusted, wonderful girls— women now—who got to experience traveling through Europe, visiting Rome, over a year in Greece, and spending a month in Denmark. I regret nothing but have one thing left to say about CAS.

I believe they are needed as so many children suffer.

But—I will never forget what that one CAS worker in Barrie, Ontario, did to my family. There should be some kind of oversight for these people. She was a travesty of the system and made sure I was aware that she *hated* men. All she did was hurt my girls that day because the CAS worker ordered them back into the abusive situation with a gleam in her eye. It took years to fix that woman's mistake. I'm not kidding—I would never make light of this situation.

That's over now …

Then another issue came up. Child support. Again, without going into it, I didn't pay any support to my ex-wife *after* I got custody in 2014 and my daughters came to live with me.

Apparently, my monthly amounts accrued for years even though the court documents were all signed and finished. Then, in 2017, I was back in divorce court for an extremely large amount owing to my ex-wife when the kids had been living with me for years. There's a process to get this changed, another motion to file, and it hadn't been done, so my ex-wife claimed—falsely—that I owed her nearly $60,000. Finally, it ended in August 2018, a decade after separating.

Still, no one told the enforcers I owed nothing in child support.

The family maintenance people in British Columbia, where I was living at the time, seized my bank account and took all the money there. They sent letters to seize my passport and my driver's license. I lost my fucking mind in anger and went after them with everything I could. I made phone calls and discovered they were trying to collect sixty thousand dollars in child support. They threatened me with jail time!

I said to the case worker that I had custody of the children and that they had been living with me since 2014.

There was a pause on the line.

"What?"

"They live with me." I fought to keep the anger out of my voice. "I've had custody for years. My ex-wife is lying again. This should be criminal."

"Then why are we trying to collect?"

I suppressed the urge to throw the phone across the room.

I faxed all the court-stamped documents to the right people, and all the seizures of my accounts and documents (passport, license) were rescinded.

So, I left that marriage in 2008 and was still fighting issues with it in court as of August 2019 (that's when these financial seizures took place). My ex-wife was never held accountable for anything she ever did.

It's finished now, and there's nothing to return to court over, as my daughters are over eighteen.

The reason I say all this (there's so much more, but it's not appropriate here) is to illustrate what Ronald Harris was going through. The black eye he had, I had one, too. The police at the door? My house, too. The officer's advice to take the punches and not defend myself in case my ex-wife got hurt when she was punching me was the exact advice a Barrie police officer gave me in March 2008, a month before I moved out.

I was told that she could beat me with impunity and that I was done for if she had a scratch and wanted to press charges.

So I moved out. I had to move out to save myself.

I'm not looking for sympathy, and by no means am I a battered man (some would say so, but like Sarah, my shoulders are big enough. I took the hits and moved on). Yes, there were times when my ex-wife got violent. Some people do. I love strong women when they're ready to fight for something. That's why I write about Sarah. But I've never hit a woman, and I wasn't going to then.

And I was never charged with a single crime during that entire ordeal.

But neither was she, even though I had the wounds to prove it.

That chapter in my life is over, and we've all moved on. We all have issues and have to deal with something in life. And if you don't heal what hurt you, you end up bleeding on someone else, someone who didn't hurt you. Often, someone who loves you the most because they're the safe one.

Man, I loved that woman with all my heart. To this day, even after everything we went through, there's still something in my heart for that woman. It's been almost three decades since we first met, and I still look back fondly on those wonderful early years. We were so happy—until we weren't.

Hey, shit happens, and here we are. Everybody goes through a breakup.

Although CAS added to the pain my kids went through in my case.

That is a fact. Forgive CAS? That'll be a challenge, but I will forgive—because it allows me to let it go.

I hope whoever you are and wherever you are, you're living the life you've always wanted. I'm serious. I truly wish the best for you.

And if you're not, think about making changes.

I did, and I couldn't be happier.

I want to thank Annemarie Willard for allowing me to use her name as Ron's friend, Belleville.

And a big thank you to Vicky Budnack for allowing me to use her name as Detective Budnack.

Until *The Delivery*, keep smiling, reading, and caring for yourself and each other.

I love all readers.

I'm *your* biggest fan.

Jonas Saul

About Jonas Saul

Jonas Saul is the bestselling author of the Sarah Roberts Series—more than two million sold!—and has written and published over sixty thrillers. After acquiring an agent, he signed several deals in Los Angeles, with MadRiver Pictures optioning his Sarah Roberts Series— over forty books!—(currently in development).

Jonas has often outranked Stephen King and Dean

Koontz on Amazon over the past decade. He's regularly invited to be a guest speaker, teacher, or workshop presenter at international writing conferences and film festivals worldwide. He hosts an annual writer's retreat in Greece, where he currently lives. He focuses his teaching on how to get tension and emotion in every scene, on every page, how he made it as a creator/writer, the path to success in this business, and the pitfalls to avoid. He also hosts a reading retreat in Greece with guest authors, yoga retreats, and hiking retreats. Visit the Imagine Greece Retreats website at www.imaginegreeceretreats.com, or email him directly to discuss an opportunity to join one of the retreats at jonas@imaginegreeceretreats.com.

Jonas is also a professional freelance editor. He works for several publishers and does private editing for clients, with many testimonials on his website at www.imaginepress.org, which details each author's response to Jonas's editing skills. Email Jonas directly for an editing quote at editor@imaginepress.org.

To book Jonas for a speaking engagement at a writer's conference/festival, to have him on your jury at a film festival, or even to say hello, email Jonas directly at jonassaul@icloud.com.

For updates on releases, hit the "Follow" button on Amazon or Bookbub, and join Jonas on Facebook, where he's most active.

Contact Jonas Saul

Linktree: Find me here

Email: jonassaul@icloud.com

9 781998 047680